HOLLOW SEASON

CAMILLA OCHLAN
CAROL E. LEEVER

OF CATS AND DRAGONS BOOK 4

Copyright

Hollow Season

Cover illustration: Samantha Key

Additional Art and Title page copyright © 2018 by
Carol E. Leever

Visit our website at OfCatsAndDragons.com

Like us on Facebook @OfCatsAndDragons

ISBN: 978-1-7929294-9-6

Dedication

To our nephews and nieces: Brittny, Chelsea, Dylan, Wyatt, Evan, Shannon, Tommy, Katie, Becky, Lizzy, Julia, Megan, Evelyn, and Marissa — the next generation of warriors, mages, scholars, and heroes.

CONTENTS

Timeline of Books

Counted from the year of the last Covenant, 14,000 years ago.

❖

14,021 *Autumn:* Night's Gift (Book 1)
14,021 *Winter:* Winter Tithe (Novella)

❖

14,022 *Spring:* Radiation (Book 2)
14,022 *Summer:* Summer's Fall (Book 3)
14,022 *Summer:* Hollow Season (Book 4)
14,022 *Summer:* Autumn King (Book 5)
14,022 *Summer:* Solstice Thyme (short story)

❖

You can get Night's Gift (Book 1 e-book) for free when you sign up for the Of Cats And Dragons Newsletter.

Radiation (Book 2 e-book) is also available for free when you sign up for the Of Cats And Dragons Newsletter.

We offer Winter Tithe as a seasonal gift for our newsletter subscribers.

Solstice Thyme will soon be available on our website at OfCatsAndDragons.com

Chapter 1: Port

OMEN

Kadana had described the port of Khreté but what Omen beheld upon their approach on that bracing, fog-shrouded morning was unlike anything he had imagined.

In the distance, a large granite islet jutted out from the mainland at a considerable distance and provided a solid platform for Khreté. The coastal town spread upward at a steep angle, the citadel winding around in a gradual spiral that reminded Omen of cinnamon snail rolls. Seamless stone walls corralled many-storied buildings from the busy harbor to the sizable fortress at its pinnacle. The stoic battlements of the fortress and four round towers took shape as the early-morning fog started to burn off.

I heard Kharakhian architecture was unimaginative. But if Khreté is any measure, Kharakhian builders have dark romance in their souls. I should write a song.

"Khreté is smelling deliciousnessness." Tormy sniffed the air. "Like adventure and shaved truffles."

"Could be, Tormy. Could be," Omen said. *I guess the wet stone could smell mushroomy. But how can he smell the city from all the way out here? Cat's like a bloodhound.*

Omen leaned a little closer, snuggling into Tormy's thick coat to protect himself from windburn. "You don't mind the wind, fuzz face?"

The cat giggled, his orange mane blowing this way and that in the rough breeze.

Kyr, also cuddled into Tormy's fur, blinked sleepily and

1

murmured, "Stone city by the sea." The sunset hues of his irises swirled slowly, seeming to change from violet to red gold.

Trick of the light, Omen convinced himself.

"Pieces scattered on the ground. Broken." Kyr studied the tall walls and the length of the causeway leading to the battlements at the highest point.

"The city isn't broken." Omen put his hand on Kyr's shoulder. "It's built to withstand the fury of the ocean. It's encased in thick walls. Unbreakable."

"The stones defend the city from the sea, but the man with the dove-grey eyes is frozen in time." Kyr's speech took on a distant lilt, as if he were not the one speaking. Omen noticed the quality of the vibrations in Kyr's voice change briefly.

A spike of some sort? Omen wondered if the fluctuating eye color and the shift in vocal quality could be markers of Kyr's odd episodes.

Maybe I can train Tyrin to notice the early warning signs. Maybe Tyrin can help pull him out of it before it starts.

"The man with dove-grey eyes? What man?" Omen asked carefully.

"What man?" Kyr asked, his incandescent eyes large and round. "Is it a joke, Omen? Like knock, knock?"

"What?" Omen couldn't hide his confusion.

"Man," Kyr said firmly and then let out a hearty belly laugh. "That's a good one, Omen!"

Though the sea had been rough at sunrise, the waves smoothed for their arrival. The grey dampness had given way to blue skies, nearly clear with intermittent dustings of thin white clouds.

2

As they glided toward port, Omen admired the water's gradual color change. Deep blues rivaling the sun-streaked sky flowed into brilliant aquamarines that in turn reached up to the fine sands of the cliffside beach.

Shalonie climbed down from the rigging, the ship's tiny monkey lounging tamely on her shoulder. "Built at the beginning of the Set-Manasan dynasty." She cleared her throat. "Khreté was the capital of Kharakhan for hundreds of years. The ramparts are twenty feet thick and have served to protect the citadel from both land and sea. This port city was the Set-Manasan seat of power—"

"Until Indee built the new capital?" Omen asked plainly.

"Caraky," Shalonie agreed. "Built for the coronation of King Khylar."

"My parents went to the coronation, but I didn't get to go," Omen said with an edge of embarrassment. "Something about slurping my soup in elevated company."

"You were ten," Templar threw in, he and Dev having joined them from below deck. Both young men were armed and wearing leather armor in anticipation of going ashore. The sigils embossed on Templar's armor blazed briefly in the sun as if reacting to the light before settling back into a dark charcoal grey that blended in with the black. "It was mostly dull. Mostly." He fell silent.

"Respectfully, I can't exactly agree with that assessment," Dev said. "Granted, my circumstances were very different."

"I thought you said you hadn't been there." Omen hoped to catch a glint of uncertainty in the spy's silver eyes.

"Did I?" Dev's lips curved into a smirk. "Must have been a lie. Or maybe I am lying now—"

"Well, which is it?" Shalonie looked as if she were mak-

3

ing a list of questions to ask Dev later.

"I was stuck with my sister," Templar admitted ruefully, ignoring the Machelli. "But according to my father it was lots of pomp and circumstance, most of it kak Indee had made up." Templar squeezed one eye shut and studied the horizon. "Of course, Terizkand and Kharakhan were barely on speaking terms at that time. My father hated King Charaathalar. Called him a burr on the rear of a donkey. Only agreed to enter into talks once Charaathalar had officially been declared deceased."

Dev's usually unreadable silver eyes flashed as if he were biting down a comment. Omen noticed Shalonie raising an eyebrow.

"Of course, my father liked Indee," Templar continued almost wistfully. "She was bold and fearless. The scuttlebutt was that Indee used wild magic to get Caraky built so fast."

Templar unwrapped a piece of hard Melian cheese and an apple from a folded handkerchief. "Mégeira gave me this. Anybody hungry?"

"I is liking cheese," Tormy mentioned casually, hope twinkling in his amber eyes.

Templar nodded. "I had a feeling." He broke a small piece of the cheese off and threw the rest to Tormy, who snapped it out of the air. Templar handed the smaller piece to Kyr, who stuffed it in his pocket.

The pocket undulated, and a tiny voice yelled out, "It's &*$!^% cheese. My favorite!" The rest of Tyrin's words were lost in hurried munching.

"Wild magic?" Omen shouted as if he'd been smacked upside the head. "Khylar disappeared from Caraky! A city built by wild magic! Maybe he's not even in the Autumn

Lands, maybe he's trapped in the city itself?"

Kyr cried out, then quickly hid his hand behind his back.

"Kyr!" Omen turned toward his brother, realizing with alarm that his careless words had inadvertently triggered the hex. Shame flooded through him. *How? What did I say? I didn't refuse the quest. What triggered it?*

"Kyr, show me your hand."

Slowly, Kyr brought forward his marred hand. Blisters were forming along the mark, spiraling up his wrist. The web of inky black lines was growing and pulsing even as they watched.

"It's the Autumn Lands!" Dev exclaimed. "Say you're going into the Autumn Lands to rescue Khylar. Quickly!"

Praying that Dev was right, Omen swiftly said the words, speaking them clearly and loudly with as much conviction behind them as possible. "I'm going into the Autumn Lands to rescue Khylar." To his relief, the mark on Kyr's hand stopped growing.

"But now the mark's bigger," Omen said, his voice hollow. "A lot bigger."

"Well, at least now we know that you can't even suggest something else happened to Khylar." Dev fished a small jar of ointment from the inner pocket of his coat and handed it across to Omen. Omen recognized the label on its lid as his mother's. Familiar with his mother's potions from a long childhood of scrapes and bruises, Omen knew the concoction would ease Kyr's pain.

Omen carefully smeared the ointment over the burn and then bound Kyr's wrist with the white bandages Dev handed to him. He nodded his thanks to the Machelli, glad at least one of them had the sense to carry such things. *Dev knows what to do to lessen the pain of the hex — either my mother told him, or he has experience with hexes himself. Maybe I shouldn't open my bloody mouth at all! How am I supposed to know what will trigger the hex?*

Templar watched with a bitter twist of his lips. "Indee's a bitch!" he spat out. "I can't even magically or psionically heal the burns."

"Indee might not even realize what she's done," Shalonie tried to defend Indee once again, though she didn't sound convinced.

Her loyalty to the Sundragons runs deep.

"I think this means we have to move faster." Omen felt helpless but determined.

"Your psionic blast already brought us here weeks before Kadana was expecting to arrive." Shalonie scratched at her eyebrow with her thumb as if deep in thought. "We should have arrived about ten days after midsummer — and instead we're arriving almost a week before the solstice."

So we'll be here for the solstice.

"Kadana sent word to her husband a few days ago," Shalonie said. "Another one of her handy magic trinkets, some sort of message box. She put a letter in; it disappeared, and not five minutes later a reply from Diatho came."

"How big was that box?" Templar asked; wheels seemed to be turning in his head.

Shalonie ignored him.

"Diatho should arrive in Khreté by lunch," she said to Omen. "If possible, I'd like to get into the fortress. Rumor has it there's a faulty portal there, and seeing it could help me with my studies. I'll need to know more about portals if we're going to be wandering around in the Mountain of Shadow — that place is filled with portals and traps and

6

doorways into other worlds. The more knowledge I have, the better I'll be able to help you."

"I don't know anything about a faulty portal, but I can get you into the fortress," Dev told them then. He'd pulled a small spyglass from another inside pocket of the metal-studded leather coat he was wearing and peered at the long stone dock they were approaching.

"Can't we ask for an audience?" Omen asked, turning his attention to the tall battlements of the massive structure at the top. The fortress had been the home of King Charaathalar Set-Manasan, and likely still was home to numerous members of his family. As prince of Lydon, Omen had always been granted full access to any castle he'd visited, and since his grandmother Kadana held some sort of title in Kharakhan, he couldn't imagine they'd be denied.

"If you ask for an audience, you'll be welcomed into the Palace Hall — that's that large stone building next to the fortress with the white tower and all the flags," Dev told him, pointing toward the building in question. It appeared to be made of a different type of stone — the outward facade's gleaming white marble designed to catch the eye. Fluttering flags proclaimed that at least one member of the royal family was in attendance. "There's nothing interesting in the Palace Hall. If there is anything to be seen it would be in the fortress, but Indee sealed that off years ago. They won't take us there. Especially not you."

Omen gaped at Dev. *He makes it sound like they have something personal against me.* He couldn't recall ever having had any sort of unpleasant encounter with the Set-Manasans. Khylar and Caythla were the only ones he'd ever met. *And Indee — but she's a Lir Drathos now.*

"Especially not me? What's that supposed to mean?"

Omen asked.

Templar and Shalonie looked at Dev with curiosity.

Dev's lips twitched upward. "The Set-Manasans don't like your father . . . or your mother for that matter. They tend to hold grudges. Wouldn't say anything to your face, but wouldn't even bother to spit on you if you were on fire either."

"Spit on you?" Tyrin piped up, poking his head up from inside Kyr's coat pocket, his little white paws looped over the side. "I is thinking that the saying is that they wouldn't p—"

"Tyrin!" Omen cut the little cat off before he could finish. "He was trying to be polite. We don't say bad words in front of Shalonie."

"Why not?" Tyrin looked baffled. "I is just trying to be accurateness. Shalonie is liking things to be accurateness."

Omen stared hard at the little cat, and Tyrin twitched his ears a few times before letting out a little sniff and sinking back down into Kyr's warm pocket.

Kyr seemed oblivious to the exchange, staring instead at the bandages wrapped around his wrist. Avarice's burn ointment was supposed to take away any pain on contact, but Omen worried the boy was still suffering. *It's not like Kyr would say anything about the pain.*

"So what was it my father—" Omen began again, turning his attention back to Dev.

Dev cut him off, his smirk widening. "You might want to ask your parents that," he told Omen. "I try to stay out of politics, and I definitely have no interest in meddling in your mother's personal affairs. You're welcome to borrow the bonding book if you want to ask her yourself."

Annoyed, Omen turned his attention back to the city.

She wouldn't answer. Would tell me to mind my own business. Avarice had never responded well to his pointed curiosity — she expected him to figure things out for himself. And if he couldn't, then — she'd told him — he'd have no business knowing.

"If you don't meddle in politics, how are you going to get us into the fortress?" Templar asked then, looking intrigued by the entire conversation.

Good question. Omen frowned and glanced back at Dev.

Dev pointed toward the fortress. "See that stone house with the red roof at the base of the battlements?" He indicated one of many manor houses ringing the fortress. "The locals call the area *Fortress Hill.* It's where lesser nobles and wealthy merchants like to live."

The neighboring abodes were all built of the same dark stone, only the tile on the inner roofs distinguishing one from another. The tile colors were quite impressive in variety — reds, blues, greens, golds. The house Dev pointed to had tiles of reddish gold — like untarnished copper. As the fog around the hilltop burned away, the roof caught the sunlight and flashed like flames.

"That's the Machelli Guild House. We can get into the fortress from there." Dev motioned toward the long stone dock the ship was approaching. At the far end, on the main causeway that surrounded the port, Omen spotted a number of carriages. "Kadana has business with the guild. They're waiting for us." He handed over the spyglass without asking.

Omen peered through it toward the dock at the carriages. *Apparently they know how many are in our group. Doubt they accounted for Tormy.* Omen couldn't really see Tormy wanting to ride in a carriage, even if he were tired. The

9

poor cat had grown so restless, Omen didn't expect him to slow down even for a second as soon as his paws hit solid ground.

Along with the carriages and the muscular horses attached to them, Omen saw two tall, dark-haired men standing nearby. *Wonder how long they've been waiting.* He strained to see as many details as possible.

Though well-dressed in the fine doublets expected of wealthy merchants, there was something wild and dangerous about them — even from the distance. Both were well-armed, swords hanging from their sword belts and gleaming daggers strapped to sheaths on their legs. Bits of shiny metal plating were woven through the fine material of the doublets and leather breeches. Omen recognized their profiles and had no doubt that their eyes would be silver. These men looked like the Machellis Omen knew — unlike Dev who, despite his uncanny resemblance to Avarice, was far more delicate and slender than the typical Machelli male.

"Relatives?" he asked, guessing Dev would know the answer. He handed the spyglass to Shalonie who was watching curiously.

"Probably," Dev agreed. "Cousins more likely. Glaive and Foil."

"Those are Kharakhian long swords," Shalonie corrected swiftly as she peered through the spyglass.

Dev laughed at that. "I meant those are their names."

Definitely Machelli.

Shalonie's brow furrowed. "I understand the custom behind the names," she said. "But do you all have actual names as well — like Armand for Omen and Ava for Avarice? And do you ever use them?"

"My mother and I have those names because the

Machelli custom doesn't go over very well in Lydon," Omen admitted. He smiled fondly when he thought of all the times as a child he'd argued with his father's mother, Queen Wraiteea, about his name. She'd finally agreed to call him Omen in private as long as he went by Armand in public. "My grandmother Wraiteea insisted we have proper names. My real name is actually Omen — that's what my mother named me when I was born. And as far as I know, my mother was named Avarice at birth. The Machellis call them hex-names, to ward off bad luck."

"What about you, Dev?" Shalonie asked. "Do you have another name?"

"Lots," he admitted with a smile that gave nothing away. "If you don't like Devastation, make one up. I'll answer to it. Not particularly attached to any of them."

Not the answer she was looking for, Omen noted, grinning at the consternation on Shalonie's face.

"Names can be stolen," Kyr said, his gaze still on his bandaged hand. "Like rings found on the ground and picked up by kings who are no more." He turned his solemn gaze on Omen, the morning sunlight catching in the violet hues of his eyes and making them seem more amber. "There's a monster inside it."

"Inside what, Kyr?" Concern swept through Omen.

The boy's eyes widened, and then he smiled peacefully. "That's a great idea, Omen! I miss fried cakes. There aren't any on the ship — Tyrin and I looked. I hope they have ones with custard inside them. Do you think they know about custard?"

Omen glanced over at Templar who raised his shoulders imperceptibly. They were both willing to take Kadana's words to heart and take more notice of Kyr's strange ram-

11

blings, but it wasn't easy when it always seemed as if he were having a completely separate conversation. "We'll check when we get to shore," he assured his little brother. "I'm sure the Kharakhians know all about custard."

Kadana and Liethan joined them on deck a few moments later, Kadana barking out orders to the sailors around them as they prepared to pull into port.

Khreté, like most port cities, possessed deep-water slips where even a ship the size of the Golden Voyage could dock — though they were limited to a small number of outer piers. Some had only floating wooden docks leading back to the main causeway, but the pier Kadana directed the ship toward was permanent, held up by enormous stone pylons embedded into the sea floor. Omen imagined his grandmother had paid quite a handsome docking fee for the slip.

Tormy started dancing impatiently as the ship glided gracefully toward their final destination. The great vessel slowed down through the elemental magic that controlled it, Kadana herself guiding it into port. The moment they neared the stone pier, several sailors tossed thick ropes to the dockworkers waiting for them, tying the vessel off as others moved to lower the gangplank.

Omen watched in fascination as workers rolled large, intricate cargo cranes into position along the pier to empty the hold. *My dad would love this.* Workers easily hand-cranked the wheels on the side of the cranes to lower the jibs by ropes and pulleys.

Numerous people lined the docks and congregated farther up along the causeway, all having watched the great ship pull into port. From the looks of people pointing toward them, Omen guessed more than one person had spotted Tormy. *A giant orange cat hopping around on the deck, tail lashing back and forth, is pretty hard to miss.* Omen tried to see his cat through a stranger's eyes. *Hope they like cats.*

Tormy's presence in Melia went for the most part unremarked — beyond the numerous people who admired him. The giant cat, while strange, was not the oddest thing to see in that city — the Sundragons dwarfed the cat, and the Melians had no fear of large creatures. And while Tormy had certainly caused a stir the first time Omen had taken him to Lydon, the citizens there had gotten the opportunity to know the cat when he was still relatively small. The Kharakhians would have no such preparations. In a few more months Omen imagined Tormy would be large enough for him to ride.

From the look of things, Tormy was not going to present himself sedately, and Omen didn't imagine that any amount of cajoling would change that.

He patted the cat on the flank and scratched him behind the ears to calm him down, but even before the sailors could finish lowering the gangplank, Tormy took one huge leap over the side of the ship and landed all four paws on the stone pier, causing the workers below to scatter. The cat took off, racing down the pier, turning at the end, and sprinting back to the ship, only to repeat the course over and over again. All the while he shouted at the top of his lungs, "DRY LAND! DRY LAND! I IS LOVING DRY LAND!"

Watching from the upper deck, Kadana roared with laughter. Kyr tittered happily from his place at the ship's railing while holding a remarkably sedate Tyrin.

"We is being a spectacle," Tyrin explained to anyone

13

who wanted to hear.

And it did seem as if all work had stopped as Kharakhians and sailors stared at the giant ball of orange fluff racing up and down the pier.

Initially, the cat gone wild had been met with sounds of concern and even terror, but the panic was short-lived. Before long, Omen saw people beginning to laugh at the sight, and numerous sailors nodded as if they could well understand Tormy's sentiments. *If nothing else he's an extremely cute giant fluffball.*

"You're going to have a serious problem if you ever want to arrive somewhere unseen," Templar remarked as they watched the cat.

So quiet, so stealthy, so cat-like.

Eventually, Tormy calmed down and trotted happily back toward the ship to sit down and wait for the others. While warming himself in the breezy morning sunlight, he thoughtfully positioned himself off to one side, well out of the way but still able to see all.

Satisfied that his cat wasn't going anywhere, Omen headed below deck with Kyr to retrieve their belongings and prepare to disembark.

He'd already packed his things — keeping track of everything he'd need for himself, Tormy, Tyrin, and Kyr for the journey. Like Templar, he wore a light coat of armor — thin, interwoven metal scales made of lightweight Lydonian silverleaf that would turn most blades. And though it was summer, the weather was more autumn-like, and the wind blowing in off the ocean was cold. Omen shrugged on a knee-length leather coat over the armor, before slipping his sword belt over his left shoulder, and strapping the enormous two-handed blade across his back. He adjusted the quick release buckle that rested against his chest, allowing him to unfasten the sword belt instantly and draw the sword from its scabbard easily. He'd learned the painful way that it was too difficult to draw over his shoulder, the blade far too long to clear the scabbard unless he'd released it from the belt.

"Do you have everything?" he asked Kyr. Omen fastened two thin daggers to his belt and tied them down to each thigh. Then he grabbed his backpack along with the lightweight saddle he'd have to coax onto Tormy's back. The larger the cat grew, the stronger he became, and the more could fit into his saddlebags.

Kyr held up the small traveling satchel Avarice had given him in Melia. Save for a few changes of clothes, he didn't have much, leaving the bulk of their supplies for Omen to manage. Kyr wore a finely cut leather coat also made by Omen's mother — Lydonian design with a high collar and inner silk lining. It was made of dyed brown and green leather and would hold up well to travel, but it offered little in the way of armored protection.

Omen worried that Kyr would need something more substantial.

He's quick; he hides well, Omen reminded himself. *And he knows to run if there's trouble. Besides, knowing my mother, she wove protection spells into that coat.*

The boy also held the thin sheathed blade Omen had selected for him before they left Melia — a Lydonian sword also made of silverleaf. Kyr seemed uncertain what to do with it, holding it out to Omen.

Omen took the blade and clipped the scabbard to the metal loop on the boy's belt. "You should always have a weapon on you," he told Kyr. "And remember that this one is sharp. So be careful with it!"

If worse came to worst, he wanted Kyr to have some means of defending himself, even though the lesson in the Melian park had still been the only time they'd practiced. *Should have worked with him during the crossing,* he scolded himself. But while the boy didn't have any understanding of how to use a sword, he was extremely skilled with his carving knife and certainly understood the dangers of sharp edges. *It'll have to do for now.*

Kyr nodded blithely, accepting Omen's word without hesitation.

Tyrin, who was watching them from the desk, leaped with grace onto Kyr's shoulder. The boy instinctively turned at the last moment to make his shoulder more readily accessible. The kitten settled contently down, tiny claws digging into the leather of the extra padding Avarice had added to Kyr's coat.

"All right, let's get going, and remember you two, stay with me. This isn't Melia. Don't go wandering off by yourself," Omen reminded them both. Kyr was not prone to wandering — he followed silently after Omen no matter where he went. But sometimes Tormy and Tyrin were harder to corral, and he feared they could manage to get the boy lost if he wasn't vigilant.

Templar, Shalonie, and Liethan were waiting for them on deck when they arrived, all of them armed and decked-out for travel. Shalonie's dragon blade gleamed brightly in the sunlight, and Omen had to grin when he saw that Liethan was at last wearing boots.

Liethan noticed the angle of his eyeline. "I do occasionally wear shoes," he told him. "The Corsair Isles are all white sandy beaches, but my mother also owns land in the heart of Kharakhan. Spent a lot of time hunting in the Kharakhian forests." Along with the long sword the Corsairs tended to favor, Liethan also carried a crossbow which he had strapped to his backpack.

Omen glanced briefly over at the dock to assure himself that Tormy was still waiting in the sunlight. The cat was eating a large fish that he'd most likely begged from some fisherman and that Omen would no doubt have to pay for. He looked to the others. "Where are Kadana and Dev?"

"Kadana is talking to the harbormaster," Shalonie told him, pointing a bit further down the dock where Omen could see his grandmother talking to a tall burly man with a bushy black beard and dark skin. "Wanted to warn him about the leviathan and the troubles with the summer route so he can pass the word on to the other captains."

"And Dev's up there," Templar added, pointing toward the long causeway beyond the docks where the carriages were still waiting. "No doubt plotting something dastardly with your Machelli cousins."

Omen glared at him. "The Machelli are merchants, the guild is a merchant's guild, regardless of whatever ridiculous stories you might have heard."

Templar laughed out loud. "Even most of the Machellis call themselves 'information brokers' and not merchants . . . They're spies, and that's the polite term."

"They're merchants," Omen insisted. "They sell stuff — food, spices, clothes. My mother designs clothing — see this nice coat she made for Kyr." While Omen was well aware that the extended Machelli clans were far more than mere merchants, he tended to ignore the more unsavory side of the family. Admittedly, their wolf-bred Shilvagi blood made them ill-suited for the more placid life of shopkeepers and tradesmen, but he didn't consider them bad people. They were rowdy, temperamental, often aggressive, and mostly mysterious. And his mother had systematically kept any darker aspect away from the immediate family in Melia.

"I like my coat," Kyr offered. "It has extra deep pockets for Tyrin. Avarice says it makes me look lovely." The plain-spokenness of his voice, as if he were imparting the weather, caused the others to burst out in guffaws. Kyr laughed along, looking only slightly disoriented.

Tyrin, still seated on top of Kyr's shoulder, preened and fluffed his tail, nuzzling his face into the boy's pale, golden hair.

"We is being the loveliest," the little kitten agreed with a purr.

"Come on then, lovely." Omen chuckled with a shake of his head. "Let's go ashore."

At the bottom of the gangplank, Tormy happily licked his chops clean of the last remnants of the fish. "People is being so nicestness here!" the cat purred. "I is telling the dockworkers that I is being really hungry and they is all throwing fish at me."

"And who said Kharakhians were dull-witted?" Templar looked around, making sure Kadana hadn't heard him. *If a giant cat told me he was hungry, I'd probably throw fish at him too.*

Kadana joined them a moment later, the harbormaster following after her. The man kept a wary eye on Tormy. "Your beasty there tame?" the man boomed out to Omen.

Tormy began spinning in circles, his large plume of a tail whacking Omen and Templar repeatedly. "Beasty, beasty, beasty? Where is being the beasty?" the cat jabbered

18

frantically, looking around with keen interest.

"He was talking about me, Tormy," Templar assured him.

Tyrin, still balancing on Kyr's shoulder, narrowed his eyes dangerously as if understanding the truth.

Worried that the harbormaster was about to be lambasted with the kitten's blistering tongue, Omen stepped forward to assure the man. "Everything is fine," he told him quickly, holding up the saddle he was still carrying. "See I even have a saddle."

The man nodded gruffly, his eyes still distrustful.

Tormy sat down and scratched at his ear with his back paw. "I is thinking the saddle is being for me, Omy? Is it being for Templar?"

The question set Templar choking with laughter; he turned away attempting to hide his mirth at Omen's dilemma.

Tyrin stood on his hind legs on Kyr's shoulder, front paws perched on the boy's head so that he could glare at the harbormaster. The tiny cat's tail lashed violently back and forth. "Hey, mister!" the little cat shouted.

Kadana fought hard to keep a somber expression but failed.

"Really . . . Everything's fine!" Omen cut in, glaring briefly at Templar and throwing his grandmother a pleading look. "No beasties here, and yes, Tormy, it's your saddle, though if Templar doesn't shut up, he's going to be wearing it. Now, are we ready to go?"

"Yes." Kadana took the reins of the conversation. "The Machellis are waiting for us." She motioned toward the causeway, before calling out a few final orders to her crew. The Corsair sailors were attaching the hook block of one of

19

the cargo cranes to the first crate of the ship's stored haul, the unloading of cargo in full swing as if choreographed.

Omen quickly ushered Tormy and Kyr forward.

Tyrin, hardly appeased, continued to glare the prickliest of his spite at the harbormaster as the lot of them hurried up the stone dock and toward the awaiting Machelli carriages.

Chapter 2: Guild

DEV

D ev headed swiftly up the stone pier, making his way toward the upper causeway where his contacts were waiting. He carried his personal belongings in a worn satchel. Save for weapons, he tended to travel light. He had a sword strapped to his belt along with numerous daggers, and the recurve bow slung over one shoulder. The bow's quiver of arrows was secured to the side of his pack. Even more deadly weapons were hidden in various pockets of his leather coat, along with blades secured beneath the thick straps of his black leather armor.

For the most part, the dock workers along the pier ignored him, their attention still on the amazing sight of the giant orange cat near the equally impressive Ven'tarian ship. But one or two Kharakhians glanced in Dev's direction as he passed, politely nodded, and then swiftly moved out of his way. While Kharakhians were not as a rule polite, his unmistakable coloring and the silver eyes, marked him as a Machelli. Kharakhians knew to avoid conflict with the guild.

Glaive and Foil both straightened from their casual poses as he neared the carriages, the two men eyeing him cautiously, sizing him up. While Dev had never met them, Avarice had told him their names via the bonding book. He recognized the type: Scaalian-raised warriors, direct from the Machelli clan's mountain fortress. Educated enough to be given positions of importance in the Kharakhian guild

21

house, they were nonetheless wild-born and savage at heart. Dev caught the feral look they gave each other and knew they were baffled by his appearance.

"Devastation," he introduced himself and saw two pairs of silver eyes widen simultaneously.

Glaive — he knew him by the crescent scar on his cheek — opened his mouth, but Foil elbowed his companion hard in the side, silencing him before he could speak.

Dev trained his gaze on Foil, recognizing him instantly as the more dominant personality of the two.

The name Devastation was well-known among the Machelli clans, though truthfully he'd spent little time with the family. He also realized that his reputation did not match his appearance. Dev possessed Avarice's refined features, and though he was taller than Avarice, he would never have the height or the muscle most of the Machelli men were gifted with. He also knew he looked far younger than he should — the name Devastation had been known in the clans since the early days of Avarice's father's rule.

"You're not what I was expecting," Foil commented, his tone slick.

Not stupid then. He knew Avarice had contacted the guild house, would have told them to afford him and those with him every courtesy. Whether they believed he was who he claimed to be or not, they were not foolish enough to directly disobey Avarice. Avarice had told him that Glaive and Foil were both clever and would serve them properly, but were at heart Machellis who would push the boundaries to see what they could get away with.

"I never am," he agreed mildly, glancing briefly at Glaive to see his reaction. Whatever momentary spike of protest might have stirred in the man had obviously been contained, and he seemed content to let Foil speak. "You have Lady Kadana's information?" Dev asked.

Foil nodded. "Back at the house. We've had one of our girls watching the tavern. She can tell Lady Kadana everything she needs to know." Foil turned his attention toward the ship.

Dev glanced over his shoulder, spotting the others moving across the pier at a fast clip.

"Didn't expect a huge cat," Foil said then. "What is it?"

"Probably shouldn't let the cat hear you call him an *it*," Dev suggested. "He's Omen's companion."

Foil and Glaive both startled at that. "Omen Daenoth? Avarice's son?"

Dev bit the inside of his cheek — Avarice hadn't told them who he was traveling with, not that it surprised him. If word had gotten out that Avarice's son was arriving, the city would have been filled with Machelli upstarts seeking to challenge the boy for the sheer bragging rights of saying they had done so. "We also have the crown prince of Terizkand, the daughter of a Melian Hold Lord, and the son of a Corsair duchess. I suggest you mind your manners. The Melian and the Corsair are too polite to do anything, but the Terizkandian is a Nightblood. And well . . . you know what Lady Kadana will do if you step out of line."

At the mention of a Nightblooded companion, both Machellis raised their right hands and made the instinctive sign to ward off evil. The two men exchanged another long glance before settling back against the side of the carriage to wait for their charges. "Who's the elvin child?" Foil asked as the group approached.

"Kyr Daenoth, Omen's brother, and he's got a smaller cat with him — don't mess with either of them, the little cat's

23

dangerous," Dev told them. If there was one thing he was certain about, any serious threat to Kyr would send the entire group into a rage.

If the men were curious, they knew better than to openly ask questions about Kyr's parentage — he might be Omen's brother, but he was definitely not a Machelli. Still, Dev could see their wheels turning.

"Don't often see elvin children out in public," Foil noted. "Might want to stop him from talking to that merchant — the pig uses psionics to make people buy his wares."

Alarm washed through Dev.

As if on cue, Kyr had stopped to look at a merchant's stall and was running his hand over the array of metal trinkets and jeweled daggers on display.

On the ship, Dev had discovered that while the boy possessed psionics — not surprising because of his lineage — he was completely untrained. An individual not gifted with psionics wouldn't even notice the merchant's meddling, but to an unshielded psionicist the intrusion would be extremely painful, if not damaging.

Fortunately, the boy wore the shielding bracelet 7 Daenoth had given to him, but Dev's concern spiked when a flicker of alarm crossed Kyr's delicate features. *Blasted unpredictable magic items!* The boy raised his right hand to stare at the bracelet on his wrist, which glowed with a white light. If the merchant continued to push, the boy could be injured despite his magical protection.

"Tyrin!" Dev shouted, taking a quick stride forward. He saw the little cat, still perched on Kyr's shoulder, swivel his ears, though his attention stayed focused on the wares on the table Kyr was investigating. "Bite the merchant!"

His words caught everyone's attention — Omen's most

notably as he immediately spun around, sparing Dev a baleful glare before sprinting toward Kyr and the orange kitten. But to Dev's surprise, the kitten didn't even hesitate — Tyrin leaped at the merchant's face, claws extended. Even across the distance of the causeway, Dev could hear the little cat's hiss and yowl.

The merchant yelped.

The cat's attack did the trick. The bright glow of Kyr's bracelet faded. And while Omen and Templar both reached for the kitten at the same time, Dev saw that Omen had noticed the flare. Instantly, he realized what was going on, and — while Templar grabbed the kitten — Omen grabbed the merchant by the front of his doublet, lifted him bodily over his stall table and tossed the man ten feet over the side of the stone walkway into the ocean.

The Kharakhian merchant shrieked as he flew through the air, and everyone nearby stopped to stare at the spectacle. The inhuman strength Omen had just displayed would be the talk of the town for weeks.

Though the commotion had caught the attention of the crowd, the Kharakhian population was instinctively leery about getting involved in anything out of the ordinary. If nothing else, Tormy's presence alone was enough to make them keep their distance.

Dev spotted several harbor patrols watching closely but making no move to get involved. They no doubt recognized Kadana's ship's flag and would have also noticed the Machelli carriages waiting on the causeway. They dreaded investigating a noble without being summoned. To help out, Dev motioned them away with a wave of his hand as he returned to the group.

By the time Dev reached their side, Omen was already

speaking to Kyr, checking for injury while the rest of the group flocked worriedly around him. Tormy's tail was fluffed to enormous proportions, his ears pulled back against his head. Surprisingly the only calm one in the group appeared to be Tyrin, who despite being grasped quite tightly in Templar's hands, was preening.

"My bracelet is warm," Kyr complained to Omen. "And I really want to buy something." He sounded confused by the latter admission.

The fact that he was speaking at all assured Dev that no serious harm had been done. He supposed that if the bracelet could shield Kyr's mind from the Widow Maker, a trinkets merchant couldn't really do any permanent damage.

"Did that man psionically attack him?" Shalonie asked, disgusted. "Why would someone do something like that? Kyr's just a boy!"

"He was trying to influence him into buying something," Dev explained. Neither Kadana nor Templar or Liethan looked surprised, but both Omen and Shalonie looked appalled.

Dev sighed. *Melians! The Sundragons should have kept all of you safely behind magical borders.* While he knew Omen wasn't technically a Melian, the young man had lived the majority of his life in the beautiful city. *And it's not like Omen would even notice if someone psionically attacked him. The attack would bounce right off.* The Daenoths' psionics were in a class unto themselves. Omen had unbreachable shields — the merchant's meddling wouldn't have even registered with him.

"Welcome to Kharakhan," Dev told them, and Kadana nodded her sentiment.

"He's right — this isn't Melia," she informed her grandson. "Why hasn't Kyr been trained?"

A mixture of irritation and remorse flashed through Omen's multi-colored eyes; for a moment Dev would have sworn they both glowed a deep vibrant red. *Cerioth's colors!*

"Because I've been too busy teaching him how to live in society!" Omen exclaimed. "How to read, how to write, how to dress himself. In the last five months, he's learned how to speak three different languages!" He broke off his angry tirade. "Nightfire! Why is my father always right? He told me—"

Templar clapped Omen on the back, looking nearly as remorseful as his friend. "It'll be fine. He'll be trained . . . Eventually."

"I'm all right, Omen," Kyr said earnestly, looking more upset by his brother's distress than the psionic attack. Dev wasn't certain Kyr even understood what had happened. "My mind is green and growing," the boy continued. "I know how to use the right fork. And the spoon is for soup. That's important. Avarice said so."

Omen smiled weakly. "Yes, Kyr."

The boy reached to take his kitten from Templar.

"Is I being amazingnessness or what?" Tyrin shouted at the crowd as Kyr placed him back on his shoulder. "I is being a fierce warrior cat!"

"You is being amazinglyestness!" Tormy exclaimed in complete agreement.

That broke the tension.

Quickly, Kadana urged them to continue toward the causeway. "Just like herding cats," she murmured the words like a chant. "Just like herding cats."

As the group proceeded toward the carriages, Dev noticed Templar eyeing the merchant's stall and then glancing toward the water's edge where the man was quietly dog-paddling to shore. The lack of shouts for help convinced Dev that the merchant realized he'd severely miscalculated. *Got off easy.*

Dev saw Templar lift a small, jeweled dagger from the merchant's unmonitored table; no doubt the table would be picked clean before the man made it back to shore. *Serves you right.* Kharakhians were opportunists. But to Dev's surprise, rather than pocketing the dagger, Templar presented it to Kyr. "Here, Kyr, a present for your troubles," he told the boy.

The boy looked delighted by the gift and smiled as he took it. "Can I eat it?" he asked hopefully.

Dev frowned at the question but to his surprise, Templar didn't seem to find it even remotely strange. "No, but I bet you can carve things with it. You like carving."

"I like carving," the boy agreed brightly. He reached into his right pocket and removed something from it. He held the item out to Kadana. "I made this for you." On his palm was a small wooden replica of the Golden Voyage, carved with the most extraordinary detail. They all stopped to marvel at it.

"That's fantastic, my boy," Kadana thanked him, leaving the boy pink-faced and casting his eyes shyly to the ground.

It was several more minutes before the group managed to work their way along the causeway and to the carriages. Glaive and Foil greeted them with polite respect as the drivers came to open the doors and stow luggage. Both Machellis kept their distance from Omen. Dev supposed that seeing the young man lift the fat merchant over his head and fling him through the air like a sack of potatoes had curbed any thought of challenging Avarice's son.

Tormy poked his head inside one of the carriages, investigating, before backing out and lashing his tail back and forth. "I is walking!" he announced, though considering he was far too big to get inside the carriage, his point was somewhat moot.

Dev caught hold of Foil's arm before he could board the last of the carriages. "I probably should have mentioned," he told the man quietly. "Kyr is a favorite of Avarice's. If she found out he'd been hurt while the two of you stood there and watched . . . well . . . I'm sure you can imagine what she'd do."

Naked fear flashed in Foil's silver eyes.

Dev sneered. "You should have warned me immediately that there was a potential threat." *They waited until it was too late because they wanted to see what everyone would do.*

The meek nod Foil gave him assured Dev he understood his error. *Not that I'll trust him not to do it again.* Though admittedly, Dev didn't trust anyone, so nothing had really changed.

Dev made certain the others were comfortable in the carriages — Shalonie in the second one, Templar and Liethan in the last — before he climbed up beside the driver of the first carriage that contained Omen, Kadana, and Kyr. "To the Machelli Guild House!" He motioned the drivers forward and relaxed minutely for the first time since the start of their journey.

Chapter 3: Machelli

OMEN

O men, seated beside Kyr in the carriage, Kadana in the seat opposite him, frowned as the door closed. The carriage was completely enclosed, even the window opening sealed with glass and covered with a small curtain. The cushions and the walls of the carriage were all thickly padded and lined with a dark red velvet that made the interior seem darker than it was. The only illumination was the bright sunlight flickering in from around the curtain — Omen imagined at night the interior would be almost completely black.

The confined space made him uncomfortable, though Kyr at least seemed content, leaning against his side as he watched Tyrin explore the small interior. The kitten climbed around on the cushions and up over the top of them, and then peered under the curtain to stare out the window.

Omen swiftly twitched back the curtain so that the sunlight could flood the space. The opening also afforded him a clear view of Tormy who was prancing alongside the carriage, seeming content to wander about the street exploring the sights. Omen saw more than one person scramble to get out of the cat's way while simultaneously making a sign to ward against the supernatural.

"Bit coffin-like, isn't it?" he asked Kadana. The carriages in Melia were not like this — they were open to the air and roomy. In the mild Melian winter months, the carriages would be outfitted with light hoods to keep off the rain or snow.

"Kharakhian gentry don't mix with the common folk," Kadana told him. "It's not considered healthy for classes to mingle."

The look of disgust on Kadana's face made it clear to Omen what she thought of the custom. *Then again she, my mother, and most of their generation were all common-born. Even Indee.* As far as Omen knew, his father 7 was actually the only member of their group who came from a royal bloodline. And while the Machellis reigned over the wilds of Scaalia, even in that land nobody would refer to them as nobles.

Omen glanced down at Kyr.

The boy was watching his kitten flipping round and round in a near silent game of chase-the-tail. The jeweled dagger Templar had given him still in hand, Kyr spun the sheathed blade around in circles between his agile fingers.

"You all right, Kyr?" Omen asked.

The boy nodded silently.

Better keep an eye on him.

"So you've taught him three languages in five months?" Kadana asked suddenly in High Kharakhian. Omen suspected she was testing Kyr to see what his third language might be.

"Yes. Well me and the cats," Omen answered back in High Kharakhian. "Melian, Merchant's Common, and Sul'eldrine."

Kadana raised an eyebrow. "Sul'eldrine, the Divine Tongue? Why? Avarice has never been particularly devout — neither has your father."

"The cats taught him Sul'eldrine," Omen responded.

31

Tyrin paused in his play, ears perked forward as if analyzing their words. As far as Omen knew the cat didn't know Kharakhian — not unless his sister Lilyth had taught him. "Sul'eldrine is their native tongue."

Kadana let out a surprised, "Huh." She glanced over at Tyrin as if reassessing what she knew about the cats. "Are the cats the reason he switches languages mid-sentence?"

Making up words and conjugating them into bizarre concoctions was the cats' prerogative; Omen had never thought about their peculiar linguistic eccentricities. He also knew they were not the reason for Kyr's strange dialect and mishmash of tongues.

"It's been only five months since I found him," Omen told her. "He doesn't have a large enough vocabulary in any one language to stay consistent. He does his best — at least he's not constantly speaking Kahdess anymore."

Worry swept over him. Many of the things his father warned were coming forward to haunt his thoughts. *I have to keep Kyr safe.*

"What is it, my boy?" Kadana asked, the warmth and concern in her voice propping him up.

She really is my grandma.

"There never seems to be enough time in the day to learn all the things my father insists I learn," he confessed. "And yet every single time I go out into the world to do something, I need to know all the things I haven't gotten around to yet. Like teaching Kyr how to use his psionics or at the very least how to shield his mind. My father told me . . ."

Kadana leaned back against the carriage wall, stretching her long legs out, and crossing her booted feet at the ankles. "Don't worry about it, kid." Her sage confidence calmed him. "Your mother and I and all the others . . . we didn't know anything when we were your age either. You'll manage as long as you keep your wits about you. And you've got good friends. Templar and Liethan are bit crazy and impulsive, but they're both loyal. And Shalonie's brilliant."

"And Dev?" Omen asked, grimacing.

"He's a Machelli," Kadana said as if stating the obvious. "He's attracted to trouble like a moth to open flame, but he's clever enough to avoid getting burned. Just like Avarice, always pragmatic." She glanced briefly out the window.

Tormy hopped about on the street, running strange zigzag patterns on the road. He swerved from one side to the other and swiveled his head around as if trying to see everything at once.

"And these cats of yours . . . A lot more useful than I expected. Brave beyond reason." She glanced down at Tyrin who was still watching her curiously. She gently patted the kitten on the head.

"What language is you speaking?" Tyrin asked, head cocked to the side, ears perked forward.

Omen tried to remember if either he or Kadana had uttered any curse words — that was typically the only thing that ever drew the kitten's attention to a new language.

"High Kharakhian," Kadana told the cat, switching to Merchant's Common. "It's the language most city dwellers in Kharakhan speak."

The kitten flicked his whiskers thoughtfully, and then leaped across the seat to land gracefully in Kyr's lap. Tyrin settled down and purred beneath the boy's fingers. "It is being very bumpy," the little cat explained.

It took Omen a moment to realize that Tyrin was speaking about the carriage ride and not about the language. The constant bounce of the wheels over the cobblestone roads was growing uncomfortable. He guessed that Tormy had the right of it — walking freely instead of being trapped inside a carriage. Were it not for the unseasonably cool winds blowing through the streets, Omen suspected the interior of the carriage would be hot as well.

Know several small spells and cantrips that could take care of that, he thought restlessly.

"We'll be there soon," Kadana told the kitten.

Tyrin gave a tiny *meow* and dug his narrow claws into the leather of Kyr's trousers.

"You know, we'll have to get you into the fortress," Kadana said abruptly.

"Why?" Omen was taken aback. "That's where Shalonie wants to go. To look at some portal. Is this about . . ."

"I don't know anything about a portal," Kadana said with a dismissive wave of her hand. "But if you want to get into the faerie lands, you are going to need a faerie-built instrument."

"Why?" Omen asked, baffled.

"There are thousands of portals in the Mountain of Shadow. The hard part is finding the right one. Easiest way to open up a portal into the faerie lands is to have a faerie bard play a faerie instrument. They can't resist that."

"Who?"

"The faerie. . . The Gate should open easily."

"What does that have to do with the fortress?" Omen pressed.

"Well, you're our faerie bard for this trip—"

Omen coughed and had a hard time catching his breath again.

"Oh yes, you are it, my boy. You have Beren's blood in

34

your veins after all. And I happen to know that one of Beren's instruments — faerie made — is hidden in the fortress. You'll need it."

"Beren's—"

"Not my story to tell. Suffice it to say that the Set-Manasans shouldn't have it. And Beren will be pleased. I think it's your duty to steal it back. And I will help you." She smiled brightly.

Unsure what to do with the information, Omen leaned back in his seat and closed his eyes. *This is getting more complicated by the moment.*

Before long, they neared the rising hill at the center of the city. The road wound like a ribbon upward to the top. When they reached the copper-roofed guild house, the carriages passed through tall metal gates into a cobbled courtyard in front of an imposing building.

Grateful to be done with the ride, Omen shoved open the door and got out of the carriage, hardly waiting for it to slow down.

A swarthy man wearing black and silver livery rushed from his post by the house's impressive entrance and held the carriage door. Young stable hands came from around the side of the house to take control of the carriages, and a handful of other men and women emerged to wait in a semicircle near the door. Omen noticed that all of them were wearing various pieces of silver jewelry that bore the Machelli wolf head coat of arms, marking them all as guild members. The keystone above the great double door entrance to the main house bore the same mark.

Dev leaped down from the top of the carriage where he'd been riding, and stood beside Omen, making no effort to greet anyone.

Glaive and Foil, however, hurried forward to greet one of the men standing near the entrance. They spoke quietly to him. The man in question was tall and well-muscled, his dark hair and neatly trimmed beard streaked through with grey, and his silver eyes marked him clearly as another relative.

No doubt another distant cousin or uncle I knew nothing about.

"His name is Feud," Dev told Omen quietly. "He knew your grandfather. He's old school."

"Old school?" Omen asked, wondering what precisely that meant. He'd stayed out of Machelli politics.

"Not happy a woman is ruling the clans," Dev explained. "Smart enough not to say anything about it though."

Omen considered. *First I've heard of that!* He hadn't had many dealings with his Machelli relatives. None of the ones he'd met had ever said anything negative about his mother. He was beginning to think there was a lot about his mother's life he didn't know.

The older man came forward then and inclined his head respectfully to all of them. "Omen," he greeted. It was customary among the Machellis to forgo the use of titles within the family. That the man had chosen to do so suggested he considered himself a close relative and not simply some distant cousin.

Omen kept his face neutral.

"I am Feud Machelli," the man continued. "Welcome to our guild house." Feud nodded a curt greeting to Dev. "Devastation, you haven't changed." Something tight in his voice gave away his unease.

"Clean living is the secret to a youthful appearance," Dev replied with a smug smile. Without further courtesy, he set about introducing the other members of the group.

At Kadana's name, Feud bowed deeply. "Please enter our halls," he said formally, quoting from a memorized passage. "We offer safety and sustenance to the friends of the wolf and her kin."

Wonder what that's from.

They were ushered through the great doors into the guild house and swiftly shown into a large parlor elegantly decorated with dark, ornate furniture and an abundance of silver and blue brocade. The dark wood paneling on the walls was etched with thin silver filigree, and the stone floor bore a thick blue rug, the Machelli coat of arms woven into the center. Along with the ornate filigrees, Omen noticed numerous artistic sigils that he suspected were hex marks and wards against a plethora of spells and curses. He knew that silver was a strong ward against necromancy, and it was poisonous to many dark creatures. He marveled at the copiousness.

And I thought my mother was superstitious and paranoid! Omen recognized some of the symbols because he'd seen them in his own house. *But never this extreme.* He saw Shalonie studying several of the marks.

"Is this typical?" she asked Omen quietly, wrinkling her brow.

"Dev?" Omen searched.

"Typical enough," the young Machelli admitted. "But some of the precautions are because it's Kharakhan. Kharakhan isn't the most stable place in the world. Pays to be prepared."

Kadana snorted. "After the first time a random portal opens up in your dining room while you're eating and killer giant squids pop out, you start warding your house," she told all of them, sounding as if she were speaking from experience. "The magic in this land is wild and unpredictable. Some would even say it's broken."

"Does anyone know why it's so . . . random?" Shalonie asked, ever curious.

"Not that I've heard." Kadana didn't seem concerned.

"My Aunt Arra did a study on it," Liethan admitted. "But every answer she ever got only led to more questions. She always called Kharakhan a crossroads, said things ended up here that just didn't belong, but she never knew why."

"Maybe Kyr knows," Templar suggested mischievously, throwing a sidelong glance at the boy.

Kyr was sitting on the floor near the unlit fireplace playing with a corded tassel he'd taken from one of the curtains. Tyrin was chasing the tassel as Kyr dangled it over his head. Tormy sat beside them, watching in fascination and ready to pounce.

Tormy would destroy the whole room. Hope he doesn't join in, Omen worried but did nothing to interfere.

At Templar's words, Kyr paused and looked up, his large eyes guileless, his face the picture of innocence.

"He knows," the boy said softly, his voice carrying through the suddenly silent room. "The face that stares with eyes that do not blink, looks upon the endless sea and whispers in our dreams."

"Templar!" Omen reprimanded sharply. *Creepy! Creepy! Creepy!*

"Sorry I asked!" Templar threw him an apologetic look. "It was only a joke."

A noise at the door drew their attention away from Kyr. Feud entered, followed by several maids who carried an assortment of trays and platters with tea and snacks: cakes, pastries, cold meats, and fruits.

The food immediately caught the eager attention of Kyr and the cats. They padded after the maids to the far side of the room where everything was set down on the large mahogany sideboard that ran the length of the wall.

A young, dark-haired woman accompanied Feud. She curtsied as Feud introduced her. "Lady Kadana, this is Misery. She's obtained the materials you asked for."

Misery, silver-eyed and blessed with warm olive skin, was charming but plain. She moved with feline grace and a fighter's strength. Despite the girl's bearing, Omen suspected she could easily get lost in a crowd.

No one would even notice her. Probably her biggest asset.

As Misery handed Kadana a small folder filled with papers, Templar chuckled under his breath and leaned toward Omen. "Right, just merchants," he murmured.

Omen glared. "Those could be shipping manifests."

Kadana leafed through the papers. "So, it *is* them then, and they're here in the city." She nodded as she scanned the information. Glancing up, she motioned the woman to the far side of the room, away from the others. "Tell me what you observed."

"Definitely shipping manifests," Templar agreed sarcastically.

Omen watched closely, his curiosity piqued. Misery, however, kept her voice low, and he couldn't hear what she was telling his grandmother.

Guess I'll have to wait until she is ready to tell me herself.

"Omen wants to see the fortress," Dev told Feud bluntly during tea service.

The young maid standing to Feud's left hurried to pour a drop of milk into his cup and neatly scampered away before the man could form a reply.

Feud's lips thinned. "You know the way, Dev," he stated. "But don't get yourself caught — that passage isn't publicly known. Princess Harla is the only family member in residence at the moment, and she's hosting a gathering of friends at the White Palace this afternoon. Her attention will be there. Stick to the side passages — they are mostly unwatched. The guards keep to the main halls — but no one will be happy if they see you. Especially Avarice. And I'd stay out of the east wing. It's cursed; no one goes there. Even thieves avoid it."

Feud shifted uncomfortably in his chair as if annoyed by the request, and for a moment Omen thought he might protest further. He set his teacup down on the table with a hard clink of porcelain and waved his hand dismissively at them. "Show him the old throne room — it's still spectacular. The entire throne and dais are made of crystal and gold. It's quite impressive."

"Of course," Dev agreed.

"Who's Princess Harla?" Liethan asked.

"King Khylar's aunt," Feud explained. "Harla Set-Manasan, sister of the former King Charaathalar. She can be difficult to deal with, so I'd avoid her." He glanced briefly over his shoulder at Kadana as if debating his next words. "Before you go . . . I received word from Avarice that I was to assist you in any way possible, so I should probably inform you that there is a rumor going around that King Khylar is missing."

Omen shot a look at Kyr who was still happily eating by the sideboard, the cats sitting beside him. *If I'm not careful*

I'll activate the hex mark again. Luckily his companions were not bound by the same restrictions.

"Missing?" Shalonie asked, laying a hand on Omen's arm, letting him know that she would ask the necessary questions. "How do you know?"

Feud stroked his chin. "As I said, it is just a rumor. But Fel'torin of Nelminor, Khylar's brother-in-law, has been appearing in public in the king's stead. And there are other rumors, dark ones, that are spreading quickly through the merchant's quarters. They say the king's highways are unsafe. The roads themselves are supposed to be warded against magic, and they're well-patrolled. But the patrols have been going missing, and there are creatures appearing where they do not belong." He paused, thoughtfully amending his words. "Well, more so than usual, anyway. They've never really been that safe. And yesterday a merchant arrived in Market Square with Goblin Fruit."

Shalonie scooted closer. "Actual Goblin Fruit? Ripe Goblin Fruit?"

Feud nodded. "The winemakers fought over it at first. But then more of the fruit showed up today. If the taverns start serving Goblin Ale in large quantities, there will be blood in the streets."

Omen leaned back in his chair, noticing that the others looked as confused as he did. *At least I'm not the only one who doesn't know what Goblin Fruit is.*

Seeing their blank looks, Shalonie hurried to explain. "Goblin Fruit is found only in the wilderness and only on one day out of the year, the autumn equinox."

"The day the Autumn Gate is opened?" Templar guessed.

Shalonie nodded.

41

"The fruit can be dangerous to eat," Shalonie continued. "It causes feelings of great euphoria, but it is often followed by mindless rage. And any liquor made from it only amplifies the effects, and tends to be highly addictive. But since it can't be domestically grown, and you can only harvest small quantities of it one day of the year, it's mostly considered a novelty. Though highly prized."

"Wonderful," Omen groused. *One thing leads to another, and it all goes quickly spinning out of control. My mother was right when she said this would all very likely go horribly wrong. I'm beginning to see why she and her friends spent so much time in Kharakhan — they would have thrived on the constant chaos.*

"What about my cousin, Lady Tara?" Liethan asked Feud. "Has anyone seen her?"

Feud shook his head. "No, not her, nor her sister Knight Tylith. The priestesses in The Lady's Temple are not happy about it either. Lady Tara was one of their strongest healers and she hasn't been seen in a while. They're starting to make noise about the subject — which means the Set-Manasans are starting to grow restless. They won't move against Fel'torin of Nelminor openly, but they won't sit idle for long."

"Perhaps, I could employ the services of the guild to inquire more deeply after my cousins," Liethan said with steel in his voice. "I'd like to make arrangements as soon as possible."

Feud snapped his fingers, and before he could put his hand back on the table, the maid who'd poured the tea returned with a scroll, an inkwell and quill.

Liethan glanced at the contract briefly, and then handed it to Shalonie for closer inspection.

"I only want to know where they are," he said firmly, looking at Feud. "Do not interfere with them in any way. When you have information, you are to send it to Lady Arra and to me."

Shalonie made the small adjustment on the parchment and returned both scroll and quill to Liethan, who signed his name to the paper before Kadana rejoined the group.

"What did I miss?" Kadana asked immediately upon seeing the determined look on Liethan's face.

Shalonie imparted the news since Omen was still uncertain what he could and could not say.

The last thing I want is to injure Kyr again with a careless word, he thought with frustration. *But if I can't talk through this, how can I figure out what is going on?*

"Of course," Kadana said after listening to Shalonie's account. "It was bound to get complicated." Whatever business Kadana had had with the Machelli spy, she kept to herself, only telling the group that she had an engagement later that afternoon and that they were all to join her.

When tea was done, Kyr and the cats having finished much of the food on the side table, Dev led them deeper into the bowels of the guild house, down several flights of stairs and into the cold stone cellars. Omen suspected the stairwell led down to subterranean tunnels under the city. But rather than take them all the way down to the bottom cellar, Dev paused three floors down and touched a worn stone on a back wall across from the stairwell.

They heard the grating sound of stone upon stone and watched in fascination as a secret passage opened into a narrow, pitch-black hallway. A sharp, dank breeze blew from the depths of the hall, like the chill breath of an ancient beast. For a moment Omen thought he heard whispers on the breeze, but as Kyr made no sign that anything was amiss, he suspected he had imagined it.

"So this is how Avarice always got into the fortress unseen." Kadana peered into the darkness.

"There are probably other passageways as well," Dev admitted. "Even the Set-Manasans don't know about this one — so keep quiet all of you. If the guards in the fortress spot us, we'll have a hard time explaining why we're there."

"Is we going into the dark? I is thinking we is eating snacks and now we is napping, is we not napping?" Tormy sounded hopeful.

"Shalonie needs to see the broken portal, Tormy. Remember?" Omen appeased his cat. *And I guess I need to get Beren's instrument.* He glanced at his grandmother, who winked at him.

The cat's ears twitched and briefly flattened against his head as if he were displeased. But they perked up a moment later. "I is 'member 'membering," he agreed. "I is not napping."

Dev reached for a small lamp hanging near the entrance of the passage. Opening the lamp's casing, he whispered the words of a simple cantrip and the candle inside the glass flared to light. In the dim flicker, they could see that the hallway beyond was coated in a heavy layer of dust — no marks or footprints to be seen, suggesting that no one had used it in a long time.

Dev led the way with the lamp. Kadana followed swiftly behind him.

Templar held out his left hand, palm upward, and a moment later a small ball of golden light appeared within it, illuminating the hall far better than the single lamp. He tossed the illumination upward, and it floated over his head as he followed after Kadana. Shalonie and Liethan followed him. Omen motioned Kyr to go in front of him. The boy, holding tightly onto Tyrin, stepped warily into the passageway.

"Can you make it in, Tormy?" Omen asked.

Tormy twitched his whiskers and ears as he spied ahead. "I is making it," he concluded. His large white whiskers brushed against the sides of the passage walls, but Omen guessed there would be room enough for the cat to squeeze along behind him.

Omen followed after Kyr while Tormy took up the rear.

The passageway led upward at a fairly sharp angle and took several twists. Beyond the light of the lamp Dev carried, and Templar's floating magic light, Omen could see no other signs indicating where they were. It wasn't long before the narrow, cold hall and the heavy darkness began feeling uncomfortably confining, and when Kyr reached back to take hold of Omen's hand, Omen squeezed it tightly in reassurance. Tormy's bulk and fur blocked the way back, and Omen could no longer see the light from the door behind them.

Luckily before too long, Dev led them to what seemed like a dead-end; but a quick press against another stone activated the sound of stone-against-stone. Another door swung open and light flooded the passage, nearly blinding Omen.

The cats squealed.

Templar quickly waved his hand at the light floating over his head, and it winked out of existence. They followed Dev into the sunlit hallway beyond.

When they were all clear of the secret passage, Dev hung the lamp on a hook and pressed another stone to close the door.

They found themselves in a long corridor with a high arched ceiling. Thin glass windows lined the far wall. Through the windows, Omen could see the city stretched out below them and the deep blue sparkle of the ocean far beyond.

A loud sneeze from Tormy drew his attention, and he laughed when he spied his cat. Tormy was coated in a thin layer of grey dust from head to paw. A string of cobwebs stretched across his ear tips.

"Come here, Tormy," Omen coaxed. He raised his hands as he drew a small amount of the ambient magic around him inward and fixed the correct magical pattern in his mind, a short musical tune serving as a mnemonic device. He uttered the words of the often-used cantrip. A moment later his cat's coat was pristine again, all signs of the dust and grime gone.

"So are you going to show us this spectacular throne room?" Liethan asked Dev as he brushed away the dust from his own clothing.

"Liethan, we're not sightseeing," Omen reminded him with a nudge to his shoulder.

"'Member, 'member," Tormy added. "If we is not getting a nap, we is doing something importantnessness — we is not playing."

"We just broke into the fortress — we're not going to look at anything fun first?" Liethan asked, sounding disappointed.

Omen cut in quickly, "We're here to see a forbidden broken portal. What could be more fun? Right, Shalonie?"

Shalonie already had her notebook in hand and was leafing through the pages; she looked up distractedly. "Right —

yes, there's supposed to be a broken wild portal somewhere in the fortress." She looked eagerly toward Kadana and Dev as if expecting them to know where it was.

Kadana narrowed her eyes, seeming to search her thoughts. "I don't recall there being a broken portal anywhere in the fortress. Where did you hear about it?"

"Hold Lord correspondence sent to my mother," Shalonie explained. "We were told that all further correspondence with Kharakhan was to be sent to the White Palace. This must have been right after Charaathalar disappeared, but still several years before he was officially declared dead. According to rumor, there was a portal in the fortress that went bad, and they had to seal off a large section of the building to protect the city."

"The only part of the fortress that was sealed was the east wing," Dev supplied.

"The cursed east wing," Templar clarified. "The one Feud told us to stay away from."

"The same."

"Lead on." Liethan's expression brightened visibly.

"Charaathalar's private quarters were in the east wing," Kadana recalled. "According to Indee, that's where he died." She turned to Omen and murmured quietly, "And that's where Beren's instrument is."

"Say what now?" Templar asked.

"Family heirloom," Omen said quickly. "A faerie-made instrument. And apparently something we'll need to get into the Autumn Lands."

"A faerie bard playing a faerie instrument?" Shalonie considered. "That is one way to get there. Though there's no guarantee which clan will answer us."

"What about this curse?" Omen asked his grandmother.

47

"Does it have something to do with Charaathalar's death?"
Never heard much about Indee's first husband. Alive or dead.

Kadana paused briefly before answering. "Maybe . . . The official story is that he was killed defending the city from a Night Lord. They built a statue in Charaathalar's honor in the city square. The Defender of Khreté."

"A Night Lord?" Dev stopped in his tracks. "Are you certain?"

Kadana motioned him to continue walking. "So the story goes."

Dev proceeded down the corridor with less enthusiasm, an uncharacteristic frown fixed on his face.

He doesn't like any mention of the Night Realm. For all his flippancy he's wracked with Machelli superstitions. Omen was somewhat amused by the realization.

"If that's the official story, what's the unofficial story?" Templar pressed.

"Unofficially — according to Indee, Avarice and 7 — Charaathalar summoned the Night Lord," Kadana replied. "I wasn't there, so I don't know if any of it's true. I know that none of them liked Charaathalar." She left the words hanging.

Surely she's not suggesting my parents killed the king of Kharakhan because they didn't like him? As far as Omen had ever known, there was no bad blood between his parents and Kadana. They considered the Deldanos part of their extended family, and with Omen's connection to them, there had never been any question of their friendship or loyalty. *Kadana has no reason to make up a story like that.*

Reading the alarm on his face, Kadana laughed and slapped him hard on the back. "Oh, don't look at me like

48

that. He was a very bad man. And whatever did or didn't happen to him, I have no doubt he deserved a lot worse."

Still . . . Regicide. Charaathalar was Khylar's and Caythla's father. I grew up with Caythla. She must have been a baby when Charaathalar died. I can't imagine that her father could be bad enough to deserve being murdered. By my parents. Omen felt an unsettling swish in his stomach. *There's got to be more to it.*

"So Indee never said anything about a broken portal?" Shalonie prodded, also looking somewhat uncomfortable by the turn of the conversation. "That was the story that reached Melia."

"If the king of a land disappears under mysterious circumstances, one generally doesn't go spreading the details of those circumstances to other world leaders," Kadana informed her, amused. "An address change due to a faulty portal sounds a lot better than, 'Our king has vanished and a Night Lord might be involved.'"

Her words sent a shiver down Omen's spine. *King has vanished . . . isn't that . . .*

"This is beginning to sound alarmingly familiar," Templar spoke the very words that were on Omen's mind. "Charaathalar vanished, and now Khylar has also vanished under mysterious circumstances."

"If Indee lied about the first vanishing . . ." Liethan looked to Omen in concern, his gaze moving briefly toward Kyr who would be the one to bear the consequences of this quest whatever the outcome. "But no." Liethan shook his head firmly and clapped Omen on the shoulder. "The one thing I'm certain about is that my cousin Tara would have nothing to do with summoning a Night Lord. This is a coincidence."

"Either way, I now really want to see what is being hidden in the east wing," Kadana cut in. "Broken portal or something else — I think we need to know."

Chapter 4: Circle

OMEN

Kadana took point, familiar with the passageways. With the exception of an occasional lone
guard, the fortress was surprisingly empty.
Once or twice, Kadana shooed the group into a side hall,
urging them to wait in silence.

*Funny how stealthy Tormy can be when he puts his mind
to it.* Omen felt a lightness in his chest. *Like playing hide-
and-seek.*

Most of the rooms they passed were filled with furniture
covered over in large white sheets, curtains drawn to protect the carpets from fading.

There aren't even any servants around. He guessed the
fortress had been unoccupied for years.

Eventually they came to a large oaken doorway that was
heavily barred from the outside, a thick beam of silverleaf
across iron fastenings that were in turn embedded deep into
the stone walls. The door led off from the main hallway, all
further passage blocked.

"This is the entrance to the east wing." Kadana investi-
gated the door's frame.

Templar touched the silverleaf bar, running his fingers
lightly over the cold metal. "It's wizard-locked," he told
them. "Prevents anyone from lifting the bar and opening
the door. Prevents anything from escaping as well."

The unspoken question hung in the air for a moment.

Opening it seems reckless, but . . .

51

Shalonie finally broke the silence. "If there's a ruined portal in there, I really do need to see it," she told them. "That's why I'm here."

Kadana gave an encouraging nod. "And this is where the instrument is."

She's curious about what's inside there as well.

"I'd have to shatter the lock," Shalonie continued, "but I can replace it with something better when we leave . . ."

"I want to see what's on the other side," Templar jumped in with great enthusiasm.

"And what if there really is a Night Lord on the other side?" Dev tried to argue, resignation coating his words. "They barred this door for a reason."

He already knows we're going in.

"Wouldn't be the first Night Lord we've run across," Templar said quickly. "Omen and I play against them all the time in the Night Games."

And that's always worked out fine. Omen looked over at Tormy, who sat up tall, long tail swishing in anticipation.

Dev blew out a dismissive huff. "Those are Night Dwellers and Nightlings who play. They're not Night Lords. There is a world of difference."

"What's the difference?" Omen asked.

"Remember those little shrimp Tormy and Tyrin were eating before we left Melia?" Dev asked.

Omen nodded. *Don't start talking about lunch.* Omen shot a worried look toward both cats and Kyr. All three were surprisingly quiet, contentedly waiting. Omen wondered if they were more subdued because of the oppressive emptiness of the castle.

"Compare those shrimp to that leviathan we met at sea, and you'll have a pretty accurate comparison. You don't want to meet a Night Lord."

It took a long moment for Dev's words to sink in.

This time it was Liethan who broke the quiet. "Is it just me, or do the rest of you really want to see what's on the other side of that door even more now?"

"I was thinking the same thing," Templar agreed briskly.

Kadana chuckled.

"Grandmother?" Omen asked, still leaning toward caution. *Kadana knows what to do.*

"If Shalonie needs to see a broken portal, and we need a faerie instrument in order to help you complete your quest and get you into the Autumn Lands, I don't think you really have much of a choice," Kadana said. "And I really want to know what happened to Charaathalar. Besides, I doubt your parents or Indee would leave a Night Lord wandering free in the fortress."

Omen nodded to Shalonie. "Go ahead and open it."

Dev muttered something under his breath and moved to stand near the back where Kyr, Tormy, and Tyrin were waiting. Omen wasn't certain if he was protecting himself or taking up a guard position in front of the boy and the cats.

To Omen's surprise, Kyr broke away from the group and grabbed Shalonie's hand, tugging on it to get her attention. Startled, she turned toward the boy. "It's just the one single moment that matters," he told her earnestly, smiling hopefully up at her. "Ignore all the rest of it."

She glanced uncertainly over at Omen; he didn't understand what the boy had said any more than Shalonie did. "All right, Kyr." She nodded her agreement. Kyr seemed satisfied and returned to his place beside Tormy.

Shalonie removed a piece of white chalk from a small

pouch attached to her sword belt, and proceeded to draw several strange symbols along the silverleaf bar, and then across the door itself.

Though unfamiliar with this branch of magic, Omen thought some of the symbols resembled marks that made up the transfer portal in his father's office. *I'm going to have to get her to explain again. I know they're powerful, but they look so much like a mathematical equation. Yuck.*

A moment later he felt a faint swirl of magic, and he realized that Shalonie had drawn the ambient energy from around them and channeled it into the marks themselves. For a second, the marks glowed blue with light before fading back into the dull white chalk. Omen heard the smallest, high-pitched sound — like glass shattering in the far distance. *She did it.*

"That was quick," Templar proclaimed. "Would have taken me at least an hour to find the correct magical pattern to undo that."

Shalonie smiled sheepishly at the praise and stood aside as Templar stepped forward to lift the heavy beam from the metal clasps holding it in place. He set it aside, leaning it up against the nearby wall, and then he took hold of the two iron door handles, turned them, and pulled open the large wooden doors. The doors swung silently outward without effort, revealing another long dark hallway, tall stone statues lining either side.

The air beyond was stale, but amid the oppressive darkness Omen could also sense a strange vibrating hum as if the air were charged with electricity. *The others sensed it too.* All of them paused before entering, and Omen noticed that both Tormy and Tyrin had flattened their ears tightly against their heads as if they did not want to listen to the humming tone coming from deep within the east wing.

"Do you hear that?" Omen asked the others, pitching his voice low.

"It's not a sound," Templar put his fingers over his ears, testing. "It's more like a vibration."

Shalonie crouched down and placed the palm of her left hand flat against the flagstones. "It's traveling through the stones. It sounds like whispering."

"Whispering?" Omen frowned. "It sounds like a musical note to me."

"It sounds like a drum to me," Liethan told them, head cocked to one side, brows drawn together. "No, more like a heartbeat."

"And I'm hearing stone grating against stone." Kadana considered. "We're all hearing something different. That's always promising."

Unnerved, Omen looked back at Dev. The Machelli's eyes had narrowed, his jaw fixed tightly as if he were biting back words. "I hear distant screams."

The cats still had their ears pulled flat against their heads, but Kyr looked surprisingly calm.

"What about you, Tormy?" Omen asked.

"We is not listening, Omy," Tormy whispered, and Tyrin, tucked away in Kyr's coat pocket with only his face peeking over the top, nodded fiercely.

To Omen, Kyr's calm was perplexing. *Considering he sees and hears things that aren't there all the time.* "Do you hear anything, Kyr?"

His brother blinked at him. "It was on the outside, Omen, not the inside. It's trying to trick you. Don't listen. The eyes are staring. If you look at it, it won't move."

"That's not even remotely creepy." Templar took a step

forward into the hallway. He shivered noticeably. "It's cold in here — like ice."

As Omen followed after him, he too felt a wash of cold air sweep over him. He glanced at the statues on either side of them. All were likenesses of different stern-eyed men with sharp, squared-off features. All the plaques beneath the statues bore the Set-Manasan name.

Past kings of Kharakhan.

They moved silently down the darkened corridor — the windows along the north wall all heavily curtained so very little of the ambient daylight seeped in to brighten the shadows. At the far end of the hallway, the path branched off in two directions. North led to another long corridor, but they could see that the south hall ended at a large door that had bright red light shining through the cracks.

The group only spared each other brief looks before proceeding south, heading toward the glowing door. The light seemed almost like firelight save that it did not flare or flicker. When they reached the door, Templar cautiously touched the surface. "Ice cold," he told them and grasped the iron latch. Unlike the other door, this one did not appear to have any magical locks. It swung open silently at his touch.

Omen and the others stared into the room. It was large, similar in size to other throne rooms Omen had visited over the years. Tall marble pillars held up the ornate web of stone arches that formed the ceiling. The floor was tiled in a colorful mosaic of interlocking patterns, and the long walls on either side of the room were covered with floor-to-ceiling scarlet curtains that blocked out all light. Along the curtained walls were dozens of pedestals with heavy glass cases all filled with an assortment of items: swords, armor, jewelry, musical instruments, horns, even a few white shapes Omen suspected were bones. But it was the glowing shapes in the middle of the room that drew all their attention.

A tall man, stern-faced, dove-grey eyes staring ahead, expression fixed in grim determination, stood in the center of the room inside a ring of red light that emanated from the floor. A large crystal globe rested in the center of the circle, half shattered so glass lay scattered about on the floor at the man's feet, the tiny shards gleaming like pools of blood in the light. A red mist leaked from the half-shattered globe, spreading outward, also frozen so that not even the natural air currents in the room disturbed it.

"That's Charaathalar," Kadana hissed, staring at the man in the center of the room.

King Charaathalar did not react, did not move or turn at the sound, but remained frozen, eyes fixed ahead at the red mist in front of him.

"Kyr, you and the cats stay here," Omen ordered as the others began cautiously moving closer. Tormy immediately sat on his haunches, while Kyr snuggled into the cat's warm, orange fur. The boy was visibly shivering in the unnatural cold of the room.

Satisfied that neither his brother nor the cats had any interest in proceeding further, Omen followed the others, keeping a wary eye on Charaathalar.

Shalonie held up a hand in warning as she neared the glowing circle. "Stay out of the ring of light," she told everyone. The light seemed to emanate from a mosaic circle in the very center of the room. The marble tiles were painted with intricate glowing sigils.

"Is that one of your Cypher Runes, Shalonie?" Omen

asked. Now that he was closer he could see that the marble pillars all around them were damaged by scorch marks similar to the marks left behind by magical strikes of lightning.

"No." Shalonie crouched down near the edge of the circle, out of range of the vertical curtain of light, and was carefully studying the patterns painted on the mosaic tiles. "And it's not a broken portal either. It's a summoning circle."

"What's the difference?" Omen asked.

"Summoning circles take their power from the summoner's will and the creature summoned," Shalonie explained. "Cypher Runes have their own power." She moved around the ring, reading the marks. "He was summoning . . . a Lord of Strife by the name—"

"Don't say its name!" Dev cut in sharply. "Names have power."

Startled, Shalonie accepted his warning without question. She continued moving around the ring, intently studying the marks.

"So, it's true then," Kadana said, her eyes on the unmoving form of Charaathalar. "That son of a troll summoned a Night Lord."

"But why?" Templar stood off to one side, staying well back from the ring of light, his gaze drawn to the red mist in the center. "What would he gain from it?"

"Immortality," Shalonie said as if it should be obvious. She motioned to the marks on the ground. "The entire bargain is written into the summoning circle itself." Her lips moved silently as she moved around the circle.

"Is that the Night Lord?" Liethan asked, pointing to the red mist.

"Can't you feel it?" Templar asked, turning his face

away. "Staring at you."

Liethan glanced uncertainly over at Omen.

I can feel the cold, but I don't sense anything staring at me. Omen looked around the room at the numerous glass cases lining the walls. A faint flash of red caught his eye on the far side of the room, and he started to move cautiously around the ring of light, giving it a wide berth, to investigate. "Grandmother, do you know what all this stuff is? What this room was used for?"

"It's Charaathalar's trophy room." She poked at one of the cases. "He collected magical artifacts — sometimes flat out stole them." She paused in front of one long case. "This sword used to belong to your mother, Liethan. It burns in the presence of the undead." Beneath the heavy glass lid, a pale silver sword had been displayed artfully upon red velvet.

"Is it valuable?" Liethan asked, surprised. He moved to Kadana's side to study the blade.

"Valuable enough, but more trouble than it was worth. It also tended to give our position away by drawing all the undead toward us," she said. "Your mother thought it was a pain in the rear and traded up. Guess Charaathalar liked it."

"The city of Khreté and all its inhabitants," Shalonie said abruptly, still focused on the marks.

They all turned to stare at her; the look of shock on her face was plain to see.

"What about them?" Omen asked, a bad feeling starting to nag at him. *What are we getting into?*

Shalonie looked up, her blue eyes filled with sheer disbelief and the first flickers of anger. "The price for King Charaathalar's immortality. In exchange for becoming immortal, he agreed to let the Night Lord destroy the city of

Khreté and devour all its inhabitants." She let out a disgusted scoff. "He was willing to sacrifice thousands of his own people so that he could be immortal."

"Are you sure?" Omen looked past her at the markings. *This is Shalonie. Of course she's sure. She doesn't make mistakes translating.*

"That sounds like Charaathalar," Kadana agreed. "Told you, he was a bad, bad man." She tilted her head, studying the figure. "Any idea what happened to him, Shalonie? Why is he frozen?"

Shalonie turned her attention back to the circle of light, continuing her way around it. "I'm not sure yet. Obviously, it didn't work out the way he'd intended. There are some marks on the outer edge of the circle that seem to be burned into the tile. They don't belong."

Her words drew Omen's attention away from the pedestal he was approaching, and he paused to run his fingers over one of the scorch marks. A familiar flare of magic brushed past his outer psionic shields, and he jerked his fingers back quickly.

"My father made these marks," he said. *Whatever happened here happened before I was born, but I have no doubt it was him.* Omen could still feel his father's psionic signature resonating off the burn marks on the pillars.

"Right," Kadana said as if things were starting to make sense. "According to Indee, she, Avarice and 7 tried to stop Charaathalar from summoning the Night Lord."

The faint flare of red off to one side grabbed Omen's attention again, and he approached one of the glass cases. The elegant form of a fifteen-string, cherrywood lute lay inside. Omen's eyes involuntarily widened at the sight of the instrument — the sounding board made of light-colored

60

wood, carved intricately and enhanced with delicate floral filigree at the center. The strings themselves gleamed brightly as if they were crafted of metal instead of the commonly used sheep's gut. It was an exquisite instrument — the tuning keys fastened with gears and locking mechanisms to hold their place, the frets across the neck also crafted from an opalescent metal instead of animal sinew or wood.

Faerie-made. This must be Beren's. Omen stared in awe. *Enchanted, no doubt. There's no warping or cracks in the wood despite all the time it must have lain here unplayed.*

A flash of red light caught his attention again, and he took a step back to figure out the source. *It's barely visible from here.* He turned his head to the side. *There! I saw the flash again.* As he prowled around the pedestal, Omen glanced over his shoulder and noticed Tormy's large amber eyes darkening with excitement. *Does Tormy see the light too?*

From the side perspective, the red gleam became more noticeable — hovering over the top of the glass case — no more than a faint swirl of red mist, held perfectly still like a mouse holding its breath while a predator looked on. As Omen looked closer, he realized that there at the top of the case was a faint line of darkness. *Is the lid open?*

"Found it!" Shalonie exclaimed.

Omen spun.

They all stared at the golden-haired girl who now knelt on the floor next to the ring of light, just past Charaathalar's left shoulder.

"The reason the summoning failed?" Kadana asked.

"It didn't fail," Shalonie said, barely audible. "He succeeded. But the summoning circle was changed." She looked up and met Omen's gaze from across the room. "You said your father made the marks on the pillars?"

"I'm certain. They were burned in psionically."

"Then he must have made these marks as well, they're burned in the same way," Shalonie pondered out loud. "Does 7 know a lot about evocation or summoning magic?"

"Can't imagine." Omen knew that kind of magic was of little interest to his father. While 7 certainly understood the workings of a broad range of magic, he was obsessed with science, or with magic that mimicked science.

He's fascinated by Shalonie's Cypher Runes because they're mathematical.

"Avarice and Indee are well-versed in both evocation and summoning magic," Kadana reminded them.

Shalonie sniffed. "That would make sense. The spell must have been their idea, but they needed someone with strong psionics to push through the summoning circle. Once these circles are closed, they're nearly impossible to breach with magic alone, but 7 managed to burn these marks right across the circle's perimeter. He changed the end of it."

"Changed it to what?" Kadana asked, urgency touching her voice.

Shalonie dragged her sleeve across her forehead. "This is supposed to read 'until the end of time,' but 7 changed it to 'and time ends.' He made it part of the condition of the bargain — he ended time within the confines of the summoning circle. 7 literally froze Charaathalar in time."

"Charaathalar and the Night Lord," Templar corrected, though there was a note of doubt in his voice.

Shalonie fumbled for the notebook in her belt pouch as she rose to her feet. "Maybe. I don't know." She flipped through several pages of the book as if looking for something specific, but her eyes kept glancing toward the circle and the glowing light within it. "It doesn't look like the Night Lord fully manifested; the thing may only be partially trapped. I can't be certain."

"So what do we do with him?" Omen asked, looking at the others. "Leave him there?"

"Yes!" Kadana insisted without hesitation. "Unless I'm misunderstanding, the spell was completed. The bargain was made. Which means Charaathalar is already immortal, and that creature has a claim on this city and everyone in it." She looked to Shalonie for confirmation.

The girl nodded in agreement, looking sickened by the idea.

"Your parents and Indee have already made the decision," Kadana stated firmly. "If we do anything to disrupt the spell, we'll be facing an immortal madman and a Night Lord. We're all better off if they stay trapped in there."

"If they stay trapped," Dev broke in, emphasizing the word *if.* "You said it yourself, Shalonie. You don't know if that thing is actually trapped. If there's a way to escape, the Night Lord will find it. And it won't care how much time that takes."

"Well, it isn't escaping today," Kadana insisted.

The aggravating flash of red light caught Omen's attention again. Sharply, he looked back at the glass case. *Would have sworn there's movement. That red mist clinging to the side of the case . . .*

"Does anyone else see that?" he demanded, pointing.

Kadana and the others drew closer, both Templar and Dev careful to avoid the ring of light in the center. Across

63

the room, Omen saw Kyr, Tormy, and Tyrin still waiting by the door. *Please stay put.*

"See what?" Shalonie asked, looking at the case and the lute inside.

"There it is! Beren's lute!" Kadana exclaimed.

"The one we need?" Liethan asked eagerly.

"Yes," Kadana said. "It has other powers as well. Played properly it amplifies magic. The greater the musician, the more powerful the effect. This lute saved our lives in battle more than once."

"I wasn't referring to the lute," Omen said carefully, his attention still on the strange, barely visible red mist. "I meant the thing clinging to the side of the lute case."

He was met by blank stares. "You can't see it?" he asked.

"What does it look like?" Dev asked warily.

"Sort of like a large bug or a lizard, made out of that weird red mist." He found himself whispering. "None of you see it?" *Why can't they see it?*

"It's a Nightling," Dev stated definitively. "They're only visible when they move."

Templar peered closer, moving around to the other side of the case as if trying to spot it the same way Omen had. He shook his head. "Still can't see it. Are they dangerous?"

"They're servants made by more powerful creatures," Dev explained. "Anything from the Night Lands is potentially dangerous. But they can be destroyed, provided you can get ahold of them. They're hard to catch."

"Especially if you can't see them." Kadana strained to make out any trace of the creature.

"You can see it when it moves," Dev suggested, shifting his head from side to side to catch a better angle.

"How can I see it then?" Omen demanded. "It's not moving. It's just clinging to the side of the case. I think it was prying open the lid earlier."

"It probably has something to do with your bloodlines," Dev said. "The more important question is, what does it want with that lute?"

Shalonie threw an alarmed glance back at the summoning circle, stepping away from the others to stare for a moment at the ring of light.

Omen glanced briefly over at her, but the moment he turned his head away from the case, he saw another flash of red. He snapped his full attention back to the faint red mist. "Every time I look away, it moves," he hissed to the others.

"Don't look away," Kadana suggested, the unease in her voice making Omen nervous.

"A state of equilibrium," Shalonie murmured, and though Omen wasn't looking at the girl, he recognized the tone. She was talking to herself — working out some problem in her head that had eluded the rest of them. "That's why 7 used psionics — the level of power needed — if they'd used magic—"

"Shalonie!" Templar interrupted. "Anything you want to share?"

Startled, Shalonie turned and blinked at them. She gestured to the summoning circle. "Summoning circles are powered by the will of the summoner and the power of the creature being summoned. To modify the bargain, 7 had to match that level of power, but without pushing it to a breaking point and potentially destroying the summoning circle and freeing the Night Lord completely. It's at a state of perfect equilibrium, but if something were to significantly amplify the magic in the ring . . ." She trailed off, leaving the rest unsaid, and they all turned their attention back to the lute.

"How intelligent are these Nightlings, and can they play musical instruments?" Omen asked.

"Some of them are very clever, and it can certainly *possess* a musical instrument — make it play itself," Dev answered.

"Can it understand what we're saying?" The very idea that this thing might have been sitting here in front of him this entire time, listening to everything they said, unnerved Omen further.

This is starting to tick me off. He took a deep, angry breath.

"Maybe," Dev looked doubtful. "Most of them only speak the Night Tongue. They're a bit like the dead in that respect."

"Wait a minute," Liethan cut in. "What's it doing here?"

"It wants the instrument," Omen stated incredulously. "Weren't you listening?"

"I get that part." Liethan's hands moved toward his dagger. "But, I meant what's it doing here, now? This summoning circle has been here for almost twenty years. What's it doing here now, today, the very instant we show up? Why didn't it steal the lute years ago?"

Good question.

"It was on the outside, not the inside," Kadana quoted Kyr's words back to them. "That's what Kyr said when we opened the outer door to the east wing. We let the Nightling in."

Omen threw a look over his shoulder at his brother. The boy was still crouched beside Tormy by the door, Tyrin perched on his shoulder. All three of them watched intently, but didn't seem interested in moving any closer.

Another flash of light drew Omen's gaze back to the case.

Liethan hissed, pointing a finger at the glass. "I saw it that time!" he called out. "It moved. Just for a second. I was looking right at it. Nasty piece of work! Like a giant scorpion. I think it had teeth or pincers."

"All right." Kadana moved forward, motioning Templar around to the other side. "Templar, you smash the glass case. I'll grab the lute. Omen, you grab the Nightling."

"It's made out of mist," Omen reminded her. "How am I supposed to grab it?"

"Just grab it!" Kadana ordered.

"Should be solid enough when it moves," Dev told him. "If you squeeze it tightly enough, you should be able to kill it. They're not immortal."

Omen resigned himself to getting Nightling bug guts on his hands. He nodded once, letting his grandmother and Templar know that he was ready. The others drew back. Templar pulled a thin dagger from his belt, holding it with the hilt toward the glass. He mouthed out a silent count for all of them, and on cue, he struck the glass case hard with the pommel of the dagger. The glass shattered in a loud crystalline crash.

Instantly, Kadana wrapped her right hand around the neck of the lute and pulled it away while Omen shot out both hands and wrapped his fingers around the red mist.

The Nightling was either smarter than they'd guessed or had anticipated their actions, for the moment Omen felt his fingers closing over the cold and very real shape, he also felt the needle-like teeth or pincers sinking into his flesh. Both of his hands spasmed, and the thing slipped away, leaping toward the heavy curtains hanging along the wall.

67

Omen cursed and rushed after it. The creature, clearly visible as it ran, leaped and scampered its way like a spider up the entire length of the curtain toward the top, at least ten feet out of Omen's reach. It skittered across the top of the curtain, leaping to the next one and racing along the wall while Omen ran after it on the ground. A second later, a streak of orange and white rushed past Omen, and sprang up the curtain in a flash, hot on the Nightling's tail.

"Tyrin!" Kyr shrieked loudly. Omen saw his brother and Tormy racing toward him, Tormy's eyes dark and dilated with hunting fever.

The others scrambled after the creature as well, all of them able to see it now that it was moving.

But at the top of the curtain, it was well out of their reach. *But not Tyrin's! The curtains didn't even slow him down!* Omen watched in amazement as the small kitten ran after the Nightling, his tiny claws shredding the curtains as he ran up the vertical surface at high speed. The Nightling led him up and down the billowing curtains that stretched around the room. Wiggling like a millipede, the Nightling scrambled over the top of the curtain rods, leaping from one rod to the next in a frantic effort to escape.

"Omen, the door!" Kadana shouted.

Realizing that the Nightling was heading around the room toward the open door, Omen fixed a pattern in his mind and reached out with his psionics to yank the wooden door shut, sealing off the creature's exit.

He heard the hisses and yowls characteristic of a catfight as Tyrin finally caught the creature. Neatly sliding down one of the curtains, front paws moving with lightning speed, the kitten slashed and tore and hit at the red ball of mist with all of his might. The eyes of the Nightling flashed flame yellow with rage as it fought back.

"Grab it!" Templar yelled to the others as they ran around frantically, all of them trying to grab either the kitten or the Nightling.

Tyrin and the creature tumbled and rolled across the tile floor, the kitten shrieking and hissing as he fought.

Somehow Liethan managed to close his hands around one of the shapes, and he swiftly lifted an enraged ball of orange and white fluff from the ground.

They all heard the loud crunch as Dev brought the heel of his boot down upon the Nightling, crushing it flat. A pale sickly mist swirled around Dev's foot before dissipating completely, leaving only a wet smear of black oil on the ground.

For a long moment, they all stared.

Omen's heart beat out strong, painful pumps as he caught his breath.

The silence was broken a moment later by an absolutely delighted Tormy. "Tyrin, you is being amazingnessness!"

"I is knowing that!" Tyrin exclaimed with utter glee. The kitten hung limply in Liethan's outstretched hands, tail still fluffed twice its normal size. "That is being two battles I is fighting today! One more and I is not being ableness to count any higher!"

Liethan handed the kitten back to a horrified Kyr.

"Can we leave now?" the boy pleaded with Omen. "I don't like it here!"

"Yes," Kadana broke in. "It's about time we get going. There's obviously no broken portal for Shalonie to study, and I think we should leave Charaathalar to enjoy his immortality in peace. Shalonie, can you do something to make certain no more of those things get in here?"

Shalonie looked disheveled from the chase. "I can ward both doors. That should keep anything out."

"The Night Lord will escape eventually," Dev warned, sounding certain. "They always do."

"But not today," Kadana stated. "And right now, that's good enough for me. This is Indee's problem. She's going to have to deal with it sooner or later." Kadana held out the cherrywood lute to Omen. "Here, this is yours now. Beren would be glad to know you have it." She casually glanced at the broken glass scattered on the floor.

Omen took hold of the instrument without a word. *That should replace the lute Tormy ate.* He winked at his grandmother.

As they hurried out, Omen spared a quick look back at Charaathalar still standing frozen in time in the ring of light at the center of the room. The mist trapped with him never moved, never shifted. *And let's hope it never does.*

Chapter 5: Tavern

SHALONIE

The Machelli carriages were already waiting by the time they found their way out of the fortress and back to the guild house. No one spoke, not even the cats.

Shalonie, once again seated in one of the closed-in carriages, scribbled worriedly in her notebook, trying to capture every detail of what she'd seen in the fortress.

While the summoning circle had not been constructed of Cypher Runes, it did technically constitute a portal of sorts between the mortal world and the Night Lands. But summoning circles were typically the product of willpower, not mathematical calculations.

Pure chaos — and uncontrollable. Though every sorcerer who summons something from the Night Lands thinks they can control the outcome.

It wasn't the sort of magic she was interested in.

"Any idea what the Machellis were doing for Kadana?" Templar asked.

She looked up, startled to find him sitting across from her. She'd forgotten for a moment that she wasn't alone, and judging from the amused look in Templar's eyes, he'd noticed. She scolded herself inwardly. *I get too wrapped up in my own thoughts.*

"I didn't ask," she told him. "I thought we were meeting Kadana's husband and sons at a tavern somewhere."

"She hired the Machellis to spy on someone," Templar

explained. "Family enemy, do you think?"

Shalonie didn't think it possible. "The Deldanos don't seem to have a lot of personal enemies. Everyone likes them. I'm sure we'll find out who it is soon enough." She was losing interest in the subject. "Have you ever done any summoning magic?"

Templar didn't seem to mind the change of topic. "Too dangerous — especially in Terizkand. Half the land is already cursed by one thing or the other, and the other half is hip-deep in necromancers and the undead. If Kharakhan is a land of wild magic, then Terizkand is a land of blood and death magic. I've seen too many summonings go wrong. Not to mention," he stretched out his legs indulgently, "I'm always worried I'll end up summoning myself."

Though she knew he was being flippant, she considered the possibility. "I don't think that's probable. You still technically belong to the mortal realm even if you do have Nightblood in you."

They heard the driver calling to the horses, and the carriage slowed down.

"Guess we made it. We're here." Templar stepped out quickly, holding the carriage door for Shalonie.

She shoved her notebook back into her belt pouch and stepped out onto the cobbled street, joining the others.

They found themselves in one of the finer merchant areas of Khreté, the street busy with foot traffic.

The noonday sunlight gleamed off the signs of various interesting shops all around them. Shalonie found herself studying the wooden sign above the nearby tavern. Kadana too was staring at it, a look of profound concentration on her face as she took in the monstrous, scaly green blob carved into the signboard. The creature appeared to be playing a golden lute under the balcony of a copper-haired maiden.

"The Green-Eyed Monster," Kadana read aloud. "This is the place." She scowled and rolled her luminous emerald eyes, the definitive Deldano family trait.

"Is that a dragon or a crocodile?" Omen asked, joining them in staring at the unusual sign.

"That's probably Beren," Kadana said soberly. "Why do I think fair Carrina holds a grudge?" Kadana proceeded through the narrow tavern door with purpose, leaving the group little choice but to follow.

What does this have to do with Beren? While Shalonie knew Kadana's eldest son Beren had spent most of his life living in Kharakhan, she really only knew him from his time in Melia as one of the twelve Hold Lords. When he'd married Nythira, daughter of Hold Lord Quintar, he'd left much of his past behind him. Now both Quintar and Nythira were long dead, and Beren held the title of Hold Lord of the Province of Litrania.

"Do you know what's going on?" Omen whispered to Shalonie as he helped Tormy squeeze his shoulders through the doorframe. They both heard a faint crack in the wood and cringed in unison. The door had not been designed with a giant cat in mind.

"No," Shalonie told Omen as she followed after the cat. "I thought we were meeting Kadana's husband here."

Shalonie shook her hair from her eyes as they entered the tavern — a large-sized dining hall filled with sturdy wooden tables, benches, and heavy oaken chairs. The establishment was far from elegant, but it felt comfortable, the stone floor well swept and the furnishings in good repair. Several latticed windows looked out onto the street, but the beveled colored glass didn't let in too much sun. Muted light glowed down from round chandeliers which were hung from the wooden crossbeams. Flames from thick beeswax candles cast flickering golden light around the room. Hearty food smells lingered in the air, reminding Shalonie that the cats hadn't eaten in a while.

Despite the busy street outside, the tavern was empty. But judging by the number of tables still messy with empty plates and tankards, Shalonie guessed the establishment had had a robust lunch hour.

Clearing the tables was a curvaceous woman in a tightly laced bodice of green velvet with a dark flowing skirt that ended slightly below her knees and showed off her ankles and small, slipper-clad feet. The woman's hair was a wild mane of copper curls, and when she turned toward them, Shalonie noticed that though she was likely well beyond her youth, her face was still fair. The woman possessed a certain voluptuous beauty that Shalonie knew appealed to men — indeed she could see that Omen, Templar, and Liethan eyed her appreciatively.

Dev shot Shalonie an amused look and winked.

That must be the tavern owner — I wonder if she's also supposed to be the maiden from the sign?

The look of anger that crossed the woman's face as she took in the group marred her appearance. Her lips thinned with displeasure, and her eyes narrowed.

"No magical beasts allowed!" The woman shouted at them, pointing a sharp finger at Tormy. "No beasties, boggets or faykin in my place!" While her accent marked her as pure Kharakhian, likely of low birth judging by the way she extended her vowels, she spoke in clear Merchant's Common. Her tone, however, was shrill and rising.

"Is that &!*#! fishwife calling Tormy a beastie, bogget or faykin?" Tyrin yelled with outrage, his orange head and paws hanging out of Kyr's pocket.

Kyr stroked the little creature's back gently.

"Let me," Kadana said, her voice smooth as glass. "Carrina, do you know who I am?"

The tavern owner rocked back on her heels. "You!" she squawked. "Is HE here too?"

Does she mean Beren? Shalonie frowned, beginning to guess what might be going on here.

While Beren was considered generally well-loved by the somewhat proper Melian population, there were certain aspects of his past that could not be ignored. The fact that there seemed to be a constant stream of young men and women who arrived in Melia and were introduced as his children was something the Melians tended to pointedly ignore. *And with those green eyes of the Deldanos, it's impossible for Beren to deny any of them as his — not that he ever has.*

Kadana pressed her lips together. "I'm here to meet my grandson."

And there it is — another one. Shalonie stifled an itch in her throat. *Thank the Dragons that Beren's current wife doesn't seem to mind.*

"About bloody time," Carrina grumbled while vigorously rubbing down the length of the wooden table she'd been clearing. "Any idea how hard it is to raise a child by yourself?"

Kadana turned her head, studying the tavern from corner to corner. The main room boasted a fireplace big enough to stand in. The white plaster walls displayed large, elaborate art pieces — some paintings, some carvings depicting scenes from Kharakhian myth and legend.

Omen pointed to a wooden icon of a dark-haired queen holding a baby in her lap.

"Is that Indee?"

Shalonie nodded. "And Khylar."

Kadana stepped closer to Carrina and lowered her voice. "Prime location in a thriving port city," she enumerated to the copper-haired woman. "Furnished with style. Expensive art. Well-stocked." Kadana waved a gauntleted hand toward the casks and bottles neatly arranged behind the smooth wooden bar. "Doesn't look like you've done so bad for yourself."

She switched to Kharakhian instead of Common, Shalonie noticed. *And that was Low Kharakhian, not High. Probably doesn't want Kyr or the cats to understand too much of this.*

Carrina huffed. "My father disowned me."

"Your father, if I remember, was a tinker." Kadana shrugged. "The way I see it, the money I gave you bought you a much better life. Congratulations."

Omen shuffled his feet uncomfortably, and Shalonie had to sympathize, feeling rather awkward herself. Whatever wild past Beren had lived, she wasn't certain she wanted to hear the details.

"Perhaps we should leave?" Shalonie whispered to Omen.

He headed toward the door. "Tormy, let's go wait somewhere else."

"Don't mind my mother." A young man emerged from a door behind the bar. He was carrying a basket of thickly sliced brown bread and an earthenware butter crock. "Everyone is welcome at the Green-Eyed Monster," he continued in the Common Tongue and flashed a big smile at Tormy. "Especially giant magic cats."

Tormy preened, and Shalonie was impressed by the young man's demeanor. While Tormy was undeniably adorable, he was also an enormous predator and most Kharakhians they'd met had kept a healthy distance from him.

"And little pocket cats," the young man added quickly before Tyrin could open his mouth again.

Kyr smiled weakly.

The young man turned to Shalonie and Omen, his smile welcoming, and Shalonie caught her breath. *Deldano eyes! No question about that.* The young man almost didn't need the emerald green eyes to mark him as a Deldano because he was the spitting image of Beren — tall, with dark wavy hair and the sort of dashing good looks that women swooned over. But there was a softness in his features that Beren lacked — regardless of the wild life Beren might have lived, it hadn't been an easy one.

And yet, despite that softness, Shalonie also noticed a rather large bruise marring the young man's left cheek, and the knuckles of both of his hands were red and split. *He's been in fights — but then again this is Kharakhan. I understand brawling is common enough among the young men of the city.*

"He looks exactly like Beren," Templar half-whispered to both Omen and Shalonie. "Just a little shorter and a little younger."

"You can't buy back my innocence," Carrina shrilled in the guttural Low Kharakhian that Shalonie guessed was her native tongue.

Shalonie cleared her throat, the Melian in her wanting to

change the conversation quickly. Such topics were not openly discussed in Melia and certainly would never arise in mixed company. But far from being outraged by the comment, Kadana seemed to find it funny. Kadana's hearty belly laugh echoed through the tavern before Shalonie could find anything appropriate to say.

"You can get out of my place right now!" Carrina shouted and put both hands on her ample hips.

"You wouldn't have a 'place' if it wasn't for my money!" Kadana returned the volley with as devastating a Kharakhian growl as Shalonie had ever heard. While she was fluent in both High and Low Kharakhian, she had never been able to master the accent that went along with it.

"What language is that?" little Tyrin inquired, his kitten eyes bright.

"Low Kharakhian," Shalonie provided quickly. "Not something you need concern yourself with."

"Oh, Low Kharakhian is soundingnessness like a wonderful language for the cursings." Tyrin stretched his fuzzy head high and addressed Kyr. "I is learning Low Kharakhian now. Set me on the bar! Set me on the bar!"

Kyr gave Omen a helpless look. While Shalonie doubted the boy understood anything the two women were saying, she didn't think he liked the raised voices.

"Look what I have, Tyrin." Dev drew a small pouch from his jacket. With quick fingers, he untied the little sack and picked a flat brown oval from it.

Beef jerky. Good thinking. Nothing distracts the cats more than food. Indeed Tyrin, Tormy, and Kyr were suitably distracted.

"One at a time," Dev instructed Kyr and handed over the pouch. "I'll be right back." Devastation Machelli swept out the tavern door before Tyrin had taken his first bite.

While Kadana and the tavern owner went on in Low Kharakhian at an impressive pace and volume, the young green-eyed man motioned the rest of them toward a table on the far side of the room, sparing only a pained look back at the two women.

"Please, ignore my mother," he urged them as if the loud exchange of insults and curses taking place near the bar wasn't happening. He smiled hopefully at them, and Shalonie and the others took pity and allowed him to steer them away from the verbal brawl.

A crash of crockery caused all of them to startle momentarily, realizing quickly that Carrina was breaking plates while shouting at Kadana.

Omen caught hold of Kyr before he could wander toward the broken pottery, and moved him to the table near the fireplace.

"Do you have any specials?" Templar asked brightly as he pulled out a chair at the table.

Shalonie noticed that while both she and Omen looked distinctly uncomfortable, Templar seemed to find this entire thing delightful. Liethan appeared amused as well.

Terizkandians and Corsairs — they probably find this exchange normal.

Carrina's Deldano son nodded, clearly appreciating the strategic diversion. "Sure. I'm Nikki by the way. I'll take care of you today." He flinched slightly as his mother let out a string of foulmouthed curses that Shalonie feared would make her ears bleed. She was fairly certain she heard the word "bastard" several times and hoped Tyrin was not taking note.

The young man, Nikki, flinched each time the word was

shouted. *He's trying to ignore the fight. His mother embarrasses him, I think. Or maybe it's something else.*

"I am working on a white fish stew," Nikki continued hurriedly as he set the basket of bread and the butter crock down on the table. "Should be ready in about twenty minutes." He pulled out a chair for Shalonie. "I could start you with some crimson pepper and sardine toasts. They have a little bit of a bite."

"I is not liking spicy," Tormy bleated out and blithely settled himself between the fireplace and Omen. Now that food was being offered, the cats didn't seem to care about the fight.

Omen leaned over the table, spread a thick pad of the soft butter on a piece of the bread and flipped it to Tormy. "Maybe a bowl of cream for him to start. We'll take the sardine appetizer and the stew when it's ready." He dug Melian coins from his pocket. "You might want to have someone run to the market now; the cats eat a lot. A haunch of beef or venison wouldn't go amiss if you have it as well."

The young server gave a polite nod, his face calculating the logistics. "Let me start you with drinks, and then I'll run out to get more meat." He tilted his head toward the bar. "Wine or ale?"

The fight between the two women cut off abruptly as Carrina stormed away through the back door behind the bar and Kadana came to join them, her face fixed in a hard expression. Kadana said nothing as she passed by the young server and seated herself at the table.

"I'll bring ale," Nikki decided for them as he hurried past the angry woman and went around behind the bar to prepare their drinks.

After her shouting match with Carrina, Kadana was unexpectedly quiet, and Shalonie shot a nervous look at Omen who busied himself hand-combing Tormy's face, obviously not certain what to say either. *Would have thought she'd throw a fit, being spoken to like that by a commoner. Then again, Kadana gave as good as she got.* Her sheer fluency in Low Kharakhian reminded Shalonie pointedly that Kadana herself was low born.

She might be a landed noble now, but Kadana understands where Carrina comes from. This is normal for her — like she's done this before.

Several more loud crashes came from the kitchen, though Carrina did not reappear. The sounds made Nikki move faster, and a few moments later he returned to their table carrying a large tray filled with heavy tankards of foamy Kharakhian ale. He passed them out swiftly, his face fixed in a pleasant smile despite the fact that he flinched with each loud crash coming from the kitchen.

Shalonie noticed the furtive glances he threw Kadana as he set the tankards on the table, though he made no effort to catch her attention. His cheeks, however, were flushed with embarrassment. *He must have understood who exactly Kadana is. I wonder why he doesn't say anything? Does he not believe that she's his grandmother? She might not seem old enough — but surely the Kharakhians must know who she is?*

"I'll be right back with your appetizers," Nikki told them. "And the cream for the cats. We have peach juice for the boy if you'd prefer, or tea. Begging your pardon, miss."

Shalonie looked up in surprise at that, realizing he was addressing her. Unlike Kadana, she was not particularly fond of ale. Kadana had already downed one complete tankard and had taken the one in front of Liethan as well.

81

Shalonie slid hers over to the woman and nodded politely to Nikki. "The juice will be fine, thank you."

"Do I like peaches?" Kyr asked Omen as Nikki hurried away. "I don't remember peaches. The trees are changing. Are they supposed to turn colors like that? I like them when they are green. Will they be green again, Omen?"

"The trees will be fine, Kyr," Omen assured the boy as he buttered more bread before Tyrin could stick his nose in the butter crock. The kitten still had his piece of beef jerky held firmly under one tiny claw but had been eyeing Tormy's bread quite curiously.

I thought cats were supposed to be carnivorous. These two seem to eat anything and everything.

The front door opened again, and Dev slipped back inside, moving silently across the room to join them. Shalonie assumed he'd gone to speak with the Machellis still waiting outside with the carriages.

"The stable you mentioned is down the road a few blocks. No sign of your sons or husband yet, Kadana," Dev told them. "I sent the carriages ahead with our belongings."

Kadana sullenly continued drinking her ale.

"So, are we going to sit here politely and drink our ale and eat our fish stew or is someone going to ask the obvious question?" Templar asked blithely. He shot a pointed look in the direction Nikki had gone.

"He's one of Beren's," Kadana said without preamble. "I suppose that's obvious enough."

"Those eyes do tend to make it difficult to hide his heritage," Templar laughed. "So, what does that make it — seventeen or so?"

"Twelve!" Kadana corrected, a look more exasperated than annoyed spreading over her face.

"You counting Omen in that number?" Dev asked curiously, and Shalonie saw Omen press his lips together. She was fairly certain Dev knew the answer to that question already, but he seemed to enjoy teasing Omen about his bizarre birthright. While Omen was not technically Beren's biological son, the Deldanos still considered him one of their own — when Beren had saved both Omen's and Avarice's life at his birth, some part of the Deldano's bloodline had been transferred to Omen through Beren's healing gift. *He even has the green eyes to show for it — well one green eye anyway.* Omen's mixed heritage was made all the more apparent by the distinct dual color of his eyes. *Heterochromia, I believe is what 7 calls it.*

"Yes, I count Omen in that number," Kadana informed Dev in a tone that indicated he should drop that line of questioning. "And four of them are legitimate, I should point out."

"Five!" Omen corrected her quickly. "There was nothing illegitimate about my birth, even if I'm not technically Beren's. My parents are married."

"True," Kadana conceded. "I've been trying to find all the others."

"You mean there's more?" Templar asked incredulously.

"Probably." Kadana shook her head as if she too couldn't quite believe the situation. "Beren had a . . . troublesome youth. And we've all done our best to set things right."

"The Deldanos are soon going to outnumber the Corsairs." Liethan laughed. "And that's saying something. My grandparents have fourteen children already, and even more grandchildren."

While Shalonie couldn't bring herself to find much humor in the subject, she had to admit that the Deldanos had

83

been nothing but a positive addition to Melia. Beren, for all his past faults, had accepted every one of these unexpected children into his household, and Shalonie couldn't deny that they were all good additions to their society. And Beren, while he counted himself a bard above all things, was even more widely known for his healing gift. *Anyone with a gift like that is blessed by the gods. And certainly, the Sundragons are fond of him.*

"A troublesome youth?" Templar asked. "There has to be more to the story than that. I could never figure out how Beren was even old enough to have so many children. The timeline doesn't seem right."

Kadana nodded curtly. "That's part of the problem," she agreed. "There are a lot of things that weren't quite right."

"What do you mean?" Omen asked. Shalonie noticed that while she'd assumed as a Deldano, Omen knew more about Beren than the rest of them did, he didn't seem to understand the reference.

Kadana took another long drink from her tankard before settling back in her chair, stretching her long legs out beneath the table. "Well, I told you a bit about the portals here in Kharakhan — they're everywhere, some disappearing and reappearing, others seeming to be stable. When I was younger, we used to ride the portals — me, Omen's mother and Liethan's mother and aunt, Indee, a few others."

"What do you mean 'ride?'" Shalonie asked, feeling somewhat alarmed by the thought. *Surely they didn't step into unstable portals? There's no telling what could happen.*

Kadana's eyes danced. "You have to understand we had a certain disregard for our safety back then — a certain disregard for everything really. If we found a portal, we jumped into it. It was fun. They'd take us to all sorts of strange and wild places, jumping us from one side of the land to another, inevitably landing us in the middle of trouble. But we always managed to get out of trouble, so I suppose we never really learned our lesson — never really learned how dangerous it truly was. And when we got into serious trouble, we had also learned how to use the portals to escape. We made our fortunes riding those portals."

"So what happened?" Shalonie asked. "You don't use them now." *When 7 and I set up the Cypher Portal to Terizkand and Lydon, Avarice had been more mistrustful of it than anyone else.*

Kadana sighed. "When Beren was about seven years old, he and I got into some trouble with a local warlord. We had to flee for our lives, and we jumped into an unfamiliar portal to escape from him. This portal was different — it seemed to hold us inside its vortex for a very long time, and when we came out the other side, Beren and I were different."

"Different how?" Omen asked. They were all listening with rapt attention, all save Kyr who was staring happily at the stained glass windows and the lights they were casting upon the tavern floor.

"I was younger," Kadana explained. "A lot younger — barely out of my teens. It seemed the greatest blessing — as if I'd been gifted with a newfound youth by the gods themselves. And then I saw Beren — and realized that we had been cursed. My little boy was all grown up — a young man equal in age to me, robbed of his childhood."

Shocked by the story, the rest of them stayed silent as Kadana took another long drink of ale. "Beren however was delighted," Kadana continued. "He didn't realize what had been taken from him, and no amount of words on my part could explain it to him. The rest of us had learned our lesson — learned the true dangers of the portals. But Beren grew out-of-control and rebellious and ran away from us, continued to ride the portals while the rest of us chased after him."

"He learned his lesson eventually though," Dev remarked, guessing at the end of the tale while the rest of them were still sitting in stunned silence. "Something happened to him. Something made him stop — made him flee from Kharakhan and settle down in Melia."

Kadana nodded, sadder than Shalonie had ever seen her. Up until now, she'd seemed somewhat stoic about her past, but this story obviously troubled her. "The Sleeping Shadows," she replied.

Shalonie frowned at that, and Omen too looked perplexed. "The ballad?" they both asked in unison, each familiar with the popular song frequently sung in the Melian taverns.

"The one about the haunted castle in the woods?" Omen clarified. "That's a children's story — Beren used to sing it for me when I was little."

"The version he sang for you was a children's story," Kadana said quietly. "But the first version he wrote was not. He jumped into a portal and ended up someplace dark — someplace that changed him far more than any other portal ever did — even the one that aged him. Maybe one day he'll tell you the whole story himself." They all took her words to mean she was not going to elaborate further, and Shalonie felt disappointed, wondering what more there was to the popular song.

"Then are all the portals in Kharakhan dangerous and

unstable?" Templar asked.

"No." Kadana brightened. "There are some that are quite stable — but no one really understands the magic that governs them. And I certainly couldn't tell you the difference between one of our portals and the Gates into the Autumn Lands or the Night Lands. All I know is that if you don't understand the magic controlling something, you can never be truly certain what it will do. They're too dangerous to use unless you have no other choice."

"My father said our Cypher Portal is safe," Omen pointed out, his tone suggesting he had absolute faith in 7's claim, though he looked to Shalonie for confirmation.

"They're not the same things," Shalonie assured him. "The Gates were created by the Elder Gods — they do exactly what the gods intended them to do. The wild portals here in Kharakhan are naturally occurring — created by wild magic. They could change or cease to exist at any moment. The Cypher Portals are constructed — the calculations controlling them keep them stable."

"And all these wild gates into the other realms are found in the Mountain of Shadow?" Templar asked.

But again Shalonie shook her head. While she was no expert on the Mountain of Shadow, she knew enough to understand why so many people believed that. "No, the Gates are more of an idea than actual gates. They are the barrier that exists between one realm and the next, created by the Elder Gods and governed by the Laws of the Covenant. But there are certain places in the mortal world where the barrier between here and the other realms is thinner — the realms touch, overlap, and it's easier to slip through that barrier in those places. At night the barrier to the Night Lands is thinner, during the summer solstice, the barrier into the Summer Lands is thinner. And in the Mountain of Shadow, the barriers into all the realms are thinner — they all overlap and touch there."

Another loud crash from the kitchen startled all of them as they heard Carrina cursing again in Kharakhian. Kadana looked over her shoulder. A moment later, Nikki emerged from the back carrying another tray filled with the promised appetizers, cream, and the jug of peach juice for Shalonie and Kyr. There was a large red mark on his right cheek that would no doubt give him a bruise to match the one on the left.

"Excuse me," Kadana told the others. She rose swiftly to her feet. "Seems I have a bit more to discuss with Carrina." She stormed past Nikki as he set the tray of appetizers on the table. The tray was piled high with baked crackers, salted sardines, several small cheese wheels, and a large plate filled with sliced fruits. Kyr and the cats hungrily turned their attention toward the food and cream, Omen scrambling to help distribute the helpings before Tormy could stick his face into all of it.

"I brought a few more things for you," Nikki explained surveying the items. "I'll be right back with the stew. Will you need rooms for the night as well? We have several upstairs."

"I don't think we're staying," Omen told him. "I'm Omen, by the way." He stuck out his hand to Nikki in greeting, and then proceeded to introduce the others at the table, giving only their first names and not their titles.

While Nikki returned their greetings politely, Kadana emerged from the kitchen, two young women trailing behind her, one carrying a stack of plates and bowls, another carrying out a large cauldron filled with the promised fish stew. The girls were both dressed in much the same manner as Carrina had been. Nikki, however, was startled to see them and turned immediately to take the cauldron. Kadana clapped him on the shoulder before he could do so, steering him back toward the table.

"Do you ride, Nikki?" she asked.

Dev rose and pulled out a chair at the table, and Kadana pushed the young man down into the seat.

Nikki looked utterly astonished. "My lady?" he asked, confirming to Shalonie that he did indeed know who Kadana was.

"Ride, my boy," Kadana went on. "Do you ride?" She gave him an appraising look. "You must be what, fifteen by now?"

"I am eighteen, my lady," Nikki said, his head held high, and his shoulders pulled back as if determined to meet the line of inquiry straight on.

He's no pushover either. Polite, but not scared of the nobles.

"Has it been that long already?" Kadana mused, caught up in her own thoughts for a moment. "I should have come sooner. No matter, I am here now." She clapped him heavily on the shoulder again when he started to rise, keeping him firmly seated at the table as she took her own seat beside him.

"My lady?" Nikki asked again, baffled by the turn of events.

"Do you know who I am, Nikki?" Kadana asked as she took two of the plates the serving girls had placed on the table and set one in front of Nikki and another in front of herself. She began loading both plates with cheese and bread while Nikki watched, befuddled.

"I do, Lady Deldano," he replied.

Shalonie noticed that while he spoke perfect Merchant's Common, he'd taken pains to smooth away some of the rough edges of his Kharakhian accent.

Kadana grimaced at the title. "I meant besides that."

Color rose in the young man's cheeks, and this time he merely inclined his head without giving a reply. He was obviously aware of their family connection. Considering some of the things Carrina had shouted earlier, Shalonie supposed Nikki had grown up being quite aware of the details of his birth.

"Good." Kadana nodded her approval. "You're of age, of course; free to go where you will, but I hope you'll agree to come with us. Your mother has already given you leave to join us. If you're worried about her, you needn't be. I've given her enough gold to replace you with three more servants and a cook."

"Really?" the young man's voice broke. His Deldano green eyes lit up with excitement.

Kadana looked pleased. "As I said, if I'd known about you, I would have come earlier. We Deldanos stick together, no matter what." She slapped Omen hard on the back with a friendly grin. "And I see you've already met your brother Omen."

"Brother?" Nikki turned toward Omen. "I always wanted to have a brother," the young man admitted, and this time Dev, Templar, and Liethan burst into laughter.

"I hope you mean that," Kadana said, not letting the laughter bother her, "because I'm afraid you're getting more than just one brother. Not to mention sisters, cousins, aunts, and uncles, but I'll let Omen explain the details to you."

Shalonie smiled at the look in the young man's eyes. She

was an only child herself, and despite their less-than-traditional circumstances, she'd always envied the large Deldano clan. *It'll be interesting to see how Nikki copes with his change in circumstance.*

Chapter 6: Stables

OMEN

Omen placed two large bowls heavy with fish stew in front of Tormy and Kyr. Then he set a small bowl in front of Tyrin.

Tyrin, however, had other ideas. The little cat ignored the bowl obviously meant for him, instead he stuck his face into Kyr's bowl and began lapping up the liquid.

Undeterred, Kyr dug his spoon into the stew and started eating as well.

Ugh.

While Omen had managed to teach Kyr basic table manners, it hadn't occurred to him to tell Kyr not to eat from the same bowl as the cats.

Took that for granted. But Kyr spent the majority of his life starving to death . . . I'll mention it later.

Omen set another bowl in front of Nikki.

What should I tell him?

Trying to buy himself time, Omen broke off a hunk of freshly baked bread and took a bite. "So, yes," he told Nikki through muffled chews, "you have a lot of new family members."

"Not us," Tormy piped up helpfully as he licked his whiskers for the bits of stew clinging to them. "We is being cats. We is not being your cousins or brothers on account of the fact that we is being twins and nobody is being able to tell us apart."

"Ah." Nikki looked from Tormy to Tyrin, seeming afraid

to speak.

"Yes, very helpful, Tormy." Omen patted the cat on the shoulder.

With a wet purr, Tormy turned back to his meal.

"So, there's me," Omen began, trying to organize the Deldano family in his head. *Better leave out the part about me and Cerioth though.* He proceeded to launch into a long and detailed accounting of the Deldano family tree, constantly interrupted by Liethan and Templar, who seemed more than eager to elaborate. *Not that Liethan has cause to talk — the Corsair family lines are just as convoluted.*

They all ate heartily while they chatted. Nikki still seemed uncertain of his position at the table. Occasionally he glanced over his shoulder as if expecting his mother to order him back to the kitchen.

Omen eyed the angry red mark on Nikki's cheek and the older bruise on the other side of the young man's face. *Probably never occurred to him to hit her back. Can't imagine. My parents don't pull their punches when we train — but they've never beaten me.*

Nikki caught Omen looking toward the kitchen. "I should have left a long time ago," Nikki said quietly, "but she's my mother. I thought she needed me."

"You've put in your time," Kadana said simply. "She made her choices. You need to make yours. Worlds to explore, my boy. It's time you get out there."

At that moment, the tavern door swung open wide, cutting short further discussion.

"Mother!" a young baritone voice cracked from the open doorway. "Glad we found you."

Tall and lean, two identical boys barged into the Green-Eyed Monster and headed straight toward their table.

93

Kadana jumped to her feet, nearly knocking over her chair. "My boys!"

Omen almost didn't recognize his young uncles Rask and Reeve — while it had been only two years since he'd last seen them, Kadana's sons had grown like weeds.

The twins moved through the tavern confidently as if it were their home, one of them continuing to address their mother. "Knew you had the Tormy cat with you when people said you'd arrived at port with a manticore." Both boys looked over at the giant cat.

Tormy sat up straighter.

While Rask and Reeve had never actually met Tormy before, they'd both written Omen numerous letters asking about the cat in detail. Both gave their mother exuberant hugs. *They're only twelve, and already as tall as Kadana.*

Omen also noticed that despite their youth, the twins also looked combat-ready. Scale armor gleamed under leather surcoats emblazoned with the green Deldano herald badge.

Not the full Deldano coat of arms. Interesting.

The young men carried swords strapped to their sides. Rask, distinguished by his wild mane of curly hair unlike the straighter mop of his brother's, also displayed an array of daggers at his belt.

I really have to teach Kyr how to fight, Omen reminded himself.

"Sit down, boys." Kadana gestured for extra chairs and more food.

The tavern door opened again, and a man paused in the doorway. Also tall, he had straight black hair like Reeve and an open smile like Rask.

"Diatho!" Kadana crossed the room swiftly and grasped

her husband's hands, a casual, warm gesture that showed great familiarity and comfort. He pulled her hands to his lips and placed quick kisses in each of her palms. A moment passed between them, and Omen found himself smiling at the warmth in their eyes.

Must be hard to be away from the family so much. If Shalonie can get that Cypher Portal created between Melia and Kharakhan, they can be together more often.

Diatho Deldano was not Kharakhian. Omen knew the tall man with dark eyes, raven black hair, and golden skin had come from the mysterious continent of Shindar, also the home of Beren's new wife, Nekarra. And while Kadana was a Kharakhian on her father's side, she too had relatives from Shindar.

Shindar was a place with unusual customs, ironclad traditions, and magics foreign and beautiful. Both Diatho and Nekarra were considered outcasts in their own lands, an outrage that made Omen mistrust the rules and regulations of the people of Shindar.

While Melia had strict customs, they had always seemed ones of gentility and kindness, designed to promote harmony among their people. The customs of Shindar seemed restrictively brutal, designed to keep the majority of society in tight check. *No wonder Diatho and Nekarra ultimately rebelled.* Both Diatho and Nekarra were of outstanding character in Omen's eyes, and anyone who would deem them *lesser* was very foolish or very wrong.

"So, what's for dinner?" Diatho asked and slid into a chair next to Kadana. Rask and Reeve both crowded around Tormy and Tyrin, ruffling the cats' fur and scratching them behind their ears. The resulting purrs — both rumbling and squeaking — told of the felines' delight and contentment.

Rask and Reeve seemed bewitched by the cats. Omen noticed that both boys took extra care to pat Tyrin gently and to moderate their exuberance around Kyr, who watched them uncertainly. *They know to be careful without being told.* Next to the twins, the half-elvin boy looked tiny and delicate. Omen wondered if his brother would ever gain back his full health or strength.

"More stew," Kadana told the serving girls, pushing Nikki back into his seat when he attempted to rise. "Not you."

Omen tried not to grin at the lost and confused expression on the young man's face as he took in Diatho, Rask, and Reeve. *No doubt desperately trying to figure out how he's related.*

"Why are the three of you so late, and why are my boys in brand-new armor?" Kadana asked, doling out warm biscuits and butter.

Diatho cupped a hand around the back of his neck. "There was some trouble on the road." Like the boys, he was dressed in scale mail over thick leather padding, a slender curved Shindarian blade at his side. He also carried a large Kharakhian broadsword which he'd set beneath the table.

"Trouble?"

"I thought the ride would be fun for the boys," Diatho said and took a drink from Kadana's tankard. "But at the bog . . . There are new critters in the bog."

"Slimy. Scaly," Rask added with exuberance. "Like tall toads or turtles walking on two legs."

"And carrying cudgels," Reeve added. "Bonked me in the shoulder good. Turned all purple."

"What did you learn?" Kadana asked without hesitation.

"I learned to duck."

The serving girls set steaming bowls of the seemingly never-ending fish stew in front of Diatho and his boys.

"Once we got to town, we went up and down the quarter looking for you. Then we spotted the gentry sigil on the door," Reeve said and tilted his head. "I clearly remember you telling us not to use the sigil."

Kadana's eyes flew to Dev, who was calmly finishing his bread pudding. The Machelli merely wiped his mouth with his coat sleeve.

"And so it stands," Kadana said firmly. "You are not to use the sigil, boys." She looked directly at Dev. "But some-times it is best for me to keep my private business private. As long as the gentry sigil is removed when we leave, so fair Carrina's customers know to return."

Omen spared a moment to look around the room. It oc-curred to him that they had spent the better part of two hours in the tavern and never once had another patron en-tered. *Gentry sigil? The nobles have a special mark that tells the commoners to stay away? And everyone follows that rule? Kharakhan has some curious customs.* While it was extremely unusual for anyone to directly approach a noble in Melia, they had no mark that forbade access. *But here the nobles seem to loathe the thought of mixing with their own people.*

"Rask, Reeve, come greet your nephew," Kadana start-ed, calling the twins away from the cats. It struck Omen how very similar in height and coloring Nikki and his un-cles were; while Omen was a Deldano as well, his copper-colored hair set him apart. His looks more favored 7.

Nikki could pass for their older brother. Besides their matching emerald eyes, the three shared a similar jawline

97

and strong, straight noses. Older, Nikki possessed a great deal more muscle than the lean, athletic twins.

"Sorry, Omen. Didn't mean to ignore you," Rask jumped in as the other twin turned his attention away from the cats to scoop Omen from his chair and close him in an unexpected bear hug. Omen laughed and clasped the boy back, pounding him heartily in greeting.

"We thought we'd be taller than you by now." Reeve chuckled, looking a little put out by the realization that Omen was still taller than them. "We're never going to catch up with you if you keep getting bigger."

"Well, there's only one of me," Omen pointed out. "I have to keep getting bigger to ward off the two of you."

"Is you being twins?" Tormy asked curiously. "Me and Tyrin is being twins, excepted that we is being identicallyness. You is not being identicallyness on account of the fact that you is smelling like apples and peaches."

"Identicallyness means we is both being orange," Tyrin added helpfully.

Rask and Reeve, identical save for the texture of their hair, both laughed at the same time. Omen supposed scent would be enough for the cats to tell them apart.

"I was just eating an apple," Rask agreed. "And Reeve had peaches earlier. They're both ripe at the same time — that's never happened before."

More out of season fruit. Omen frowned at Shalonie. *Doesn't bode well — the apples shouldn't be in season for months yet. Wonder what else is messed up.*

If Kadana was worried, she didn't show it. "I didn't mean Omen; come greet your new nephew," she corrected. "Boys, this is Nikki." She stood up and put both hands on Nikki's shoulders. The young man stood.

"Beren's?" Rask asked, approaching swiftly to shake Nikki's hand.

They're taking that in stride. I suppose they're used to it.

"Yes," Kadana said, "though he hasn't actually met Beren yet. No matter. His mother has given him leave to join up with us and—"

Yet another crash sounded from the kitchen.

Nikki shot a startled look toward the doorway.

Kadana patted his back. "Perhaps you had best get your things together now, Nikki," Kadana decided, sweeping aside the awkwardness. "We'll be off immediately, I think."

Nikki's green Deldano eyes sparkled with excitement. "I'll be right back," he promised and headed toward another door on the far side of the tavern.

While they waited for Nikki to return, Rask and Reeve happily recounted their adventures traveling to the city, describing their bog encounter in detail. Both seemed intent to impress their mother as well as the others. They spoke in rapid Kharakhian, their native tongue, and neither Kyr nor the cats took much notice — Kyr's attention held by the colored light coming in through the window, and Tormy and Tyrin still fully occupied with the fish stew. They claimed to be on their third helping, though Omen didn't believe it. *More like five or six.* Templar, Liethan, and Dev, however, enjoyed the tale. Omen noticed the pensive look on Shalonie's face as she listened, no doubt worried about the journey ahead.

"And then Dad cut through its arm, and it plunged back into the bog," Rask finished, eyes gleaming.

"But the arm started crawling, slow at first and then really fast, after its body," his twin added excitedly. "The stump was all blue and veiny and left these smears of black blood behind. I almost got sick! It was so wicked!" The brothers chortled.

"Bower Dames," Kadana said. "They don't normally slither out of the bog. It's very odd for them to attack travelers on the King's Road."

"That one won't do it again any time soon," Reeve insisted.

"Well," Kadana considered. "One Bower Dame isn't so difficult. It's when they start hunting in packs that you have real problems."

"There are more troubles coming from the northwest," Diatho inserted cautiously. He spread out a crude map drawn on a torn piece of linen and pointed to an area he'd labeled *wilderness*. "Had reports in Hollow's End that Skerlings have been rampaging between last light and moonrise."

"Skerlings," Kadana shuddered. "Hate those things."

"The Wyrding Woman brewed some poison to keep them away, but we might have to find an exterminator." Diatho ran his hands through his straight black hair. "We'll tell my father to look into it when we get back home. He has a lot of friends in the Chain, and he loves conducting official business."

Nikki returned before too long, carrying with him a small leather satchel which he slung over one shoulder. He'd also grabbed a worn woolen cloak, but Omen noted that he had no armor or weapon with him. Kadana too eyed him critically, but said nothing, nodding her head to him as if satisfied by what she saw. Nikki let out a visible sigh of relief.

"We better get to it then," Kadana announced. She scanned Diatho's crude map. "Four days ride, if we stay away from the portals, and if nothing gets in our way." She traced her finger over the charcoal lines demarcating the Bay of Khreté and ran it west toward the dot identified with the abbreviation D.K.

"Is that where the Deldano Keep is?" Nikki asked, holding his breath.

"Your ancestral home," Kadana said, a slight smile on her lips. "Such as it is," she added as if amused by a private joke.

It's got to be so strange for Nikki. To be dropped into this family without any warning. Changing stations from commoner to . . . What? A noble's illegitimate son? And what does that mean in Kharakhan? Wouldn't make a difference in Melia. When Hold Lord Jothfree adopted Skendar as his heir, no one blinked an eye.

"Has the keep been in the family for many generations?" Nikki's voice quivered with reverence.

"Just one. Mine." Kadana answered and clapped her newly discovered grandson on the shoulder. "I took the castle from someone who didn't deserve it."

Omen's eyes bugged out. "What?" he sputtered. *Never heard that story before. Doesn't that technically make it someone else's ancestral home?*

"Another rule of Kharakhan: If you can't hang on to it, you don't deserve it," Kadana said, having noticed Omen's visceral reaction. "Which is why I protect things I want to keep. Which is why Diatho and the boys won't join us on the ride back to our lands."

Diatho took in a short breath. "The ship?"

Guess that's news to him.

"Right." Kadana's tone was neither one of asking nor one of demanding. "The summer route isn't safe, so instead of continuing along our trade route, I want to move the ship to safe harbor now."

"Corsair Isles?"

"I sent messages ahead."

"Done." Diatho eyed his sons. "Guess our little trip to Khreté is going to turn into an ocean voyage to Mitraius."

Rask and Reeve whooped with joy. "Swimming in the sea! Cliff diving! Beach! Mierloje casserole! Going barefoot!"

"Sorry we won't be there to shield you from Caia back home," Rask said and nudged Nikki in the ribs. "She's six, and she never stops talking."

"And Tokara is ten, and she will follow you around like a puppy and eat all of your dessert."

Diatho's face spread into an indulgent smile. "Wait and see, boys. We'll be gone for months. You're going to miss your sisters."

Rask and Reeve didn't look too perturbed. "Are we really sailing to the Corsair Isles just like that, without going back home?" Rask asked Kadana, barely able to hide his excitement.

"Yes," Kadana assured him. "The ship will be safer there, but the autumn doldrums could slow you down. It might take longer than usual." Kadana gazed thoughtfully back down at the map as if plotting their course in her head. "The girls and I will catch up as soon as this Autumn Gate business is straightened out. And then we'll head out again. Ven'taria by winter solstice. Like I promised."

Then Kadana hugged her sons and her husband fiercely. At Omen's urging the rest of them gathered up their belongings and headed outside, leaving Kadana to bid her family goodbye in peace. Nikki, Omen noticed, didn't say goodbye to his mother, nor did he look back as he stepped from the tavern he'd grown up in. Omen bowed his head in sympathy.

Outside, Dev reached out to rub away the dark chalk mark he'd drawn on the door. But before he could do so, Shalonie stopped him. The girl peered intently at the mark, her hands scrambling for her notebook and the lead stylus she wrote with. She flipped through her notebook to a blank page and began copying the mark down. "Where did you learn this?" she asked Dev excitedly, the others watching her with curiosity.

Omen took note of the mark — a circle with several smaller sigils inside it.

Dev shrugged. "It's the nobility mark," he explained. "It's simply a general coat of arms indicating the ruling families. I don't think anyone even knows whose family it originated with. Been in use in Kharakhan for years. Hundreds of years I would imagine."

"At least," Nikki agreed as he moved somewhat closer to Shalonie so that he could see what she was writing. She'd already managed to copy the entirety of the mark down in her notebook with great accuracy and was now scribbling down what looked to Omen to be mathematical calculations.

"It's not a coat of arms," Shalonie told them. She turned her blue eyes on Nikki, her gaze turning sharp. "What does it mean?" she asked him swiftly, holding out her notebook and all but shoving it under his nose.

He flushed red at the attention. "As he said, it's the nobility mark," he told her.

She shook her head. "No," she insisted. "Look at it again. What does it mean to you? What do you think the moment you see it?"

He glanced down at the mark in her notebook. "Keep away," he said uncertainly.

She grinned, and then shoved the notebook at Omen. "You ever seen it before?" she asked him, motioning Templar to join him in staring at the mark. Both men looked at the notebook, and then at each other, uncertain why Shalonie was so excited.

"No," they both admitted.

"Looks a bit like a warding mark you'd see in Hex," Templar added. "The city walls are covered in them."

Shalonie looked delighted by the discovery. "It's a Cypher Rune," she told them. "And it probably means exactly what Nikki said — 'keep away.' It never occurred to me to look at merchant marks or coats of arms. Did you notice the liveries Rask and Reeve were wearing?" She looked eagerly at Omen.

He nodded. "A simplified version of the Deldano coat of arms."

"Yes, all the flourishes around the edge of the shielding were missing." She turned her attention inward, and Omen recognized the look she got on her face when she'd begun talking to herself, her quick mind going in directions even he couldn't follow.

"I'm going to have to look at the original coat, and all the others from Kharakhan," Shalonie said quickly. "Who knows what's hidden in them? That means that the second mark has to be a derivative of the elemental particle . . ." She wandered away from them, heading out into the street before Liethan caught her arm and steered her back toward the side of the roadway. She seemed to take no notice, her gaze once more on the pages of her notebook.

"Think it's all right to erase it now?" Dev asked Omen, a baffled look on his face. He motioned toward the mark on the door.

"Probably," Omen agreed. "She copied it down perfectly."

"Did I do something to offend her?" Nikki asked, his gaze fixed on Shalonie's bowed golden head as she scribbled away in her notebook.

"That's just Shalonie for you," Omen assured the young man. "Don't worry about it."

"She's beautiful," Nikki said, barely taking a breath. Both Templar and Omen started to laugh at the dopey look on his face.

"And way out of your league," Templar warned him with a chuckle.

Nikki blushed fiercely and turned his gaze away from her. "Of course, begging your pardon," he said hastily.

Templar clapped the young man on the shoulder. "I didn't mean it like that," he assured him. "She's out of everyone's league. And not because of her highborn status."

Nikki clearly didn't understand.

Omen took pity on him and explained. "Shalonie is a genius — more than that, she makes other geniuses look like idiots. She's something of a national treasure in her own kingdom."

"I see," Nikki said with difficulty. "I can read, and do my sums, but . . ." He trailed off as if realizing how that must sound. Omen could sympathize considering his father was one of the few people he knew who could follow Shalonie's fast thoughts and quick mind. *And when he teaches me, he expects me to catch on quickly.*

Kadana and the others joined them a moment later, the

two boys still looking excited, though Omen noticed Diatho did not seem quite as pleased.

He isn't ready to split up again. Kadana looks worried as well. But then considering the trouble we ran into on the ocean, I can't blame her. The sooner we get the Autumn Gate closed, the safer we'll all be.

They followed Dev down the road toward the stables where the Machellis were waiting for them with supplies. Several stable hands were saddling horses and preparing them for travel. Omen noticed the finely stitched saddle he'd had made for Tormy hanging over a stall gate — no doubt the stable hands weren't certain what to do with the odd contraption since it wasn't designed to fit a horse.

"Deldano Trotters," Templar exclaimed, moving forward to take the reins of one of the horses — it was a large, sturdy looking creature, with a thick fuzzy coat and a placid manner. "Mountain bred, I understand. Good pack animals. Solid draft horses too." He nodded his approval. The horse flicked his ears and stamped his iron-shod hooves.

They sorted their supplies, helping the stable hands finish up the preparations while Kadana said her last goodbyes to her family. The heavy haunches of meat Omen had asked Nikki to order had been delivered to the stables and neatly wrapped up for travel.

"Listen to your father," Kadana told her boys, her gaze moving swiftly over both of them as if memorizing the way they both looked. "And don't do anything I wouldn't do."

The boys laughed as if the joke was one they'd come to expect from their mother, but it never failed to amuse them.

My dad says that one too. And it always is funny.

Kadana walked a few paces with her husband; they said their farewells quietly.

Omen handed off the rest of his packs to one of the stable hands and went to retrieve Tormy's saddle.

"Come on Tormy, time to get ready," he called to his cat. Kyr was standing next to Tormy, clutching a handful of the cat's fur pensively as if uncertain what to do amidst so many stomping and snorting horses. Tormy's presence was making the Trotters uneasy, and Omen could hear horses in the stables snorting and neighing in fear. *At least the Deldano Trotters are bred for the battlefield — they'll adapt quickly enough to Tormy once they realize he's not going to eat them.*

Little Tyrin, poking from Kyr's pocket, was watching with eager curiosity while Tormy was sitting down on his haunches on the dusty ground, long fluffy tail twitching with nervous energy. The large cat pressed against the side of one of the horse stalls, while he gazed contemplatively up at the stable's hay-filled loft.

Omen sighed. He knew that look — any minute now Tormy was going to spring forward and climb into the loft, no doubt insisting that he needed a nap and *no* he wasn't going to wear the saddle. *This is going to be fun.* Omen tried to prognosticate the best way of handling his cat.

"We leaving you behind then?" Dev asked Tormy pointedly, having guessed the looming problem. "It's going to be a long walk for poor Kyr."

Both Tormy and Kyr looked astonished, and Tormy immediately rose to stand on all four paws. "I is not staying behind!" he protested.

Kyr grabbed large handfuls of the cat's long orange fur and scrambled like a monkey up his back. He clung awkwardly to the cat's body, grip white-knuckled as he started to slide off the other side.

107

"We is needing the saddle!" Tyrin shrieked from Kyr's pocket as Omen rushed forward to catch his brother before the boy could crack his head open on the gravel-covered ground.

"Right," Omen agreed. "Let's get the saddle on." He shot a look toward Dev who winked at him while aiding Shalonie with her supplies. The girl was trying to pack her things with one hand while still reading the notes in her book.

Omen helped Kyr down and then settled the saddle firmly on Tormy's strong shoulders.

"You're not riding him?" Nikki asked. He stood nearby, his hands gripping the reins of a horse that had been assigned to him, but he made no move to mount.

"Tormy's not full grown yet," Omen explained. "My father said I should wait at least another six months before riding him long distances."

"I is being strong!" Tormy objected, and Omen bit back his mirth as he cinched up the straps of the specially made saddle.

"Yes, very strong," Omen agreed, lifting Tormy's paw so that he could get one of the shoulder straps under his body, taking care to keep his fur smooth against the soft leather. "But your bones have more growing to do yet."

Omen cinched up the underbelly strap and then adjusted the bags so that they lay flat against the cat's body. "Are your straps tight enough, Tormy?" he asked doubtfully. If Tormy had been a horse he would have kneed him in the ribs to make him let his breath out, but Omen couldn't bring himself to knee the cat. *Not to mention, I'd never hear the end of it!*

"Yes, they is," Tormy agreed quickly. Too quickly. The

108

cat wasn't looking at him, which was telling.

Omen sighed again. "Tormy, if your straps aren't tight enough, your saddle will slip and Kyr will fall. And he will hurt himself."

He saw the cat's ears droop. Tormy lashed his tail from side to side several times, before turning to gaze solemnly at him. "Omy, my straps is not being tight enough."

Omen adjusted them again until finally the cat gave him a nod of confirmation. "Right then, Kyr, up you go," he told the boy who paced nervously beside him.

Kyr looked wary but dutifully reached up to grasp the silver pommel attached to the saddlebow. Omen lifted him into place, setting his booted feet in the stirrups. He squeezed Kyr's ankle to get his attention. "Remember, keep your feet in the stirrups, heels down." A few feet away he noticed Nikki watching them closely as if trying to fix Omen's advice in his mind. He held the reins of his horse as if they were snakes — tightly clenched but away from his body. He didn't look any more eager than Kyr had.

"My horse doesn't have that many straps," Nikki pointed out. "Won't my saddle slip?"

"You're riding a horse not a cat," Omen reminded him. "They don't need as many straps — horses are not as likely to twist or curve the way a cat can, and they most certainly won't suddenly leap into a tree and start climbing vertically."

Nikki's complexion took on a greenish tinge. "Ah, I see . . . is the little guy going to be all right?"

"I is being fine!" Tyrin replied from Kyr's pocket. "I is being a great tree climber!"

Omen chuckled and patted the kitten on the head through the material of the coat. "I think he meant Kyr."

Satisfied that Kyr was safely seated, he turned his attention back to Nikki. Dev had picked out a horse for him earlier, a calm, sturdy-looking gelding that waited patiently beside him, seeming unbothered by the large carnivorous cat only a few feet away. Indeed most of the Deldano Trotters had relaxed their initial distrust of the obvious apex predator and now seemed surprisingly unperturbed by Tormy's presence. The horse Dev had chosen for Nikki appeared to be the calmest of the bunch.

"You doing all right there, Nikki?" Omen asked, taking a guess that while the young man probably had worked in a stable at some point in his life — he likely hadn't done much riding.

Nikki nodded, turning his pale face determinedly toward the horse. He sighed, caught hold of the saddlebow, and fixed his left foot in the stirrup. Cautiously he swung himself into the saddle, balancing precariously. "All right," he breathed out. "What do I do if I have to stop?"

"You is saying 'Whoa, horsie. Whoa!' That is how you is stopping," Tyrin answered obligingly.

"Don't worry about it," Omen assured the young man. "Your horse will follow the others. Keep your seat and you'll be fine." He swung expertly up into the saddle of his own horse, and they all began moving out into the stable-yard. They called out their farewells as Diatho and the boys bid them goodbye before heading down toward the docks and the Golden Voyage.

"Come on then," Kadana called out. She tugged on her horse's reins, and kicked him lightly in the side, taking off down the cobbled road at a fast clip. The others fell into place behind her. Tormy trotted dutifully alongside the group though he was more inclined to move chaotically through the street, frequently stopping to investigate things and then having to run to catch up. Omen watched worriedly as Kyr blithely rode the cat, seeming unconcerned by his unruly mount. *I'll be glad when we get out of the city. Too many things here to distract Tormy.*

They exited the city through the King's Gate, the Kharakhian guards on duty sparing them only a nod as they rode onto the main highway. While the city roads had all been cobbled, the highway was not — though years of travelers had left the ground hardpacked and firm. The stone wall of Khreté gave way to the great Kharakhian woodlands, and the main highway branched off in several directions not far from the gate. Numerous wooden signs had been posted, showing the directions to other cities.

It was late afternoon and more people were making their way into the city than out of it. Merchant wagons, rolling along the road toward the gate, pulled to the side to avoid the group. More than one person pointed toward Tormy, some nervously, some enchanted. In the afternoon sunlight, the cat's orange and white fur stood out like a flame against the dark green of the surrounding forest.

Kadana directed them to stop as soon as they had crossed over to the main highway. "Twilight should still be hours away, but the light is shifting already," she pointed out to all of them. Her face was fixed in a worried expression. "These are autumn skies."

Shalonie lifted her head and shaded her eyes. "But the sun is in the right place for summer."

"It is odd," Kadana said, ambivalent. "Regardless, we'll continue west, away from the ocean and into the heart of Kharakhan. We have a lot of ground to cover before supper tonight."

111

"Supper?" Tormy sounded hopeful.

"We just had lunch," Omen tried to head the cat off.

"The stew?" Tormy's ears flicked back. "That is being hours ago!"

Nikki shifted uncomfortably in his saddle.

"Nikki did a nice job with that stew," Omen responded quickly. "It was very filling, and it wasn't hours ago. You can't possibly be hungry again."

"Nikki's stew is being very good," Tormy agreed. "But traveling is being very hard, and I is being goodnessness with the saddle and all. I is carrying two entire peoples."

"That is being true!" Tyrin piped up in agreement. "He is carrying me and Kyr. That is being at least two, maybe even three or four."

"We are traveling, Tormy," Omen said gently. "And we just started. Sometimes our schedule can't be helped."

"Oh, I is helping the schedule," Tormy replied agreeably. "When we is stopping at the inn for the night, I is ordering supper for everyone."

"There's no inn tonight, Tormy." Kadana studied the road ahead. "But don't worry. I have a plan. We'll be fine — now come on cat, put your back into it. We have a road to travel!" She set heels to her horse, Tormy taking off after her as if swept up by her words.

"We is &^!@$! adventuring cats!" Tyrin shrieked, and the rest of the group hurried to catch up.

Chapter 7: Road

OMEN

Despite the unnatural encroachment of autumn weather, it was still the height of the growing season, the solstice less than a week away. The days were at their longest, and though they'd left Khreté in the afternoon, there were still many hours of daylight ahead of them. Kadana pushed them hard, and to Omen's relief, Tormy stayed quiet through much of the journey, his attention focused on keeping up with the horses' steady clip. While cats were not endurance animals, Tormy trotted alongside the horses with ease, his orange and white fur flouncing in the summer breeze.

Given their late start, Kadana didn't allow much opportunity for rest, insisting on only brief stops to water the horses as they passed streams along the way. *She's anxious to get home to her daughters,* Omen thought as he spied his grandmother studying the map more than once as if plotting and re-plotting their route. From what he'd understood, Diatho's father was currently looking after her girls and the keep. *But it's not the same as being home with them.*

The road through the forest was well-traveled — the hard-packed dirt making easy ground for the horses. Occasionally wagons passed them on the way into Khreté, but as twilight began setting in, the number of travelers dwindled to nothing. When night finally fell, Kadana led the group to a clearing off the main road and announced they'd be stopping for the night.

Tormy surprisingly said nothing; instead he moved off to one side and lowered himself belly first onto a patch of grass, tucking his front paws underneath his chest.

Concerned, Omen dismounted quickly, tossing his reins to Templar so he could check on his cat. Kyr, who'd slid from Tormy's saddle the moment the cat lowered himself to the ground, was tugging at one of the buckles on the saddle, trying to remove it. Fortunately, the boy didn't seem unduly alarmed by Tormy's somewhat unnatural stillness, and little Tyrin sat calmly beside Tormy's front paws and watched the others dismount.

"You feeling all right there, Tormy?" Omen asked, placing his hand on the cat's large head. Resting as he was, Tormy's head barely reached Omen's chest.

"My paws is being tired, Omy," Tormy replied, tilting his head so that Omen could scratch his ears. "Is we stopping now?"

"Yes," Omen assured the cat. "You did really good carrying Kyr." He glanced at the boy who was still working on the straps and realized that with the saddle on, Tormy couldn't easily stretch out on his side like he preferred. Kyr had gotten one strap undone, but was struggling with the next. Omen moved quickly to help the boy, expertly undoing all the buckles and then lifting the saddle away from the cat. The orange and white fur beneath was matted down. Omen retrieved the large brush he kept in one of the saddlebags. He handed the brush to Kyr, who grinned at him and set himself to brushing out the cat's long fur.

Tormy's probably hungry as well, Omen thought to himself, surprised the cat wasn't raising more of a fuss about food after his protests earlier that day. While both cats could be troublesome on occasion, they also both seemed

114

eager to help.

The others were well on their way to setting up the camp for the night. Templar had already unsaddled Omen's horse for him and had led it to the far side of the camp with the other horses, where Liethan was seeing to them. Kadana and Shalonie lugged bucketfuls of water from a small nearby stream. Dev, armed with an axe, motioned Nikki to help collect firewood. The young Deldano moved gingerly, but followed Dev without complaint.

He's not used to riding. He's got to be sore.

Omen gathered the large sacks carried by the pack animals and set about sorting their provisions. *Meal prep.* He'd made certain they'd brought along plenty of meat for the cats for the first night, so they wouldn't have to go hunting. *All I need is some water and to get a fire going.*

Nikki and Dev returned with armfuls of firewood, and in no time a bright fire burned in the middle of the clearing, the light warding off the cool darkness.

Kadana motioned Nikki over and handed him a small flask. "It'll take the edge off, my boy."

Nikki took the offering, quickly bringing it to his lips and taking a full pull of the liquid.

That's either a healing potion, or some strong grast.

"It still feels like everything from my calves to my waist is one huge bruise," the young Deldano told Kadana, sounding grateful. "But now I don't think I care so much."

Grast.

Omen made a mental note not to ask Nikki to take watch. *He's either going to be too sore or too tipsy. Either way, he should just rest.*

After a few quick adjustments, a thick haunch of beef turned on its makeshift spit; Omen meticulously seasoned the roast, making sure to cover every bit of the surface. *Salt. What's better than salt?* He checked on the cast-iron pot filled to the brim with his favorite childhood meal — Chicken Scaalia, which his mother would make for him regularly as he was growing up and still made on special occasions.

He'd been taken aback to find the ingredients, including containers with chopped up Scaalian olives and dried plums, in their supply bags. *Thank you Machelli kin.*

At first he'd been unsure how to cook the familiar recipe over a campfire. But once he'd determined that browning the chicken pieces in the cast-iron pot was easy, it only took a moment to start adding ingredients. He borrowed Kadana's wineskin for a splash of dark Litranian red and sprinkled the bubbling concoction with a handful of sugar. *Let that sit on the flames for an hour.* He added another pinch of salt, then he checked on the flat bannock bread in the skillet next to the pot. *Almost looks like a loaf. But it should taste good.*

Catching the scents of cooking, Tormy perked up. Omen could hear loud purring coming from the cat while Kyr dutifully combed out the tangled orange fur. The mellow purr set Omen at ease.

What a perfect night.

The travel and the fresh air of the summer woodlands had whetted everyone's appetites, and they all gathered around the fire hungrily.

Once both the cats were gnawing away on meaty bones, and he was certain his brother was eating enough of the hearty chicken, Omen retrieved the lute. He'd been dying to play the instrument ever since they'd rescued it from the Nightling in the castle.

He set about checking the strings for damage. Under normal circumstances, the lute should have needed restringing after sitting idle for so many years. But one strum of the fifteen metal strings declared them in good form and finely tuned.

It's still tuned to Beren's voice, Omen marveled to himself, recognizing the key Beren preferred. He fiddled briefly with the tuning keys, testing out how readily they changed the pitch and tone of each string, before setting his fingers against the neck of the lute and running through a series of warm-up exercises. *It's been a while since I've had time to practice — or had a lute to practice on.* He peered over at his large orange cat, but Tormy was still happily nibbling at his meal. *If Templar tricks Tormy into destroying this lute, I'll destroy those bone blades he's so fond of. Or I'll cut his hair when he's not looking.* Omen threw a warning look at his friend and found Templar watching him, amused, as if he knew exactly what Omen was thinking.

"Go on then," Templar urged. "Give us a tune. Been a while since you've had an instrument of that caliber."

"Whose fault is that?" Omen shot back, still sore about the loss of his favorite lute.

Templar placed his right hand over his heart. "I swear on my honor I will not attempt to damage this lute in any way." Though the mischief in his eyes belied his words.

Omen held his stare, unrelenting.

Templar reached for another helping. "I didn't actually mean to damage the previous one, honestly," he assured him. "I had no idea Tormy was that hungry."

"He's always hungry," Omen reminded him.

"That is being true!" Tormy piped up, lifting his head

117

briefly. "I is always being hungry on account of the fact that my belly is being emptinessness. Is you going to play for us, Omy? I is liking a song. I is not eating your magic lute, Omy, I promise." He extended the 'o' in promise for several long seconds as if lengthening the sound would assure Omen of his sincerity. It was hard to stay mad in the face of such sincere remorse. *Makes up for Templar's non-apology apology.*

"Do you think the magic in the lute is dangerous?" Omen asked Kadana. While he could feel the power in the instrument, the few chords he'd played hadn't seemed to do anything unusual.

Kadana cocked her head to one side. "I think you have to activate it somehow — Beren never explained the mechanics behind it — not that I know much about bardic magic."

With the others watching expectantly, Omen quickly decided on a fairly well-known tavern song about a wishing well. He played several bars of the song before he started to sing, his voice blending harmoniously with the sweet tone of the lute. The music rose above the crackling flames.

As he sang, he could feel the hum of power beneath his fingers thrumming through the body of the instrument as if waiting for him to touch it. He made no attempt to activate it or interact with it, unsure what precisely it could do, but he let his psionic senses probe it tentatively, testing the source of the power. *It's the music itself,* he noted with surprise. *A sour note would break the spell — it's responding to both the strings and my voice.*

He didn't try to awaken the magic, but he noted that as the music drifted over him, his mood lifted considerably, rejuvenating him, making him feel energetic despite the long ride. *I can see where that alone could be valuable,* he thought. He couldn't help but wonder if playing the instrument could cure a psionic reaction headache. *My psionic and magical patterns take the shape of musical tunes — I'm certain I could learn to use this lute to amplify them.*

The tune he played was familiar enough to the others that after a few verses both Shalonie and Liethan joined in on the chorus. While Liethan was no musician, he had a pleasant enough voice, and Shalonie, being Melian, had been studying music since she was a child and added harmonies that Omen enjoyed. The real surprise was when Nikki joined in after a while — his strong tenor blending perfectly with Omen's.

He's feeling better. Definitely Beren's son, Omen thought with something akin to pride and threw a look over to his grandmother. Kadana chuckled to herself — there wasn't a single one of Beren's children who didn't have a beautiful voice and the musical talent to match it.

Omen played several more songs, choosing tunes he was certain both Nikki and Shalonie would know. They all had a good laugh when Tormy insisted on joining in, happily singing in his off-tune fashion and making up the words of the song as he went. *And he does it so earnestly,* Omen thought mirthfully and played a couple of tunes he knew the cat especially liked.

"It's an exquisite instrument," Omen pronounced after a while.

"You play it well," Kadana agreed. "You'll have to get Beren to show you how to access all of its magic."

"Why do you suppose Charaathalar stole it?" Omen wondered. "He wasn't a musician. Was he?"

Kadana took a drink from a different wineskin. "Sheer

greed — he was an unpleasant man."

"The king?" Nikki asked, looking surprised as if he were uncertain he'd heard them correctly.

Figuring Nikki would likely hear the story from someone else sooner or later, Omen briefly recounted the tale of their encounter with Charaathalar in the castle earlier that day. Nikki listened in stunned silence.

"So he sold us out?" Nikki asked when he'd finished. "Our king bargained away the souls of everyone in Khreté in exchange for immortality?"

"Bargained away lives, not souls," Dev corrected. "You can't give away someone else's soul — just your own. He bargained with the lives of his citizens, not their souls. There's a difference."

"Not much of one," Omen protested. "Dead is dead. Does it really matter how it happens?"

"Yes, it matters," Dev insisted emphatically. "Death isn't the worst thing that can happen to a person. It's not even in the top ten worst things. In some cases, it's even a blessing. Charaathalar was a fool for asking for immortality."

Unease stole over Omen. He'd never heard such a sentiment before — not that he'd thought overly long about it. At fifteen, he'd never had much cause to contemplate death, and even if he had, immortality was a gift he'd been born with. *Same with Templar, Liethan, Kyr, and Nikki — though Nikki probably doesn't know it yet. Not like the Deldanos go around bragging about their inhuman heritage. And it's certainly nothing the Corsairs openly advertise.*

He looked at the cats and then his grandmother, a cold sinking sensation hitting the pit of his stomach. He knew his grandmother, while youthful in appearance due to a quirk of magic, was completely human, and thus mortal.

And he knew next to nothing about the species of creatures the two cats came from, or how long-lived either of them might be. *Not like regular house cats surely — with only a decade or so of life. Tormy is so big!*

"I thought immortality was a great blessing bestowed by the gods?" Nikki asked in confusion as if equally baffled by Dev's words. "Is it not?"

"No. Dev is right," Kadana told them all firmly. "Immortality is no blessing. Most immortals come to a very bad end."

"A bad end?" Omen protested. "But that's the whole point. If you're immortal, you can't die."

"Of course immortals can die," Kadana scoffed. "It doesn't look the same as a mortal death, but it's an ending nonetheless. But death wasn't what I was talking about. Death is the last thing an immortal should worry about."

"Most immortals end up slaves to someone more powerful," Dev told them. "Look at what happened to Charaathalar. He didn't even get a single moment to enjoy his immortality before he was trapped. And even if he should be freed, that Night Lord will never leave him in peace. The moment he even thought of making that bargain he was already doomed. And what happened to him is the norm, not the exception. Most immortals end up longing for a death that will never come."

Omen looked across the fire toward Shalonie to see if she was accepting these words as truth, but to his surprise, her gaze was resting on Kyr, a soft sadness in her eyes. She looked up at him then and gave him a quiet smile as if she understood. *She's not immortal — Melians are long-lived, but not immortal and yet . . .*

He turned to look at his little brother who was staring up

at the night sky with rapt attention, his thin body resting back against Tormy's warm belly as he and the two cats talked quietly to one another. Omen thought about the years of torture the boy had endured before Omen had rescued him. *He wouldn't have survived any of that if he hadn't been Cerioth's son.* Though Omen didn't want to even think too long on what it must have been like for Kyr, he couldn't help but realize that Dev was probably right. *How many times did Kyr wish for a death that would never come? If I hadn't found him . . .*

"Immortality is one of the reasons the Gated Lands exist," Shalonie told them then. "If you live long enough the world around you changes too much, to the point that you can no longer endure it. That's what happened to all the people in those lands — they went into worlds that don't change, that remind them of what this world once was."

"Not the Night Dwellers," Dev corrected. "They didn't go willingly. And they will never stop trying to reclaim this world."

Omen threw a quick glance at Templar who was listening with a dark frown on his face. Liethan too was unusually quiet, clearly never having contemplated the repercussions of having inhuman blood. In the flickering firelight, Templar's face was cast into shadow, and the inhuman yellow in his eyes stood out all the more as it flashed with the fire. "You know just because someone has Nightblood, doesn't make them a bad person," Templar objected.

Dev laughed at that, his mood shifting again as he fixed Templar with a bemused smile. "Really? You certain of that? How many Nightbloods do you actually know personally?"

"Three," Templar shot back immediately. "Me, my father

and my sister."

"Three." Dev exaggerated the word. "Tormy can even count that high."

Tormy, who had not been following the conversation, still more focused on the quiet words being exchanged between Kyr and Tyrin, looked up at the sound of his name. "I is counting to three!" he agreed happily. "I is learning lots of numbers. Is somebody needing me to do the countings?"

"No, that's all right, Tormy." Omen patted the side of the cat's belly before turning his attention back to the others.

"Three or not," Templar argued. "That still proves my point." He looked toward Omen as if for confirmation, and Omen nodded encouragingly.

"Three out of millions, perhaps billions of creatures?" Dev pressed. "And of those three you know, one is the Warlord Antares, Conqueror of Terizkand—"

"My father liberated Terizkand!" Templar protested immediately, quick to rise to his father's defense. "He's still fighting to rid our lands of the giants who had enslaved us."

"Terizkand would be a nightmare if wasn't for Antares," Omen agreed.

"He's still terrifying," Dev pointed out.

Omen had to concede that point. *Antares is terrifying.*

"The second — your sister — is the High General of Terizkand," Dev continued. "Equally terrifying. So that leaves the third — you . . . Do you count yourself a hero?"

Templar blanched. "Well, no, Omen's really more the hero type. I simply go along with him because it's less boring that way . . . Oh!" His face lit up then as a thought occurred to him. "We play Nightball! That's fun! Those Night Dwellers are fun."

Omen had to agree. *Nightball is fun. Insane, but fun.*

123

"I've seen Nightball," Dev sighed. "Do you really think for a single moment that if either you or Omen fell in the midst of one of your games that your opponents wouldn't literally tear you apart?"

"No, of course they would," Templar scoffed as if the idea were ridiculous. "That's what makes it fun."

"Wouldn't be Nightball without the fear of dismemberment." Omen grinned at Templar.

Kadana started laughing, and Omen gave his grandmother a confused look, only to realize a moment later that Dev's point had been made. Of the three Nightblooded people he knew, all were . . . *Crazy, terrifying, unsafe?*

"Templar might have Nightblood," Omen snapped at Dev, annoyed that the Machelli was disparaging his friend, "but he's also the first to come to any of our defense." *Machelli superstition. But my mother doesn't mind Templar.* "And while we're on the subject, you certainly seem to know an awful lot about Night Dwellers." Omen desperately hoped to catch Dev in some subterfuge.

The Machelli didn't even blink. "I've had a few unpleasant run-ins with Night Dwellers. It pays to learn as much as you can about the people and things you're up against. I don't like surprises."

"That's enough talking for one night," Kadana interrupted curtly. She rose to her feet. "Probably best not to talk so much about Night Dwellers while it's . . . you know . . . nighttime. And in any event, dawn will come early and we all need to get some sleep. Dev, take first watch. Wake me in a few hours. The rest of you, get to sleep. Omen, Templar, you'll both take a turn at watch as well."

"Tormy would hear anything before it got close to camp," Omen assured her as he rose to his feet. The loud snore that followed his words caught his attention. He realized with chagrin that his cat was already sound asleep, Kyr half-buried under the cat's large paw, also snoring. Tyrin had climbed on top of both of them and was curled up on Kyr's head, nose tucked firmly under his own white paws. All three were insentient to the world.

"I'll take a turn at watch," Omen amended immediately and smiled sheepishly at his grandmother.

She nodded and headed toward her own bedroll for the night.

Chapter 8: Bears

SHALONIE

S halonie was up with the sun the following morning and watched, quietly amused, as Kyr begged and prodded Tormy to wake from his torpid doze. The boy looked flustered, unable to break through Tormy's refrain of, "I is still sleeping."

But once the truly mouthwatering aroma of breakfast — bacon-wrapped trell, Omen announced — wafted through the camp, the cat grew lively, as did his miniscule double.

"How did you manage this, my boy?" Kadana scraped at her plate, trying to spear the last bits of flaky fish as the very satisfying campfire breakfast drew to a close.

"With a little help from my brother." Omen nodded toward Nikki.

Nikki blushed slightly. "We prepared the fish at the Green-Eyed Monster. Just before we left. Salt, pepper, sage. Omen said to stuff and wrap the fish with bacon. Done in a snap."

"A little domestic cantrip to keep them fresh . . ." Omen eyed Shalonie as she took a careful bite. "Doesn't taste frozen? Does it?"

"No," Shalonie answered while chewing. "Delicious!"

Omen nodded with satisfaction, finishing off the remnants.

Tyrin happily licked up bacon crumbs and bits of fish that had fallen to the ground around where Dev sat.

That Machelli sneak dropped food for the cat on pur-

pose, Shalonie thought. *Why . . .*

"Campfire fish bacon is being the bestest!" Tyrin squealed with delight.

She noted the amused look on Dev's face as the little cat hopped over his legs to get to another bit of bacon. *Creating a positive association. Clever.*

"Don't expect more of that." Omen picked up the cast iron pan. "Any other fish, we'll have to catch ourselves."

Shalonie felt the tingle of the third Tevthis Pattern sweep over the pan, cleaning the surface.

Magical kitchen shortcuts. Must be shying away from domestic psionic use. I wonder . . . She made a mental note. *My psionics don't match up to the Daenoths', but I bet I can work out the patterns to suit the purpose.*

"No time for fishing," Kadana said as she stood. "We have to get started. Long day ahead."

Omen's relief was obvious when Tormy made little fuss as Omen began to saddle him. *Full belly. Helps make the cat cooperative.* Shalonie observed with delight that Tormy even offered helpful suggestions while Omen fastened the straps. *And he's committed to keeping Kyr safe.*

"We're going to have to get you some armor one of these days, Tormy," Omen remarked as he adjusted the saddlebags. "I'm sure I can find someone who can make armor that will fit a cat." He gave Tormy's ear a quick pat. "Even a big cat."

"They make armor for horses," Templar added, seeming to consider the possibility. "Don't see why they can't make some for a cat."

"I is being a fierce fighting cat," Tormy declared, seeming captivated by the suggestion.

"I is getting armor too," Tyrin declared from his perch

atop Kyr's shoulder.

As Shalonie gathered her own things together for the day, she smiled warmly at Kyr, who was waiting dutifully off to one side while Omen finished with Tormy's saddle. The boy wore his sword at his left hip, and the dagger Templar had given him strapped to his right leg. Shalonie saw Omen give his brother a nod of approval.

He's so proud of Kyr for the slightest thing.

"We is both being fierce fighting cats," Tormy told Tyrin. "So we is needing armor . . . and a horn . . . I is wanting a battle horn."

"I is wanting a battle horn too," Tyrin agreed. "We is blowing our battle horns and racing into battle."

Omen shook his hair out of his eyes as he fastened the under-strap of Tormy's saddle. "How are the two of you going to blow battle horns?"

Sometimes, I don't think those cats remember they're cats. Shalonie gave Nikki a mirthful smile. The young man dropped his backpack and blushed.

He sure can be clumsy.

"Kyr is blowing the battle horn," Tyrin corrected. "We is taking Kyr with us when we is riding into battle, and he is blowing our battle horn."

Kyr cocked his head to one side like a befuddled puppy faced with the inexplicable. "The trees are on fire," he declared solemnly.

Shalonie and Templar, who was saddling the horses nearby, both glanced at the tall trees surrounding them, then over at the campfire as if trying to second-guess what Kyr meant. *Kyr frequently sees things we don't.*

"Nikki already put out the campfire," Omen told the boy.

"I did," Nikki affirmed. "Don't worry, Kyr."

128

"See, it can't catch the trees on fire—" Omen stopped speaking. "Oh, do you mean . . ." He threw a worried look at Shalonie.

It occurred to her that the boy was being metaphoric. Since leaving Khreté they had passed any number of trees that were already changing their colors to the reds and golds of autumn as if confused by the season. Plenty of fruit hung ready to be picked, ripened too early. And Kyr had already professed some alarm at the changing colors.

"The trees do that every autumn, Kyr," she told him slowly, "change colors. The leaves fall off in winter, but they come back every spring. It's the natural cycle." *But it's not autumn*, she thought with anxiety. *And this is anything but natural.*

Kyr twitched his brow, bewildered, but he nodded obediently, accepting her word without question.

Shalonie checked Omen's reaction, worry nagging at the back of her brain. *I hope it's not more than that. Kadana said to listen to Kyr.*

But Kadana seemed unconcerned by Kyr's words, ready and mounted, waiting for their small party to get going. "All right, let's get moving," she barked from the far side of camp. "We have a lot of ground to cover before nightfall."

"Blow your battle horns!" Tormy shouted with startling excitement. He, Tyrin, and Kyr raised their faces to the sky and yowled loudly and tunelessly in unison before collapsing into a fit of giggles.

Kadana too roared with laughter at the clamor while the others did nothing to hide their grins.

"Good thing we're not aiming for stealth," Dev remarked coolly, though he seemed tickled by the antics of cats and boy as well.

"Up you go, Kyr," Omen said, helping Kyr into the saddle before grabbing his own horse's reins. They rode out of the clearing and headed back to the road.

❖

The King's Road narrowed after a while, as a rising cliff penned them in on one side and a brush-filled ravine on the other. For several miles, they were forced to ride single file. Shalonie kept a keen eye on the great forest sprawling below them. It stretched out beyond the horizon. *Kharakhan doesn't seem like a land that has been tamed, despite the generations of Set-Manasan rulers. I've read the population is low too, considering the size of it.* She gauged the road, noting how it gradually snaked through the green hills, situated — she estimated — with measured precision between the rise and the drop, taking them on the most expedient route through the wilderness. *Someone knew exactly what they were doing.*

"How old is this road? Shalonie yelled, hoping Kadana, who rode at the front, could hear her.

"Don't know," Kadana tossed back. "It's always been here when I've needed it."

Which is all that really matters to her. Shalonie had to concede that Kadana's interest in the engineering of the kingdom of Kharakhan was bound to be minimal. *Silly to ask her. But somebody has to know the answer.*

"At least the narrow path keeps my horse from trying to graze," Nikki called over his shoulder and gave Shalonie a pained smirk.

He sounds nervous.

"Just don't keep a tight hold on the reins. Your horse will want to fight you if you hold too tight." She held up her own hands, demonstrating her loose grip. "It goes against instinct, but you'll have more control if you go easy on the reins."

Nikki's smile warmed, but a slight slip in the saddle forced him to quickly turn back to face the road.

He looks just like a Deldano. Shalonie noted the hard muscles of Nikki's back. *But he's so different from Beren's other children. Unsure of himself. Sweet, but he always seems to be looking for permission. He's definitely seen hard labor, but he's had no real schooling or training — not in fighting, magic, music . . . riding.*

Now tilted slightly to the side and hunched over, Nikki rode like he'd never been on a horse before. *He clings on valiantly, but he's got to still be sore from yesterday . . . And there won't be enough grast to fix the accumulating agony.*

"I is smelling badnessness!" Tormy cried out abruptly and spun his body toward the ravine. Kyr clung to the saddle horn with both hands.

"Whoa." Omen brought his horse to a halt. "Watch it Tormy!" He leaned back, trying unsuccessfully to capture the cat by the fur. "Don't let Kyr fall!"

Startled, Shalonie's horse took a few high steps forward as Templar's mount, encouraged by its rider, blocked the path to keep the other horses from bolting.

"It is being &$#@ stinky!" Tyrin squealed from his perch on Tormy's head.

Shalonie smelled nothing but a pleasant blend of rich, deep forest scents: wood, wet earth, moss, mushrooms, and the floral tones of a myriad of wildflowers warming in the sun.

Shouldn't golden hearts bloom in early autumn? she thought, absently acknowledging the round golden heads of the scattered flowers.

Tormy gave out a clicking chitter that Shalonie associated with cats who wanted to hunt but were confined inside.

"Tormy, don't—" Omen barely got the words out before Tormy took a giant leap and landed on the slope side of the ravine. Omen vaulted off his horse and sprinted after the large cat, who started crashing through the vegetation, heading downward, both Kyr and Tyrin — either willing or unwilling — passengers on their runaway mount.

Unsure what drove her, Shalonie sprang from her saddle as well, reaching the side of the ravine before Omen did. She dove down into the brush and stumbled after Tormy while trying to avoid tumbling to the ground.

"Meet you at the bottom!" Kadana's shout penetrated the rushing of blood in Shalonie's ears. The thunder of hooves followed, but Shalonie didn't look back at her companions.

She had managed to stay on her feet when she'd hit the ground, but she could feel the pull and scratch of thorny branches on her face and hands. Omen was beside her momentarily, then passed her — both of them running as fast as they could, following the wide swath of bent shrubs and vegetation left in Tormy's wake.

Her eyes fixed on the orange, plumy tail waving like a flag, she saw the moment it disappeared.

She nearly crashed into Omen who also stopped without warning. He pivoted to face her, his eyes gleaming with intensity. "Shh." He placed his index finger across his lips.

She nodded and gestured ahead. Quietly, they crept forward, passing larger trees as the grade of the slope lessened. It did not take long for Shalonie and Omen to catch up to where Tormy crouched, nearly hidden behind a line of trees. Both cats — large and small — and Kyr, who seemed no worse for the abrupt gallop, silently gaped at the scene at the bottom of the ravine, even as Omen gently lifted the boy from Tormy's back and set him on the ground.

Pressing herself against the trunk of a young Kharakhian oak, Shalonie regained her rational sense as the bark pushed against her skin. Never in her life had she acted without thinking. Her chasing after Tormy and Kyr hadn't been rational, it had been instinctual. *Reckless.* Shalonie couldn't help the smirk that played across her face. *Reckless.* Her mother always called her father reckless. *I'm like him. When it counts. I'm like him. Not like her.*

"What is that?" Omen whispered, the question directed at her.

Shalonie tried to focus on the shapes below them, but what she saw made no sense to her, so she focused on the movements themselves. "It's a couple of trees swaying over a hole in the ground," she answered quietly.

"They is bears," little Tyrin supplied in a smaller voice than she'd ever heard escape the cat. "I is smelling they is bears."

"And rotting badnessness." Tormy wrinkled his nose, the soft fur around his whiskers rising.

Shalonie still smelled nothing unusual.

"The green is green," Kyr added. "The green is not slime or decay or rot or stink. The green is green deep in the ground."

"That clears things up." Omen stood from his crouch. "We should get back—"

A deep-throated roar ripped through the quiet of the woods. The sound made Shalonie realize how very silent it had been all around. *As if the forest itself is holding its breath,* she thought.

133

The large shapes that had looked like swaying trees covered in autumn leaves turned from the hole in the ground and lumbered to their feet.

"Bears," she heard herself say what seemed ludicrous. *Can't be bears. They're trees. Shaped like bears.*

Standing nearly ten feet tall, foliage instead of fur covering their bodies, two massive bear creatures stared up at them with shiny eyes, their coal-black noses twitching.

"Is the leaf bears thinking we is smelling like hot lunch?" Tyrin asked almost meekly.

"Bears are faster than you think," Omen murmured. "Take Kyr. Tormy and I'll hold them off." He unsheathed a broad dagger.

Shalonie stood slowly, reaching for Kyr's hand. "Don't use a knife. We don't know what those are."

"Peel the potatoes," Kyr suggested helpfully but wiggled out of Shalonie's reach.

The leaf-covered bears swayed back-and-forth for a moment as if deciding between the hole they'd been digging at or the upward slope.

Shalonie couldn't tear her eyes from the creatures, fascination keeping her pinned in place. "Are they plant or animal?" She yearned to pluck a few red and orange leaves from their frames. *Do they have skeletons or branches?*

"They is being hungry bears." Tormy growled menacingly as the piles of leaves that made up the strange bears' faces opened in their centers to reveal purplish grey gums and long, pointed teeth.

Next to Shalonie, Omen tensed as he directed a surge of energy toward the creatures.

The great bears stumbled back from the force of his psionic push as was expected, but their stumbles were accompanied by a mighty tremble in the earth.

"What did you do?" Shalonie didn't want to believe Omen had caused an earthquake. *He really has no control!*

"The second Otharian Pattern," Omen shouted, panic in his cry. "I just meant to push them back so we could get away. It doesn't have the power to quake the earth."

At that moment a large reptilian head shot from the hole in the ground. The grey and brown scales of its head and neck were laced with streaks of bronze, and its long snout was ridged with spindly fangs. Two horns curled from its head, and its body circled around its center axis, lifting itself up high in a snake-like spiral. Narrow wings fluttered on either side of its broad back, keeping it upright.

"Dragon?" Omen spat out.

"Never!" Shalonie countered. "It's hideous!"

"&#@$ stinky dragon!" Tyrin howled. "That @$&% smells like dead feet!"

The awful waft hitting her nose now too, Shalonie couldn't disagree.

The scaled beast lunged forward like a spring and wrapped itself around one of the leafy bears, squeezing through its foliage down to a trunk no thicker than a man's leg.

Tree underneath. Shalonie tucked the information away in her brain.

The second bear swiped at the great reptile's body with gnarled claws, cutting deep, bloody gouges through the dark scales and spattering the bronze markings with crimson gore.

"Autumn's a thief!" Kyr stumbled back, hands waving at the scene below.

A third bear had appeared from behind the trees and ran

135

toward the hole with mighty bounds.

"They *are* fast." Shalonie heard Omen marvel.

The third bear shoved its upper body into the hole, comically kicking its legs for a moment, then it emerged with an oblong blue and green shape held aloft in its left paw.

Dragon egg, Shalonie realized. *They were trying to steal eggs from the nest.* Beside her Omen shifted his stance.

"It's not a dragon," Shalonie insisted, her emotions in conflict with her intellect. *It could be a dragon. There are multiple classifications of dragons. Sundragons are special. Other dragons are—* Her mind raced in all sorts of different directions.

The eggs are greenish, Shalonie realized as Kyr pointed at the egg being carried off by the leaf-covered bear.

The serpent creature whipped from side to side, breaking the bear in its grasp to kindling with wide, erratic lashes. It wailed a high-pitched screech, then closed its giant mouth over the other bear's entire head. The not-a-dragon bit down. The bear fell backward next to its already destroyed comrade, its parts dropping and spreading like autumn leaves falling from a tree all at once.

On the other side of the hole, the last bear fumbled with the stolen egg. Desperate, it clamped its jaws around the shell and bounded toward the distant trees on four paws, leaving a trail of gold and red leaves behind as it ran.

The dragon worm spewed out the clump of leaves that had been the slain bear's head and let loose a foul spray from its mouth.

"There's the vomit smell," Omen groaned.

Hit in the hindquarters by the foul substance, the thieving bear howled in pain and dropped its prize, the shell cracking and releasing a gloppy black and bronze mass.

"It's a little green," Kyr commented breathlessly. "Just a little, but still green."

The hatchling lay on the ground, limp but giving out tiny squeals. Summoned by its baby's cries, the giant worm slithered to retrieve it. Its long tongue snaked out and cleaned the gunk off the little worm's scaly skin.

"That's almost sweet," Shalonie murmured. "If it weren't so—"

"Utterly disgusting and lethal." Omen tilted his chin in the direction of the last bear. Whatever poison the dragon worm had let loose, it had eaten through the bear's leaves and branches. The creature crumpled to the ground.

"We is better going now," Tormy remarked. "The dragon mommy is taking the baby dragon back into the nursery."

"It's not a—" Shalonie stopped herself, knowing she was being irrational. *It doesn't really deserve to be called a dragon. Winged lizard maybe.*

"This is about as close as I want to get," Omen agreed. "Let's get out of here."

Four of them on foot, Tyrin riding on Kyr's shoulder, they started scrambling along the plateau instead of choosing the uninviting climb back up to the road.

"If we get back on the road now, we'll be too far behind the others. Can't imagine they'll appreciate waiting for us," Shalonie reasoned. "But breaking our way through the wilderness . . . I don't know."

"We may be able to make up some time if we take the ravine down," Omen suggested. "Kadana said to meet at the bottom."

I think I heard her say that.

The decision made, they managed to follow worn animal paths that wound through the brush. Shalonie was surprised

137

at Omen's keen instinct for finding tracks and his exceptional sense of direction. They were making good time until they ran up against a major obstacle in the form a deep crevice that cut into the plateau they'd been traversing. They could go up or down, but not across.

"This way," Omen called after studying their surroundings. He headed farther down to where the trees and vegetation grew denser, Tormy staying close to Kyr's side and helping the boy steady himself when needed.

"Do you hike much?" Shalonie asked after Omen led them directly to a mighty tree that had fallen across the crevice. *How did he know that was there?*

"My dad likes us to make a good showing outdoors," Omen replied, testing the thick log before sending Kyr and Tyrin across. "He's taken us to Scaalia and Lydon for some week-long hikes." He waved Tormy away from the log. "You should be able to jump across. The log won't hold your weight."

"I is not being too heavy." Tormy sounded slightly stung.

"Never said that." Omen pointed at the log. "It's just not very sturdy."

"All the other four-foots is taking the bridge." Tormy stuck his nose down to the ground.

For the first time, Shalonie noticed the plethora of tracks in the soft earth. *This is how Omen knew to come here. He followed the tracks.*

"If it's too far to jump, maybe you can fly to the other side," Omen suggested. "Like you did on the ship."

"I is being a mighty flying cat!" Tormy exclaimed, new excitement in his holler. Tyrin cheered him on from the other side with a series of squeaky meows.

Tormy took a prancing step toward the edge of the drop,

but when it came time to leap, his feet remained firmly on the ground. "My flyingnessness is being all broken, Omy!" The cat's ears drooped.

"Try again," Omen suggested.

Tormy scooted back to gain a running start and bolted toward the crevice. He took off from the ground, and it seemed to Shalonie that the cat was indeed flying as he had on the ship. But less than halfway to the other side, the cat's feet clawed the air and his large body began to drop.

Standing at the other edge, Tyrin screamed louder than Kyr, who had to snatch the kitten up to keep him from hurtling himself after his plummeting brother.

A rush of power erupted from the crevice then, like a great gust of wind. Shalonie's hair blew back as the burst pushed her hard enough that she had to take a step back.

As if burped up by the crevice, Tormy popped high into the air and then softly landed on the ground next to Kyr. "Whoohoo!" the cat squealed exuberantly and padded around in wild circles.

Flat on his stomach, Omen groaned slightly and started struggling to his feet. His chin had a scrape that bled freely.

"Let me get that." For the first time, Shalonie noticed the downiest red-gold stubble on Omen's cheeks.

"It's already healing." Omen waved her off, out of breath.

She handed him a cloth to wipe up the blood. "Never boring with you, is it?"

"Got to work on my Seudthil Patterns," Omen murmured. "Using my psionics to levitate something shouldn't push me down."

Shalonie agreed but said nothing. *He's going to berate himself anyway. But, that pattern should be so easy for him. I've seen Lily use it a hundred times without any trouble at all.*

Omen didn't speak to her as they made their way across the crevice and down to the farther plateau. But she heard him arguing with himself. "It worked on the ship. But that was catching not pushing . . ." He continued under his breath, mumbling words of spells she recognized, as if he were trying to compare the syntax of the incantations. *But that's not psionic.*

She thought of trying to get him to talk about it, but when he started humming and quietly singing she decided that Omen had to work his difficulties out for himself. *I'll help if he asks, but sticking my nose in his business would just annoy him. It's personal, let him get the hang of it on his own. It probably just backlashed because of the adrenaline rush when Tormy fell. He sure reacted fast though.* And so her thoughts continued until they finally reached the road at the bottom of the range.

They hadn't walked the King's Road for very long when they heard hoofbeats behind them.

"It's Grandma Kadana!" Tormy announced before Shalonie could worry about the dangers of encountering strange riders.

"Well met!" Templar greeted them. "You made good time."

"Traveling in a straight line can have its advantages," Omen quipped, taking his horse's reins from Dev.

"By the dirt on your face and clothing," Kadana eyed their appearance, clearly evaluating, "I'd guess the straight line wasn't exactly nogwirts' delight."

"Just stinky dragon &%$#, leaf bears, and almost falling into a hole," Tyrin exclaimed with great enthusiasm. "It is being hero &%$#@ and we is being heroes."

"That about says it all." Omen made a face, watching closely as Kyr climbed back on Tormy via the saddle. He adjusted a loose strap before swinging onto his own mount.

"Well," Shalonie couldn't help qualifying. "It wasn't exactly a *dragon*."

"Do say." Kadana gave an encouraging nod.

Getting comfortable, grateful to be in the saddle again after their long walk, Shalonie tried to choose her words carefully. "We witnessed a deadly encounter between what looked like bears made of autumn leaves and a giant lizard with a dragon head that spit poison."

"&$#@ poison," Tyrin specified.

"He's not wrong," Omen agreed. "It really smelled like decaying rot, but that spray reduced those leaf bear things to slime."

"Did it have horns?" Kadana asked unexpectedly.

"Yes." Shalonie saw the cats nodding their furry heads fiercely.

"Dark scales with some sort of metallic streaks?"

"Yes."

"Don't know about your autumn leaf bears, but your lizard was a dragon."

Shalonie's stomach lurched.

"Before you get too upset." Kadana laughed a little as she spoke. "It's a lower species of dragon. One of those offshoots that goes its own way. Kharakhan used to have many more of them, but Diemos made such sport of hunting dragons—" She cut herself off. "Well, that was a long time ago."

The group rode in silence, Shalonie certain that Kadana was trying to take back the words she had spoken about

High General Diemos.

Wonder if the Sundragons know. Indee obviously knows. Another secret.

"So," Kadana said after a while. "The dragon you saw, it's called a Giver."

"Why's that?" Dev interrupted.

"Because they give you nothing but trouble," Kadana said dismissively. "And I've never heard of them having little ones."

"Maybe because they hide so they won't get hunted by warriors with great big swords," Shalonie said more sharply than she had intended.

"And maybe that's because Givers slide into unprotected villages and gobble up the innocent humans who live there," Kadana countered without malice. "The world's a big place, and most of it's dangerous."

"What about those bears made of leaves and sticks?" Omen finally joined the conversation. "Have you seen those before?"

"The Autumn Gate had no lock, has no key," Kyr confirmed what Shalonie had been thinking all along.

"That's just great," Kadana said with some frustration. "Let's just hope nothing else has snuck in. We'll be crossing into my lands soon." She turned her head to look at Nikki. "Our family lands . . . If woodland creatures are already slipping through from the Autumn Lands, there's probably far more trouble coming our way."

Chapter 9: Lizards

OMEN

The rest of the day passed slowly, though they kept a steady pace throughout, stopping only for short breaks to rest the horses and Tormy. The long hours of travel after the excitement of the morning made Omen gloomy, and he thought he could distract himself by getting to know his new brother.

Nikki, while he appeared somewhat awkward and shy at first, relaxed the longer they talked. He was eager to hear stories about their lands: Templar told him of Terizkand, Omen of Lydon and Scaalia, Liethan of the Corsair Isles, and Shalonie spoke of Melia, though Omen and the cats had plenty to say on that subject as well.

The young Deldano had shown a great deal of concern for Shalonie after their unplanned side-trip. And Omen noted with mirth how eager Nikki was to listen to Shalonie's account of what had happened and what thoughts the encounter had triggered in her.

I was there too . . . I don't even know what she's on about. Plants. Animals. Does it matter what their digestive system is like?

Nikki was clearly quite smitten by the young woman — a turn of events that made Omen, Templar, and Liethan snicker among themselves. While Shalonie was largely clueless of the attention she garnered, Omen knew Nikki would face serious competition in Melia if he remained enamored with the girl. *There are likely Sundragons interest-*

ed in her, Omen thought, feeling vaguely sorry for his new-found brother.

Omen could see that Nikki was genuinely curious about Shalonie's academic interests, but he doubted the Kharakhian understood even a fraction of the capacity of Shalonie's mind. *I don't understand half of what she talks about. Poor guy doesn't have a chance.*

"What exactly are these Cypher Runes?" Nikki asked after Shalonie had mentioned her current field of study in relation to the autumn bears, as she had termed them, escaping the Autumn Lands.

"It's a form of representational magic based on mathematical calculations and ciphers," Shalonie explained — something Omen had heard frequently enough that he could have answered the question himself, parroting the words without having any idea what they really meant.

"Are they like magical patterns or psionic patterns?" Templar asked, attempting to categorize.

"Well . . . no . . ." Shalonie hesitated. "Or rather that is to say that any pattern can, of course, be represented mathematically — but the magical and psionic patterns are really just conduits for your own energy. They all get internalized to something personal to the caster — like for me, it all becomes drum beats."

"Magical patterns all turn into colors for me," Templar admitted.

"For me it's all music — psionic and magical both," Omen told them, catching on.

"That's a Deldano trait," Kadana informed him. "You get that from Beren — it's the same for him. Always music — even his healing gift."

"But these Cypher Runes," Dev cut in, his attention focused on Shalonie. He'd been decidedly quiet for the majority of the day but the conversation about magic had captured his attention. "They're not internalized — not unique to the caster. Does that mean the marks themselves have power?"

"Not exactly . . ." Shalonie tilted her head to one side thoughtfully. "Or rather some of them do, but only because they represent things with intrinsic esoteric power in other magical systems, like the name of a god for example. But for the most part the magic is in the intent of the marks, the symmetry of the calculations, putting order into chaos, or chaos into order."

"You can't mathematically represent chaos," Omen argued.

"You *can* actually," Shalonie corrected him. "Or at least a close approximation of it — but what I meant is that the calculations themselves build something. You see, every single particle in the entire universe can be represented as a mathematical rune . . . though obviously the majority of those runes would be meaningless since the universe is made up of a lot of dust and empty space. But the point is, everything can be represented as a mathematical calculation. But like everything else in the universe, it usually needs some sort of catalyst to give it meaning or focus."

Omen glanced around at the others, wondering if any of them had understood her explanation any better than he had. By the blank looks they were giving Shalonie, he guessed, they hadn't.

Shalonie's expression fell. She pressed her lips together in either frustration or disappointment; he couldn't tell which.

"Is it being like the makings of a battle horn?" Tormy

asked innocently. "On account of the fact that I is wanting one so I is asking Lily to make me one when we is getting home."

Shalonie's eyes lit up with excitement. "Yes!" she exclaimed eagerly, much to Omen's surprise.

He was fairly certain Tormy wasn't even following the conversation, let alone understanding any of it.

"It's exactly like building a battle horn," Shalonie said, her speech racing again, "or a sword or a cup or a saddle. I mean, think about what goes into making those things — with a sword you combine metal and heat and the force of a hammer along with the artistic intent of the sword maker, water, steam, fire, a sharpening stone, and when you combine all those things you get a sword, which has intrinsic meaning unto itself but doesn't actually do anything unless someone wields it."

They stared at the girl.

"Omen?" Kadana looked as if it had just occurred to her that Shalonie could potentially be out of her mind.

Omen hesitated a few seconds before asking, "What does any of that have to do with mathematical calculations?"

Bleak resignation washed over Shalonie's features. "You make the right mark, push the right amount of power into it, and stuff happens," she said tonelessly. Her shoulders sagged.

"Oh!" They all elongated the sound in unison, nodding their heads as if it all made sense now and throwing each other conspiring looks, silently agreeing to let the subject lie.

Shalonie wasn't fooled. She threw her hands up in the air and whispered a Melian word that Tyrin seemed to find very interesting. Shalonie twisted in her saddle, fiddled with the bag behind her, and fished out a large leather-bound notebook, which she handed across to Nikki.

"If you really want to know, you could read that — these are my original notes on the subject when I was first learning it," she told the young man before setting her heels to her horse's side and riding a few paces ahead.

"Thank you!" Nikki called after her, looking pleased by the acquisition of the book.

Templar, riding beside Omen, barely suppressed a snicker at the look on the young man's face. "Only girl I know who requires homework if you want to flirt with her."

"We did try to warn him," Omen agreed. *Wonder how far he'll get into the book before giving up . . . or falling asleep.*

"She showed me that book on the ship," Liethan told them, pulling his horse up alongside them. "I couldn't get past the first sentence. Something about derivatives."

"The really ironic thing is that the book is probably priceless," Omen said. "There are sorcerers the world over who would literally kill to get their hands on it. Nikki has no idea what a gift she's given him."

They all looked at the young man. Nikki stared down at the book in silent awe, a sappy smile on his face as he studied the cover. His entranced expression made the three of them chuckle.

"Then again." Omen shrugged. "Maybe he does."

"Poor Nikki." Liethan sniggered blatantly. And while Omen adored Shalonie, he had to echo Liethan's sentiment.

❖

They rode until true twilight surrounded them. The trees of the forest changed as they traveled — the oak and aspen giving way to neat rows of apple trees.

"Is we going, going, going all night?" Tormy put forth with a smidgen of concern.

While the cat had been remarkably compliant as the day wore on, Omen imagined Tormy had to be growing tired. *So am I, to be honest. And I'm not carrying anyone on my back.*

"Just a little farther," Kadana assured him. "The Barton farm is ahead past the orchard. They're good people. We'll spend the night there. I want to check on them with all that's going on. They'll have news if there's any trouble in the area."

Through the near dark, the sudden pounding of hooves alerted the group to quickly approaching riders.

Without hesitation, Kadana drew her long sword, the blade glowing pale-blue in the twilight as if frosted with ice. An instant behind her, Templar pulled his long white bone blades from the leather sheaths at his side even as he controlled his horse with practiced ease. The two of them moved in front of the group. Dev shifted to one side with equal speed, grabbing his bow and nocking an arrow. A fraction of a second later, Omen snatched his sword from where he'd strapped it across his saddlebag, freeing the large blade from its scabbard. Liethan snatched up his crossbow from his saddle.

"Are we fighting them?" Kyr asked, pulling his dagger from his belt and gripping tightly to the hilt. His violet eyes darkened with alarm.

"Not worried about them," Kadana spat out.

"It's what's behind them that we have to worry about," Dev completed her thought.

Omen heard a crackling hiss coming from the dark road

148

before them. Illuminated in the rising light of the moon he could see the shapes of riders on horseback. A plume of red fire rose, revealing the riders and the creatures giving chase.

The riders, two average-sized men and one frail woman, were easily identified once the firelight grew — farmers fleeing on unsaddled workhorses that seemed as terrified as their riders. But the predators behind them were wildly unrecognizable, at least to Omen.

Lizards, he thought at first — but huge, taller than a man, with golden scales that glowed like hot coals and teeth and claws that flashed in the firelight. Flames spewed from the monsters' gaping mouths, setting alight the world around them.

"Those things are fast," he threw over to Templar, hoping his friend had a guess to what the scaled horror could be.

In unison, Tormy and Tyrin let out excited hisses.

"Fire lizards," Kadana answered through the cat noises. "Really big ones. Don't let them bite you."

"Or breathe fire on you," Dev added without humor. "Their fire sticks to skin. Water can't put it out."

Two creatures chased after the fleeing riders, both fiery nightmares sporting glittering hoods that flared at their ridged necks as they ran upright on long spindly legs. Their front arms waved through the air as they ran. Bone-shaking shrieks rang out from their scaly throats, terrifying the already galloping horses into a life-or-death sprint.

"Out of the way!" Shalonie grabbed the reins of Nikki's horse and pulled both horse and rider off the road in time to avoid a collision with the fleeing farmers.

Spying Templar and Kadana closing ranks to block the

way forward, the fire lizard on the right dug its thick claws into the hard-packed dirt and unfurled its sparkling hood with a loud snap. The other over-sized reptile leaped to one side of the road and roared savagely.

Music rang through Omen's mind as psionic patterns began forming, and without thinking, he flung the first lizard backward with a wide psionic sweep. The creature stumbled, its hood blowing back like a small sail in a windstorm. The second lizard's belly glowed with sudden white-hot intensity, and it opened its mouth to spit flames at them.

Templar growled out a spell in convoluted Nightspeak and a bright circle of blue light appeared around the scaly beast, blocking the red-hot blast of sticky flame and igniting the ground at the reptile's clawed feet instead.

Dev's arrow flickered through the dusk, finding its home in the belly of the lizard Templar had trapped. A second arrow followed and buried itself in the beast's thigh. One of Liethan's crossbow bolts pierced its neck a moment later, and the creature staggered and fell backward.

At the same time, Kadana charged the other eight-foot tall reptile head-on. The scaled beast had recovered from Omen's shove and was racing forward again, jaws open to meet Kadana's attack. She knocked it back with a strong blow of her blade, both lizard and horse twisting on the path and dancing around each other. But the moment the creature was turned away, Tormy leaped toward it. "I is got you!" he shouted, landing on the fire lizard's tail.

The long tail separated from its body like it would have for any variety of small lizard. The black scaly tail wiggled fiercely, inviting Tormy to jump up and down with glee. Kyr clung to Tormy's saddle, white-faced and thin-lipped. Tyrin crowed triumphantly from the depths of Kyr's pocket.

The giant lizard lost its balance and stumbled about as if the bones of its hind legs had become jelly. The effect would have been comical, if the creature hadn't burped up a plume of bright flame in its panic, setting the nearby undergrowth ablaze. The canopy of leaves above them caught fire, and Omen feared they'd become engulfed in the flames in mere moments.

Water, I need water! Omen thought, recalling several domestic spells to produce the liquid in various amounts. He raised his hand to cast the first one to come to mind, aiming for the nearest patch of spreading fire — too near to Tormy and his bright orange fur.

Kadana swung her sword at the lizard caught in Templar's magical circle. Her sword cut through the creature as if the scales were no barrier to her icy blade. The giant reptile's head tipped to the side, a small tendon still connecting the thick neck to its scaly body. The large form crumpled to the ground.

"Good one!" Liethan shouted, and he shot another bolt toward the tailless fire lizard nearest Tormy. A fluorescent substance squirted through the lizard's black scales, spraying outward. All the horses danced away in terror, moving themselves and their riders out of the path of danger. And though distracted by the wiggling tail, Tormy instinctively skittered away as well, leaping to safety and carrying Kyr and Tyrin with him.

The minor domestic water spell Omen had directed at the nearest flame simply coated the ground in a fine layer of mist that hissed and evaporated, having no effect whatsoever. The acrid smell of char and sulfur pervaded the air, making Omen gag.

"The fire's growing!" Shalonie shouted.

151

"Water doesn't put out their flames," Dev repeated his warning — directly at Omen.

Right! He said that already! Omen cursed himself for forgetting.

"The fire!" Shalonie kicked her horse forward, moving closer to Omen. "It needs oxygen."

Science lessons? Now? Omen shot her a confused look, vaguely remembering the term "oxygen" from his father's many, boring lessons.

"Air!" Shalonie bellowed in frustration. "Smother it!"

Both Liethan and Nikki leaped from their horses and scrambled for the woolen blankets stashed on the pack horses; the animals had moved toward the relative shelter of the nearby trees. But Omen knew it would be just a matter of moments before all the trees were on fire. *Blankets won't be enough!*

"Templar! Cast that spell again around all the fire!" Omen hollered, while Kadana moved to block the remaining lizard from advancing.

"Back, bug breath!"

"It's just a temporary shield, it won't smother the flame!" Templar shouted back over Kadana, but he raised his hands to do as Omen asked, a nimbus of blue light already forming around his body as he channeled the magical energy around him into his spell.

"I'll take care of that!" Omen called back, his internal music rising as he focused his mind into a single psionic pattern.

Two more arrows from Dev struck the remaining lizard, sending it crashing to the ground amid the blaze of fire lighting the area. Templar shouted out in Nightspeak once more, the blue glow around him flaring as he cast his spell wider, encompassing all the flames on ground, bush, and trees.

Omen concentrated on the area within the blue shielding spell, opening his senses to the ground beneath the bubble of light; he focused his thoughts into the psionic pattern his father had taught him. He pushed his mind deep into the earth, extending his thoughts downward, allowing the force to build within his pattern, growing until he thought he might burst. And then with one mighty pull, he ripped upward, pulling the dirt from the very earth itself. An explosion of soil burst upward in a column. Contained within the light of Templar's shield, it ripped tree and bush from the ground and flung everything upward. A moment later, it all came raining down in a shower of dirt and mud and gravel, finally settling into a haphazard pile, flames snuffed out in a vertical avalanche of earth.

"Catch his horse!" somebody shouted. *Kadana?*

Omen snapped back to reality, his head pounding with pain as fatigue crashed into him. The fire was out. The ground before him was a jumbled chaos of ripped trees, bushes, and dirt turned completely upside down as if torn apart by a giant shovel. The bodies of the two lizards were buried beneath the pile of earth, only the still wiggling tail remaining off to one side. The ground settled and shifted as the light from Templar's shield faded away.

Omen, having slid off his horse while lost in concentration, would have hit the ground hard if Kadana hadn't leaped from her own mount and grabbed him around the waist, holding him upright as he panted with exhaustion, his body drained from the effort.

Templar and Shalonie stood nearby — Templar looking smug, Shalonie gazing at Omen, disbelief in her wide blue eyes. "Dirt?" she asked. "That had to weigh several thousand pounds!"

Omen felt too tired to even nod. "That's what you meant, right?" he asked. "You said to smother it."

"I actually intended you to move the air — not the dirt, create a vacuum," she explained. "But I guess dirt works too."

"Air?" Omen stared at the upturned earth, broken charred trees and bushes in the heap before him. "That would have been easier. Air is . . ."

"Much lighter," Shalonie finished for him, looking impressed nonetheless. She patted him on the shoulder. "Worked though. Well done!"

"Anyone injured?" he asked sheepishly, turning to look at the others. Nikki and Dev were retrieving the horses. Liethan was prodding at the lizard's wiggling tail with his crossbow. Tormy, with Kyr still perched on his back, cautiously crept closer. "Kyr?" Omen called. His brother's face was white as milk.

"The beds are burning," Kyr stated clearly from Tormy's back. "The lace is my mother's. Oh, my beautiful curtains. Where are the geese?" he rambled without taking a breath. "The door is opening! There are cracks, so many cracks! We will run, we will scamper, we will eat, we will burn!"

"Kyr?" Despite his exhaustion, Omen ran toward his brother, alarmed by the look on the boy's face and the words falling from his lips.

"Leave the critters," Kadana bellowed. "I see flames ahead."

Omen turned to look — beyond the charred area, through the darkness of the tree-lined road, he saw red light down along the path the lizards had raced. *That must be where those farmers were fleeing from!* The farmers had disappeared down the road, gone from sight.

As one, the group remounted and set off down the road after Kadana. They encountered nothing else, but soon they could smell the undeniable stink of fire.

Following Kadana, they veered onto a dirt road and up a shallow incline. In the fading twilight and the ghostly light of the rising moon, they could see a wide clearing surrounded by the neat rows of apple trees. The centerpiece of the abundant orchard was a modest farm stretched out before them. The main house and barn were intact, but a small shed blazed red with flames, illuminating the barnyard. A straight line of flame bisected the orchard, engulfed the shed, and licked at the porch of the main house.

Omen's heart sank as he took in the swath of fire. *No way I can move that much dirt or repeat what I did earlier. I'd destroy the buildings.* He spun toward Shalonie, but she clapped him on the back before he could explain.

"Air this time!" she told him. "Not dirt. And Templar, you have to make the shield as solid as possible."

"Omy, Omy, Omy!" Tormy cried. "The nice farm people is losing their house and all their apples. Omy, Omy, Omy!" The cat's giant round eyes shimmered gold in the glow of the encroaching inferno.

Nikki vaulted off his horse with surprising ease and caught Kyr who had suddenly leaped from the cat's back and dropped to all fours on the ground, digging his fingers into the earth amid the trampling hooves of the terrified horses.

"The eggs!" Kyr screamed hysterically as Nikki pulled him away from the frightened animals. "There's hundreds. I hear their whispers. Omen, they're hatching!"

155

Instantly covered in cold sweat, Omen slid out of his saddle and stood in the middle of the barnyard, eyes on the fire's writhing fingers. The flames threatened the farmhouse, swelling and reaching toward the porch with each passing heartbeat.

"Templar!" Omen shouted.

"A shield this size . . ." Templar dissented. "I can only contain it for a few moments!"

"Doesn't matter!" Shalonie insisted. "You only need a second or two if you time it correctly. The fire will be extinguished instantly."

Omen faced the flames, taking the girl's word as Templar came to stand next to him. Kadana and the others moved the horses back and away from them, leaving the area clear to work. Templar raised his hands, the blue nimbus of light forming around his body. He nodded grimly to Omen. "Tell me when," he said.

Omen focused, music rising in his mind, the same familiar tune that he'd used to uproot the earth, but lighter this time, filled with sharp clear harmonies. The pattern formed, and he drew on the wellspring of energy inside him. It was much depleted — exhaustion making his limbs shake and teeth chatter. *Just the air this time. Light, easy, I can do this!*

Geometric structures and bonds flitted chaotically in front of his mind's eye like lightning bugs made of sparklers and liquid diamonds. They buzzed and hummed, frantically crashing into each other. He caught hold of the uncountable entities, pushing and pulling at them, trapping them all as one chaotic invisible mass.

"Now!" he shouted to Templar and sensed the familiar flare of his friend's magical power exploding outward. The blue light of his shield burned against Omen's closed eyelids. He pushed upward, forcing the elusive specks of air out of the circle of Templar's shield. His mind hummed as the tiny, infinite frequencies took hold of the pattern in his mind and energy poured down the open lines.

There you are! So many — have to hold on to all of it! He pulled again, upward, outward, luring the specks from the heat of the flame, leaving emptiness behind. Their fragile song of movement vibrated his eardrums. He flung the acrid abundance into the sky, its invisible presence scattering and re-bonding elsewhere.

"They're cracking!" Kyr shouted, his voice cold as ice, breaking with hysteria.

"No, Kyr," little Tyrin called out. "The fire is being out! It is being fair and fine. Omy and Templar is saving the house and the barnsnessness!"

Omen fell to his knees. For a moment his lungs felt as if they'd been glued shut, only the thinnest stream of air coming through. Beside him, Templar hit the ground, equally exhausted. The two of them exchanged brief disbelieving looks as they sat, drained, in the dirt.

Kyr howled like a wraith and stomped his feet on the ground. "So many! Get them through the door! Too many, too many! Back home with you!"

Omen took a huge gulp of air as if saved from drowning. His lungs filled to their normal capacity, and his vision cleared. "Kyr?" Omen tried to push himself upward, grateful when Kadana offered both him and Templar a hand to pull them up.

They made a sorry sight, congregated in the barnyard — Kadana holding Omen by the shoulders; Templar and Shalonie pale as the moon; Kyr stomping his feet frantically in the dirt while Tyrin and Tormy watched over him worriedly. Only Nikki and Liethan still seemed to have their wits, corralling the horses into the center of the yard.

Kyr suddenly stopped his frantic stamping, his body growing calm and still as he looked up, his face relaxing. "The door is closed," he said simply.

The sound of horses' hooves caught their attention a moment later, and they looked up to see the farmer, his wife, and their son returning along the same road they'd fled down. Kadana raised a hand in greeting.

"Will the beastie eat us?" the farmer called out in fear. It took Omen a moment to realize they were referring to Tormy.

"Only beasties were the lizards," Omen called back in assurance. "And they're dead."

"The cat is tame," Kadana added.

"I is not being tame! I is being a fierce fighting cat! I is catching the nasty fire lizard by the tail! You is seeing that, Grandma Kadana, I is being fierce!" Tormy protested loudly, his tail swishing back and forth.

Kadana smiled indulgently. "Yes, Tormy, you are very fierce. I was very impressed."

"You killed the fire monsters," the farmer said, awe in his voice.

"And you saved our home and our land," his wife added.

Their son, barely out of his teens, looked red in the face — flushed with anger and embarrassment. "We ran." He looked down at the ground.

"You did the right thing," Kadana said somberly. "Those fire lizards are not of this world."

Shalonie tilted her head. "You've fought them before?" Her voice sounded hoarse.

158

"Not here," Kadana continued quietly. "In the Mountain."

"There was a small portal," Dev spoke, surprising Omen who realized in that instant that Dev had been missing from the yard, having failed to follow after them. The young Machelli swaggered from the orchard, leading his horse by the reins down the row of burned trees. "I followed the fire to the source," he said, matter-of-fact. "There was a nest with hundreds of eggs, and an open portal. I tried tossing them back through the portal, but they started hatching."

Frowning, Omen glanced briefly at Kyr who was now leaning calmly up against Tormy's right shoulder. "You smashed them?" he asked Dev.

"Didn't have much choice," the Machelli admitted. "They would have burned everything."

Relief washed over Omen. "What about the portal?"

Dev patted his horse's neck as he tied his bow back down to his saddlebags. "It closed — one minute it was there and the next it was gone. I looked around, made sure there were no more eggs."

"Wi . . . ill the monsters c . . . c . . . ome back," the farmer's wife stuttered, fear still making her shake.

Kadana's eyes traveled over the family. "Emilee, Goodman Barton, I don't want you to worry," she said, after a while. "We will stay here tonight, if your family can spare the space. In the morning, we'll search the orchard." She tipped her chin to Dev. "Dev Machelli doesn't make mistakes, so I am certain the lizards are gone."

Emilee and Farmer Barton tensed at the Machelli name, but neither said a word. The son squinted warily at the silver-eyed spy. "Machelli? From the guild?" he stammered, curiosity laced with apprehension.

159

The Machelli name does mean something in Kharakhan.

"I'm pretty sure I got them all," Dev said simply.

"Will the lady take our room?" Emilee Barton quickly offered with a curtsy, her eyes on Kadana.

"The ladies will share," Kadana accepted, nodding toward Shalonie. "The boys can sleep wherever there's room. And Tormy? Do you ever sleep in trees, cat?"

The giant cat's reaction astonished Omen. "Can I Omy, Omy, Omy? I is always wanting to sleep in a tree."

Omen scratched his head in bewilderment. "I didn't know you liked sleeping in trees, Tormy."

"It is being our most favoritest," tiny Tyrin answered instead. "After the featherbed and the lambskin rug by the fireplace."

Omen looked at the little cat. "We don't have a lambskin rug at home, Tyrin."

"I know," the kitten answered mysteriously.

Omen let it drop.

Chapter 10: Orchard

OMEN

S unrise came with the rooster's crow. Omen leaned against the open farmhouse door and watched Tormy and Tyrin sleepily scramble into the barn, padding after the farmer's wife who was milking the cows. He expected a scream, but the woman — Emilee — raised no alarm at the sight of the giant cat.

Not far from them in the yard, Dev and Kyr were shooting arrows into several stacked hay sheaves. Beyond them, the sky gradually shifted from velvety darkness to the pinkish haze of dawn.

Dev's archery practice had caught Kyr's attention earlier, and the boy had wandered over, watching in fascination as the young Machelli shot arrow after arrow into the hay. Eventually, Dev had handed the bow to the boy and started instructing him in the proper technique. The Machelli, despite his somewhat taciturn personality, was surprisingly patient with the boy — seeming to take Kyr's oddities in stride.

Movement in the barn caught Omen's attention, and he saw the farmer's wife emerging with a heavy pail of milk, followed closely by the two cats. He took the milk bucket from her as she entered the house and placed it on the large kitchen table where Shalonie and Kadana were seated. The table was already laden with a morning meal of eggs, ham, and thick hearty bread with honey.

He walked back out the door to see the cats calling to

Kyr before entering the house themselves, urging the boy to come eat. Omen grinned at them, noticing white rivulets dripping down Tormy's muzzle as the cat belly-crawled through the narrow doorway of the farmhouse.

"Got something on your face, Tormy," Omen teased. Having slept soundly the night before in a pile of hay tucked away in the barn, he felt much refreshed, his headache gone.

Both cats giggled.

"I is good at catching the milk right in my mouth," Tyrin announced proudly.

"I guess you have pretty good aim," Omen remarked to Goodwife Barton, who was setting more plates on the table for the others.

"'Twas nothing," Emilee replied shyly. "The barn cats always come out when I do the milking. It's a game to shoot milk into their open mouths. I've been practicing my aim since I was a wee one." She blushed as she moved to check the fire in her stove and the pots heating on top of it. "Not that your faerie cats are close in resembling my plain barn cats."

Faerie cats, ha. That's a step up from manticores. Omen appreciated the warm ease the woman had with the creatures. *Not a lot of people are so brave when confronted with the beasties. These Kharakhians have mettle.*

Kyr, having handed the bow back to Dev who was retrieving the arrows from the hay, hurried toward Omen, no doubt as hungry as the cats.

"Have fun?" Omen asked the boy.

Kyr nodded, his eyes glinting brightly in the dawning light. "I like shooting a bow." He clambered past Omen to join the cats at the table.

The familiarity of the phrase ticked by and for a moment Omen was back again in the Melian park shortly after their first sword lesson. "So you've said," he agreed. *It's like he has conversations out of order.*

Omen accepted a cup of hot, spicy apple cider from Emilee as he joined Kyr and the others at the table. "Quiet night," he said to his grandmother who'd been studying her map once again. Shalonie was scribbling away in her notebook while Kyr licked a swath of sticky honey from his fingers. Omen placed a plate in front of the boy, hoping to encourage him to use it instead of eating directly from the serving dishes.

"What do you think, Grandmother? Are the fire lizards all gone?" Omen asked.

"We'll inspect the orchard before we move on," she replied, folding her map and setting it aside. Kadana's words seemed to reassure Emilee Barton who had looked to her as well. The others entered the house through the open kitchen door, no doubt lured by the scent of cooking food. Farmer Barton and his son each carried in a crate of ripe apples, which they set off to one side while Templar, Dev, Liethan, and Nikki crowded around the table, ready for breakfast.

Kadana reached for the hand-painted ceramic pitcher of hot cider that Emilee had placed in front of her. Approvingly, she studied the green and gold dragon-horse painted upon the pitcher. "Emilee, this is a perfect copy of the Quilin from my coat of arms. Your artist did fine work, especially with the horn."

Emilee blushed a deep purple this time. "Thank you, Lady Kadana. I work hard to do us proud."

"That's beautiful work. How did you match the Deldano

163

green so perfectly?" Shalonic askcd with keen interest.

"Copper," Emilee replied, keeping her eyes down politely. "The glaze turns green on the second firing."

"I like green," Kyr announced, looking over at the pitcher with interest. He had a smear of butter on his nose that
Tyrin was helpfully trying to swipe away. "The silver's hidden under the dawn stone."

They all stared at the boy for a moment, perplexed, waiting to hear if he had something more to say. But Kyr just
stuck his fingers back into the honey jar, and then shoved a
large drip into his mouth again, smiling in delight. Omen
patted him on the shoulder and gave a weak grimace toward the others.

Farmer Barton was studying the red apples, worriedly
turning one after the other in his hand. "Never seen them
ripen this early. 'Tis not natural."

"Nothing about this is natural, Roderick," Kadana
agreed. "The Autumn Gate has opened out of season. If you
have Haunter's Eve wards to stave off the Autumn Kin, you
best get them out."

Emilee loudly sucked in a frightened breath, then cast
her eyes down in apology.

"We have pumpkins we can carve." Roderick patted his
wife's hand. "They've ripened out of turn as well. And
we've a good supply of blessed candles to light."

"The lizards won't be the only threat," Dev stated ominously.

"No, they won't," Kadana served herself another slice of
ham. "The council of the Chain will have to get organized
quickly. I will send patrols out once I get home, but your
best defense is the defense of your neighbors. You have to
stick together. The fire lizards may be the first intrusion,

but they won't be the last."

"I'll take my son down to the village later on and tell the Elder." Roderick Barton gave Kadana a respectful nod and sat down at his usual place at the head of the table.

While Omen knew Kadana was the landholder and could have commanded the position of respect, his grandmother had made no move to usurp the man's place of honor in his home. *She shows them respect, and that makes them respect her. Guess she understands the common people because she grew up as a commoner.*

Omen watched his grandmother as she continued the conversation, including young Nealen Barton, Liethan Corsair, and Devastation in a discussion of the merits of archery versus hand-to-hand combat. To Emilee's obvious relief, Dev and Liethan made numerous suggestions about other wards and customs to protect against the Autumn Kin during the fall equinox. The Corsairs were famous for the nightly balefires, fueled by a scented oil that supposedly appeased the Autumn Kin. Dev, the consummate superstitious Machelli, described various sigils and hexes that might be used.

All too soon, Kadana called an end to breakfast, and they all stood to gather their things and make ready to leave. Unfazed, the cats continued to slurp up large bowls of warm milk while the others saddled the horses. Tormy was just finishing his milk when Omen urged him back outside.

With great satisfaction, Tyrin let out a final, humongous burp. "I is being ready to nap," the tiny cat announced as Omen and Kyr readied Tormy's complicated saddle.

"You is napping while I is walking?" Tormy sounded slightly put out.

"Tyrin is smaller; he needs more sleep," Omen reassured the giant cat.

"I is not being smaller," Tyrin huffed. "I is being compact for going through the small spaces. I is being very valuable. And I is being very tired."

Tormy's ears perked forward with sudden understanding. "Is you patrolling the farm all night, Tyrin?"

Tyrin cleared his throat as if to shush Tormy. "I is making sure all is fine and fair."

Omen raised an eyebrow. "Were you out in the dark by yourself?"

Tyrin looked at him with big, innocent eyes but didn't reply. Kyr picked the little cat up and placed him in his coat pocket.

"We'll follow the burned-out swath through the orchard," Kadana broke in, "and back to the road. Need to make sure there are no more active portals or other nasty surprises."

"Begging your pardon, Master Omen." Emilee approached Omen and handed over a large canvas bag. "For your journey." He could smell the scent of baked apples, and when he peered inside he saw numerous small baked folds of piecrust fresh from the oven. Gratitude filled him, but he tried to return the offering. "You need food for yourself and your family—"

"Spinners and spools!" Emilee replied. "We have too much ripe fruit all at once. You help me by taking some." She hesitated. "May I ask though . . . What did the elvin lad mean about the dawn stone?"

Omen watched as Kyr worked to climb, unaided, into Tormy's saddle. "Do you have something called a dawn stone?"

She gave a swift bob of her head. "It's what we call the stone in the well where the morning sunlight hits."

"Are you missing some silver?"

"My mother had some silver jewelry that went missing after she died," Emilee said.

Omen shivered and glanced toward his young brother. *At least he wasn't speaking in Kahdess. That's something at least.*

"You might want to look under the dawn stone," he told the woman. "Just to be sure." He didn't really want to stick around to see if Kyr was right or not. *Next time he tells you the trees are on fire, take it literally.*

A short while later, fortified and prepared to continue the journey, the group took their leave of the Bartons. Walking the horses through the ruined orchard, they soon came upon the area Dev had discovered the night before.

"See." The young man pointed to a nondescript patch of earth.

On the ground, scattered in a chaotic jumble, were the broken shells of beige eggs the size of melons. Amid the smashed wreckage, Omen could make out the shapes of small lizard bodies with glittering golden scales, though from the looks of things scavengers had already cleaned out much of the mess. By the sheer number of cracked shells, he guessed that there had been several hundred eggs.

"The portal was still open," Dev continued. "I tossed a lot of them back through before they could hatch. But when the portal vanished, I had to smash the remaining ones."

"Good thinking," Kadana approved. "That many fire lizards would have destroyed the entire area."

"Where was the portal?" Shalonie asked.

Dev ran his foot over a bare patch of ground that looked

like it had been dug up and churned. "Here," he explained. "A curtain of light — about ten feet tall, half again as wide. I couldn't see what was on the other side, but the eggs vanished when I tossed them through."

"Rolling portals?" Shalonie suggested, looking to Kadana for confirmation.

"Not uncommon in Kharakhan," she answered with a frown. "We used to seek them out and jump into them for fun. Never knew where you'd end up."

"There's a lot of magic still hovering in the air," Templar supplied. Omen reached out with his senses and found he could feel it too — a sharp tingling in the air that reminded him of lightning storms.

"Well, that can't be normal!" Liethan announced and they all turned toward him. Liethan had led his horse away from the group and was paused on a small hill. He was looking downward past their line of sight. They hurried to join him. "Don't see that every day," he marveled as they crested the hill.

Below them, past the neat rows of the Barton apple orchard, was a second orchard that Omen suspected hadn't been there the day before. But this orchard was unlike anything Omen had ever seen — it was filled with a kaleidoscope of colors — red, green, gold, orange, pink, white, silver, purple — breathtaking in its diversity. Half the trees were in full bloom — blossoms covering their branches; the other half had changed to the colors of autumn, shades and hues in competition with one another. And all of the trees were heavy with every imaginable variety of ripe bounty.

"That tree looks like it's bearing five different types of fruit," Shalonie exclaimed in delight. "Apples, pears, cherries, plums, and apricots! All on one tree."

"And that row over there is just flowering." Liethan pointed to several dozen trees covered in delicate white blossoms.

"And beyond the little creek," Kadana waved a hand toward the horizon, "the trees are lousy with fruit, but the leaves are turning red and gold."

"All the seasons dance together," Kyr said, perplexed. "Too much green now. Too much green."

"I is smelling roasting peaches." Tyrin sniffed and wrinkled his little pink nose. "They is sweet and good and warm. But I is liking pancakes better."

Several trees at the foot of the hill had shed their leaves but their branches were densely filled with large orbs of silver and red. Omen took a deep breath. "Something smells like fresh strawberries."

"And apple brandy," Kadana said. "This region is known for it. But . . . that . . ." She gestured to the fragrant tree. "No matter how wonderful it smells, is downright unnatural." The fruit she was indicating was nothing any of them recognized — round like a peach, but silver-colored with tiny bright red seeds coating the skin.

"I think we're looking at a faerie orchard," Shalonie said, grimacing.

"It sure is pretty," Templar said. "But freakish. This can't be good for anyone." He grinned. "I like it."

They continued walking, leading the horses through a wide stretch of the curious orchard, marveling at the ripeness and abundance of the fruit.

"Can't be sure it's safe." Kadana's voice sounded hard. "We might have to burn it down."

"Can't be sure it's safe unless we taste it," Liethan said.

169

Before anyone could say anything at all, he reached up into a tree and plucked a reddish-pink apple and bit into it with a crunch.

They all stared silently as Liethan chewed and swallowed.

"I'm fine," he said after a moment. "Just fruit. Delicious fruit."

"Fruit that ripens regardless of place and season?" Omen said, half-convinced Liethan was about to grow wings and a tail. *Audacious,* Omen thought with a mix of admiration and concern.

"The powers of the seasons . . ." Nikki said, his brow in knots. "It will throw everyone into turmoil. And despair."

"You're too serious," Templar told him. "It's just fruit. Nothing to be superstitious about."

Nikki shifted uneasily. "I'm not superstitious. I grew up in a tavern. People in turmoil drink. And drink leads to despair. And despair makes everything worse. And trust me, mead made from faerie fruit isn't going to help matters."

"I think there is being mouses nibbling on the fruits," Tyrin piped up shrilly, interrupting the conversation.

"Mice?" Kadana demanded of the little cat.

"I is thinking I is seeing nibbly teeth marks on all the apples and pears and peaches and plums." The little cat was sitting on top of Tormy's head, his nose raised into the air as he sniffed at the fruit in the nearest tree.

Omen picked a red apple off the ground. Many shallow marks covered the skin, like tiny teeth marks.

"These bites aren't from mice," Dev said.

"Well &@*#%*! @#*!" Tyrin huffed in annoyance. "I is wanting to eat mouses and there is being no mouses?"

"These marks are made by very sharp teeth," Dev said,

studying a plump peach.

"We're heading out," Kadana said firmly.

Unease settled over Omen. *Now what?*

Chapter 11: The Chain

OMEN

They had traveled along the King's Road for hours without incident, even Tormy falling into a silent, bored cadence as the miles passed, when Kadana motioned to a slight widening of the road. "This is where the King's Road and the Chain run together for a bit. The Deldano lands start here. And the Chain is our best way home." She looked over her shoulder at Omen. "But I'll have to make some stops. It'll add time."

"Doesn't the King's Road keep going straight to Caraky?" Dev raised himself up in his stirrups, looking west.

"It does," Kadana said, a sour note in her answer.

"Which is not far from the Mountain of Shadow."

"Omen?" Kadana didn't answer Dev but gave Omen a quizzical look.

Am I supposed to control him somehow? With a bit of a start, Omen realized that Dev was in fact his to manage. *Scales and toenails!*

Templar loudly cleared his throat, and Omen thought he heard a distinct, "Don't listen to Dev" through the dislodging of phlegm.

"Are you worried about the hex?" Omen was curious to puzzle out Dev's angle. *Maybe he's just trying to be a burr in Kadana's—*

"Aren't you?" the Machelli spy replied smoothly.

"Look, Omen," Kadana said without the slightest irritation, "you have a couple of options if you're in a hurry. You're under no obligation to me. You can continue along the Chain to the Deldano castle. Or you can head straight to the Mountain of Shadow. It's up to you if you're worried."

"Or we can cut through the Marroways and get to your castle before dark," Dev added casually.

The Marroways?

"Or you can cut through the Marroways and your bones will never be found," Kadana snarled.

"What are the Marroways?" Omen couldn't keep himself from asking.

"The woods the Chain winds around," Kadana said simply. "The Chain surrounds the Marroways like, well, a chain. Or a fence. Keeping things in that shouldn't wander. Things that won't wander," she gave Dev a sharp look, "unless they're reminded that there's an outside."

"Does this have anything to do with the Autumn Gates?" Shalonie asked quickly. "Or the wild gates?"

"Gates have nothing to do with it," Kadana told the girl. "The Marroways were put in place centuries ago, and it falls on the people of the Chain and the ruler of the lands to keep the Marroways protected."

"What lives in the Marroways?" Omen's curiosity poked at him. *Another puzzle. It never ends.*

"Never mind who lives there." Kadana swept a peremptory look over the band of young adventurers. "No one would even know anything about the Marroway folk," Kadana continued, "except for an incident that happened during the last war. *Someone* tried to take refuge in the Marroways. And those who live in the Marroways briefly decided to join the rest of Kharakhan. Of course, they arrived to find war and chaos, so they didn't really enjoy it very much."

"What were they like?"

"Just people," Kadana said simply. "People who've lived by the ancient rule since the time of the old gods. People who could never adapt to the way things are now. People who know how to live in harmony with the other creatures of the Marroways."

"What happened when they came to Kharakhan?"

"I convinced them to return home," Kadana said. "Part of the reason I was given these lands by Indee. She likes things to remain uncomplicated."

Omen noticed that Dev, who had started the conversation, had grown oddly quiet as if he'd said his mind and felt no further need to continue. When Omen looked to him, the Machelli spy just stared down at the ground as if the horses' hooves had grown suddenly fascinating. *He's leaving the decisions up to me — which is good . . . I guess.*

"We have time," Kyr blurted out, joining the conversation after a prolonged silence. "Kadana knows the secret ways."

Kadana's eyes narrowed. "I know a lot of secret ways to the Mountain, but none I'd recommend to you unless we're desperate."

Kyr gave her a joyful grin, his golden hair catching in the breeze. "Yes, exactly."

"All right, if we're all in agreement," Omen said at once relieved and uneasy. "No Marroways. No King's Road. No traveling ahead. We stay together and help your people first."

"That's the only choice, really," Templar agreed readily. "Leadership is responsibility. Our immediate duty is to those who are in immediate danger. There could be more

174

fire lizards."

Kadana gave Templar a look Omen could not interpret. *Suspicion? Satisfaction? Confusion?* Then something shifted in her green eyes. "I'm going to guess your grandfather raised you, Templar."

Templar waved her off.

"I always liked Shauntares." Kadana laughed. "We'll get to Anke, Taldeen, Birkeen first. Then Boven is the last town on the joint stretch with the King's Road. Once we're on just the Chain, it'll be smaller and smaller villages." She gave her horse a firm kick and proceeded ahead.

As promised, they arrived in Anke before too long.

The little town was arranged around a wide cobbled street, the community made up of shops and pretty cottages with well-tended gardens.

"Taking my horse to the farrier," Dev announced. "Threw a shoe."

He was *looking at the hooves. I have to stop being so suspicious of him. He's been a good help. So far . . .*

"I is being hungry, Omy." Tormy let out a grumbly *mur.*

Omen noticed how townspeople were already gathering and pointing at the large orange cat. He saw equal parts fascination and fear. Some pointed to Kyr and Tyrin seated on his back.

"He's friendly," Omen announced to the folk milling about.

"I is being friendly," Tormy agreed as he lay down on his belly in the middle of the road, giving Kyr the opportunity to climb down. "I is being Tormy." The giant cat shook out his mane, looking magnificent and golden in the brilliant sunlight. "Tooooooorrrrrrmmyyy!" he repeated, drawing his name out with the familiar exaggerated pro-

175

nunciation.

"I'll leave you to whatever *this* is going to turn into." Kadana urged her horse ahead to a large building at the end of the road.

"She's going to the Elder House," Nikki supplied eagerly.

Is he happy to share that he actually knows something? Omen glanced at the young man only to see him gazing at Shalonie. *Just happy to have a reason to say something to her. Poor sap.*

Omen slid off his horse and joined Kyr, who returned the people's stares with deeply inquisitive bafflement.

"Guess they don't see too many giant talking cats." Omen playfully elbowed Kyr.

Kyr giggled unexpectedly.

"Don't be being afraidnessness." Tiny Tyrin pulled himself up out of Kyr's pocket and climbed the boy's shoulder. "We is mighty, but we is nicenessness too."

Omen was pretty certain he heard sounds of marvel erupt from the crowd, but all else faded as a group of children approached Tormy hand-in-hand. Their eyes large, their mouths curved up into bright smiles, they took cautious steps forward.

"Can we pet you?" a girl of about six spoke for her companions.

Brave little thing.

"I is liking the pettings and the brushings." No sooner had Tormy announced his agreeableness when the gaggle of little ones swarmed him and snuggled into his orange fur.

"Looks like you've made friends," Shalonie said as she and Templar passed by.

176

"I'll get your horse," Templar said to Omen as he headed toward the stables.

Liethan gestured in the direction of Anke's one and only tavern. "Meet us there when you're done. You'll probably be a while."

Omen took in the sight of the swarm of children around him. *Such anticipation. Such joy.* "Who here has a cat at home?" he began, wondering what seeds of adventure their unscheduled performance would plant in the hearts of the young ones.

❖

"The Elder was very receptive," Kadana said when they were back on the road. "They've had no troubles yet, but he's agreed to raise patrols just to be safe."

It was clear to Omen that Kadana routinely kept a close eye on the inhabitants of her lands, and in return she was well-loved by her people.

They reached Taldeen two hours later, and Tormy enjoyed a similarly enthusiastic reception from the townsfolk. Omen watched with pleasure as Kyr took over managing the impromptu meetings — mostly taking his cues from tiny Tyrin who was a hit among the younger children. Apparently, Lilyth wasn't the only little girl who wanted her own talking cat.

"It's the Tormy and Tyrin carnival show," Templar remarked as they watched the cats frolicking for the town's youngsters.

"You are *never* going to slip into anywhere stealthily," Dev huffed, sounding more concerned than put off, though he avoided the groups of children as if they carried disease.

❖

"Some very purposeful planning went into the placement of these towns," Shalonie noted as they rode the next link of the Chain. "Towns usually spring up pretty randomly, mostly based on a water source. There are quite a few rivers around here, but people don't usually like to stay around an area that's so . . ." She gestured at the increasingly marshy landscape on either side of the road.

"You'd be surprised," Kadana said. "This kind of farming is all about gathering and drying peat. The turf here is soil but also rotted vegetation—"

"Hence the funk," Dev interrupted.

"They sell the peat for burning — heat during the winter — and for fertilizing the fields," Kadana went on. "Bog stretches out pretty far. The farmers do well here." She scanned the sky. "We'll stop in Birkeen for the night. Make sure they aren't being harassed by the Bower Dames."

"I was under the impression," Shalonie dug further, "that this part of Kharakhan was developed very deliberately by the first Set-Manasan dynasty, almost five hundred years ago."

"Is that what your history books say?" Kadana threw over her shoulder, unimpressed. "The Set-Manasans liked to get into everyone's business, even when I was growing up. Praise the Dawn, that's over."

"Didn't you have something to do with breaking the old Set-Manasan stranglehold on the country?" Dev inquired casually, clearly already knowing the answer.

Haven't heard a lot about what actually happened. Just what my tutor made me read. Omen recalled his first and only private tutor, Agnetha Terbithae. The old Melian woman had also been the one to waken his interest in the culinary arts.

Being savvy and inventive, the lifelong teacher had discovered, after days of chasing a five-year-old Omen along the beach, that he was quite motivated to study if pastry-making was held up as a reward. Agnetha made certain Omen learned both his history lessons and how to make the perfect caramel tree cake, a difficult Melian specialty that involved baking over an open fire.

Agnetha would have loved to hear the real story of the rebellion, Omen thought with a twinge of melancholy. His tutor had been gone for several years. Even though Melians lived a very long life, they were hardly immortal. He missed her gentle voice and impetuous sense of humor.

"I heard you led an irregular campaign across the south which some argue won the war at the last minute," Dev pressed on, returning Omen to the present.

Kadana gave Dev a dark look. "General Diemos won that war. Not me." She raised herself in her saddle, studying the road winding into the quickly rising mist. "Being on the winning side of an uprising. That's luck. I got lucky. I followed a good leader."

She glanced in Omen's direction. "For all her imperiousness, Indee really is a force of nature, a titan. She was born to rule. And she whipped this country into shape like a drover breaking a horse. You'd do well to stay on her good side."

Omen flashed back to Indee throwing the hex on Kyr. "Don't know if she has a good side," he carped. Despite Kyr's assurance that the hex caused him no pain, Omen worried constantly.

Instead of scolding or warning him further, Kadana let out a hearty laugh. "You are your parents' child. That is certain."

❖

179

Birkccn lay dark and shuttered when they arrived at twilight.

"Up there!" Kadana hissed as soon as the Elder House came into view. The narrow two-story building with Deldano green double doors and a thatched roof was situated at the end of the main road.

Against the dusky sky, Omen could make out three figures, each larger than a grown man, crawling over the gables like four-legged spiders. With long claws, they dug into the straw that covered the roof.

"They're trying to get in from above," Kadana barked.

One of the shapes turned its oversized head in their direction at the same time as a burst of light streamed ahead. Templar's light spell quickly revealed a wrinkled face, scaly pleats folding over the turtle-like features. Two round eyes, placed proportionally on either side of a wide nose, gleamed as the light hit and reflected off alabaster-colored eyeballs. The creatures flinched back from the light but seemed unhurt by it.

"Bower Dames!" Kadana spat out as she drew her sword. "Brazen. And they're hunting in packs."

"What kills them?" Liethan rapidly aimed his crossbow.

"They regenerate," Kadana countered. "And they're mean. Really mean." Kadana leaped from her horse. "Omen, get Beren's lute."

"What?"

"You're going to play them a little song."

"What?"

"You're going to tell them — no — you're going to suggest to them that it's time to go home."

"I don't know a song like that." Omen felt a swell of panic well inside him. He understood what his grandmother was asking. Beren was known for using bardic magic in battle. But beyond his psionic patterns, Omen had never tried something like that.

Kadana looked at him as if he had suddenly sprouted wings. "Make one up."

"What?" He sputtered at the mere thought.

"Improvise!"

"But writing a song takes time. I haven't—"

"Never took Beren any time," she said, sounding perplexed. "He just made them up on the spot."

"It doesn't have to be good," Shalonie said in exasperation. "She just wants you to use the magic of the lute. It's the idea more than the song itself that's important."

"Better \$&#@ hurry," Tyrin called out from Kyr's shoulder. "The \$%#& is getting in!"

Apparently having discovered a weakness in the roof, the hideous Bower Dames were tearing at the structure with claws and teeth, straw raining down onto the street.

"Hurry, Omy. Sing!" Tormy squealed. "The naughty beasts is ruining the roof."

"Go on, Omen," Templar urged, looking more amused than worried. "Tormy and I will help you if you get stuck."

Tormy's eyes widened, his concerns about the roof melting away. His amber eyes glowed with excitement. "I is helping!" he agreed joyously.

This is going to be . . . Omen grabbed up his lute and strummed the strings. Improvising music was easy — that he had no trouble with. He often improvised harmonies with his father as they played together. But he preferred to spend days working on the words themselves, meting them out with perfect rhythm and meaning. And he'd certainly never performed a song he had not perfected.

181

"Oh, Dames of the Bower, it's time to go home," Omen sang cautiously, picking the theme his grandmother had asked for. The tune came easily to him. "Return to the bog . . ." *Has to be something that rhymes with 'home'.* Nothing came to him. In desperation, he looked to Templar for help.

"Like a fat, little gnome," the Terizkandian supplied with a smirk.

Omen repeated Templar's ridiculous words, trying to add a flourish to the melody line to make up for the horrible lyrics. He felt the magic in the lute throbbing again beneath his fingers. The first time he'd played it he'd cautiously avoided the magic, noticing it but not touching it. This time he reached out his senses and let the magic flow directly into him. The three Bower Dames on the roof paused in their rampage and turned their pale white eyes on him.

Next stanza! Think of something!

"The hunt and the chase, no more do they thrill—" Omen sang. He played a quick rift on the lute, searching for the next words.

"And Omy is cooking on a piping hot grill," Tormy finished with gusto.

Unable to diminish his cat's enthusiasm, Omen reluctantly sang the line. *It's about the intent, not the words,* he reminded himself. He focused on the magic of the lute. The instrument seemed eager to be of use, playing almost joyfully as he plucked away at the strings. *Focus on home — focus on going home!* He pushed the thoughts into the magic, sending it with as much intent as he could toward the Bower Dames.

He searched for his next line, wanting it to be something better than he'd managed so far.

"Flee from this town, it's time to go back," he sang as he

182

plucked out the harmony on the higher registers of the strings. *Next line! Focus!*

"Return to your bog, and put on a sack," Templar offered.

Omen rolled his eyes skyward as he repeated the words. *That is awful!*

He focused again on the magic in the lute. He could see the Bower Dames were watching closely. One of them had moved toward the edge of the roof and was looking toward the bog. *I think this is actually working!* The magic of the lute had taken over, flowing through him now with ease.

Go home! Go home! he thought, pushing the intent into the music.

"The call of the swamp and the peace of your bower," he sang, pleased this time with the words. *Mess that up Templar!*

But it was Tormy who chimed in with the next line. "And fishies smell bestest than pink little flowers."

Omen added another harmony to his lute playing as he sang Tormy's words with only a faint grimace on his face. All three of the Bower Dames had crawled spider-like toward the edge of the roof and were swaying from side to side, white eyes blinking slowly.

Omen decided to throw in a chorus — something he could repeat as he pushed harder and harder on the magic of the lute. This time the words came easily.

"Fly away home, oh fly away home,
For night has now fallen, and it's no time to roam."

He sang them again, pushing outward with the lute's magic, his fingers dancing upon the strings of the instrument. It sang beneath his hands, its magic flowing swiftly now. *A faerie made instrument played by someone with faerie blood in his veins.*

The Bower Dames listened to the chorus once more, then cast longing looks toward the bog spreading far behind the Elder House. They let out mournful whimpers, unable to refuse the magic surrounding them or the intent in the song.

All at once, each of the turtle-faced frights scampered to the ground, knobby joints clicking. The Bower Dames disappeared into the darkness.

When they were finally gone from sight and Omen had repeated his chorus for the fourth time, Kadana clapped him proudly on the shoulder. He let the music die away. "Well done!" she exclaimed, sheathing her sword.

Worst song ever! Omen sighed heavily.

Tormy danced in place and nuzzled Omen's neck. "Bestest song ever!" he proclaimed. "That is being my favoritest song!" Omen scratched his ruff and risked a glimpse at his companions. All of them were laughing, particularly Templar.

"I have to agree," Liethan chortled. "I cannot wait to tell my folks back home about this."

I'm never going to live this one down, Omen realized with some chagrin. Word of this would reach both his father and Beren eventually, and they'd no doubt have a good laugh. *They'll write a dozen more verses mirroring mine. This song will be spread from one end of the land to the next in no time.*

"Song aside, that's some powerful magic," Templar nodded toward the lute. "Made me think of my days in the temple listening to my grandfather read The Redeemer's Lament to me."

"Made me miss home too," Nikki added. "Which is silly

since I couldn't wait to get out of there!" He shook his head as if trying to shake off a memory.

"Hurrah &@%*$ dinner time!" Tyrin proclaimed.

Omen winced. *Could have been worse. Could have been Tyrin helping me instead of Tormy.*

❖

After spending the night in Birkeen, to the delight of the townsfolk who couldn't get enough of the cats and the story of how Omen had driven off the Bower Dames with music, their road took them past the edge of the great bog itself. They'd left before dawn, and as the world woke up around them, Omen's sharp hearing picked up sounds of creatures rustling through the bog.

"Omy?" Tormy asked again, expectantly.

"No, Tormy. You have to stay on the road."

"But, Omy, the soundings is being full of creakers and flitters. Why is I having to trot on the road when there is being so many things to chase?"

"Your job is to stay on the road, to carry Kyr." He tried to think of a reason good enough for the cat.

"Don't worry, Tormy." Kadana encouraged a faster pace by putting heels to her horse. "You'll have plenty of things to chase before too long. I have a feeling Autumn isn't done with us yet."

Chapter 12: Orclets

OMEN

The long day's journey marred by only a few stops, they arrived at the Deldano castle just as the sun, flaring crimson and sienna, dove beneath the horizon. Through the dense woodlands, Omen caught his first glimpse of the tall towers.

Raised on a hill, the castle was a four-tower stone monument encased by an outer wall. A large keep lay between two of the towers along the inner wall.

"Your keep must have stood a very long time," Shalonie remarked with the tone of a scholar. "The architecture is thousands of years old. It far predates the Set-Manasans."

"The keep is from Beren's father's side," Kadana said. "Like I said, I took it from someone who didn't deserve it."

"The Straakhan line?" Omen asked quickly, hoping she'd shed a little bit of light on his never-discussed grandfather Rillian and his elusive lineage. *Don't even know if we are related to the Spring, Summer, Autumn, or Winter Dwellers. Kadana must know.*

"Best not to talk about it," Kadana said evasively. "The rocks and trees still know that name." She seemed more serious than he'd ever seen her.

More secrets.

"Kadana?" Tyrin piped up, excitement rising in his voice. "Is that being big mouses crawling up your castle walls? Can I eat them?"

As they emerged from the woodlands, the full view of

186

the castle became clear. Through the impending darkness, everyone's eyes pivoted to the castle's outer fortification, which seemed to sway with odd undulating movements.

"That's not mice," Templar blurted out. "What is that?"

Omen strained to see.

Compact, bristly shapes swarmed from the dark forest and scaled the outer wall with a speed Omen would have expected from the Golden Voyage's monkey.

Yelling out an abrupt battle cry, Kadana drove her horse toward the minute invaders. The sound ripped through Omen's ears and quickened the blood flowing through his veins. He kicked his heels hard into his horse's ribs, lurching ahead, Templar at his side. Tormy, caught in the excitement, leaped ahead like a wild thing, tail fluffed. Kyr clung tightly to his saddle's pommel while Tyrin whooped with excitement.

The creatures scaling the outer walls of the castle were of varying heights — some as small as rats, others nearly the size of hunting dogs. They were compact and fast, their thick skin a mixture of green and pale red. Though they walked upright, they seemed as comfortable using their muscled arms as a means of locomotion as they were their cloven feet. Long claws at the end of each hand dug into the stones of the castle as they climbed upwards. The larger ones jumped to gain height; their short but sturdy legs ended in thick hooves, which seemed capable of finding even the slightest purchase on the rock walls. Their wide gaping mouths were offset by the red glow of their enormous eyes. And though to Omen they looked like a cross between a lizard, a goat, and a pig, he noticed that they all had long trailing antennae like insects. Certainly, they swarmed with the same intensity of insects — the chattering rattle ema-

187

nating from their hungry mouths terrifying.

Realizing that he'd have trouble hitting the creatures from the back of his horse — they were low to the ground and moving fast — Omen snatched his great sword from where it was strapped to his horse's saddle and then leaped to the ground into the midst of a cluster, clearing out a wide swath with one powerful push of his mind, the familiar battle song flooding through his thoughts. A heap of the creatures flew back like leaves in the wind, but a dozen more raced toward him.

His horse was a willing accomplice once he'd prodded at the animal's brain with a quick push of his mind, a sharp mental suggestion triggering the animal's primitive ability to fight. The horse, encouraged to trample anything underfoot, stomped and huffed as if breathing out fire. It spun and stamped deadly hooves down on soft flesh.

The scampering, swarming movements all around them were far too much for Tormy to endure, and the enormous cat started leaping and spinning. His great paws came down on creature after creature as he swatted and snapped at them gleefully, trying to catch as many of the things as possible. Like mice, they squirmed away from him, but Omen feared some of the big ones would bite back, injuring the cat.

Undeterred, the giant cat reared and danced in delight while scratching and biting the tiny monsters charging him. Omen saw Kyr holding tight to the pommel of Tormy's saddle, balancing his body to keep up with the cat's erratic movements. Though Kyr possessed elvin grace, Omen resolved to keep both cat and boy in sight, readying himself to run to their aid should anything happen.

"Don't let Kyr fall!" he called out to Tormy.

"I is catching the mouses!" Tormy shrieked, too caught up in the excitement for caution. "They is pig-mouses!"

"Orclets!" Kadana blasted out. She swung her sword from horseback, but the blade was less effective against the creatures, and she ended up driving her horse at the group to trample them like hard-boiled eggs.

"They shouldn't be this big!" Dev cried from a nearby hillock. "Not this time of year!" He'd climbed the small rise to let go his arrows as he picked off the larger orclets who'd managed to get a good footing on the castle wall. Liethan and Shalonie hovered nearby, armed with cudgels of wood taken from the forest floor. Both defended Dev's position fiercely, leaving him free to fire while also blocking the terrified packhorses who were stomping and rearing in terror.

Nikki had grabbed most of the reins and was trying to keep the horses together to prevent them from racing off into the woods and being swarmed and devoured.

"And there shouldn't be this many!" Dev shouted.

Chaos followed their fervent defense of the castle. While Omen couldn't see the entirety of the battle, he stayed in constant visual range of Tormy and Kyr throughout the clash. Templar remained nearby, guarding Tormy's other flank; the double bone blades he used were better suited to slicing at the creatures than Omen's enormous great sword.

On the battlements, Kadana's soldiers hailed their arrival with shouts of warning as they continued a campaign of dropping rocks from the crenels directly overhead. One boulder-sized rock, heaved over the merlons by what must have been four men Omen guessed, scraped the outer curtain clean of a half dozen clinging beasties and then smashed down on three more as it bounced off the ground and shattered.

189

Don't get too close to the wall! Omen reminded himself.

Arrows rained down through narrow loopholes in the upper section of the wall, their feathers guiding the dangerous flock toward their intended targets. Omen counted on the competence of Kadana's archers.

They better not hit Tormy.

"Look out below," a bright, young voice hollered from the top of the wall.

Just in time, those nearest the wall scrambled out of the way as a barrel of flaming pitch flew from the battlements and crashed down into a dense grouping of orclets. The red-eyed orclets squealed and rolled on the ground, trying to put out the flames that had caught their bristly hide ablaze.

"Burning Pig-Mouses!" Tyrin shouted over the clamor. "Smells like &$%# bacon!"

Due to the diminutive size of the orclets, the two-handed sword was a poor weapon, and Omen resheathed it. He drew the two thin daggers from his belt instead. Kicking the nearest orclet high into the air, he sliced through two more as he spun toward Tormy's location, trying to keep the cat within easy reach.

To Omen's horror, he saw Tyrin leap in a wide arc from Kyr's shoulder and onto the head of an orclet that was about to sink its claws into Tormy's hind leg. The little cat covered the orclet's eyes with both paws and pulled back, claws extended. The critter screamed and stumbled back. Another orclet ran at Tyrin like a woodland boar, its claws extended toward the tiny orange kitten.

Omen instantly positioned himself in the way of the charging beastie and delivered a swift kick into the orclet's side, caving in its ribs and shattering its spine. A tiny weight flew to his shoulder, and he spun around instinctively.

"Just me," little Tyrin breathed into his ear while digging needle claws into Omen's leather coat for a more secure hold.

A voice rang out across the battlefield — one amplified and echoing with the raw energies of magic. *Templar! That's Sul'eldrine!* Omen recognized the tongue instantly, despite the fact that nearly every spell Templar had ever uttered had been done in Nightspeak. This was the first time he'd ever heard Templar using the Language of the Gods to cast his magic. Templar had taken up a position on the far side of Tormy, his white bone blades in either hand raised and pointing at the night sky.

Instantly a great light exploded all around them. They all instinctively flinched away from the brightness. The sky from one side of the castle to the next was lit up as brightly as the noonday sun. It was hot and warm, joyful in its intensity and filled with the scent of sweet summer peaches and wildflowers. The flash lasted only a few brief seconds and then vanished again, returning the darkness of twilight and the red glow of the castle torches.

When Omen's eyes adjusted, the companions stood alone by the keep's outer wall, scores of autumn leaves piled all around them. The orclets were gone, and it took Omen a moment to realize that somehow, Templar's spell had destroyed them.

"Sunburst spell," Templar called in explanation, lowering his arms and panting heavily.

"Orclets shrivel up in bright light and turn into dried leaves." Kadana sounded grateful and relieved. "Well done Templar, my boy!"

"Yeah, but that's all I've got," Templar croaked out. "Sul'eldrine doesn't come naturally to me and casting it that wide . . ." He trailed off looking exhausted as he sheathed his twin blades at his side once more.

"The Gates are opening!" Kyr squealed. "Don't let them come in. Don't let them come in!"

The castle's portcullis creaked as it was drawn up, allowing the companions to make their way to hurried safety.

"The orclets are gone for now," Kadana yelled out. "But I'm guessing Kyr's words mean they'll be back. Hurry up."

Through the last glint of twilight, Omen spotted Nikki, Liethan, and Shalonie handling the horses. He turned his attention toward Tormy and Kyr.

The cat, tail still fluffed with excitement, was waiting next to the gate, confused. "Omy, Kyr is saying not to go through the gate. But Grandma Kadana is saying we is supposed to go inside. And now it is being dark. I is not knowing what to do."

Walking slowly up next to Tormy, Omen tapped Kyr's leg. "We have to go inside Kadana's castle now, Kyr."

The boy looked at him, eyes wide. "The underneath snakes. They're falling from the trees. We had better get inside until the sun is high in the tower."

Omen patted Tormy's shoulder, beckoning him to pass through the castle gates.

"This is being very excitinglynessness," tiny Tyrin whispered, still perched securely on Omen's shoulder. Omen could feel the tight hold Tyrin had on his leather coat, tiny claws digging fast.

"I is biting and scratching like a hero?" The little cat sounded unsure, and despite his bravado, Omen could feel the delicate feline shivering.

192

"Yes, Tyrin." Omen meant it. "You are a hero. You are very fierce. That orclet would have bit Tormy if you hadn't attacked it."

The kitten relaxed his grasp on Omen's coat. "And I is thinking a hero cat is getting dinner at the castle?" He pitched his voice up into an urgent question.

"Yes, Tyrin." Omen reached up to scratch the kitten's chin. *The little guy was scared, and now he's coming down from the battle. Guess mass numbers of carnivorous mice would scare him.* Omen wondered if they were expecting too much from the cats. Tyrin, for all his tiny stature, was proving to be just as impetuous and recklessly brave as the rest of them. He feared the little creature would get injured. "I'm hungry too. I'm sure they'll feed us."

"That is being good." Tyrin groomed the side of Omen's ear with two quick licks. "This is being an epicnessness quest." He purred noisily and settled down.

Chapter 13: Kadana's Keep

DEV

Rows of torches illuminated the darkness as Dev followed the others into the courtyard of Kadana's keep. He kept his bow firmly in hand, though at this point he was nearly out of arrows. *Hopefully Kadana has a good supply.*

The castle, as Shalonie had suggested, was ancient. He recognized the square construction and the distinctive lack of pointed arches as a remnant of centuries-old architecture. The stone itself was a mystery to him. It wasn't the usual hard chalk, flint, or limestone. He couldn't help testing the texture and ran his hand over the nearest wall. It was smoother than any rock he was familiar with, and while the flickering fires obscured the true color, the stones seemed rosy brown, internally veined like crystallized flower petals.

His gaze flicked quickly over the others as they walked — Nikki and Liethan had gathered their mounts and pack animals and were leading them in one long line through the main gate. No one seemed wounded as far as Dev could tell. *Orclet got a good grip on my calf, but didn't break through my leathers,* he noted. There was a slight twinge in his leg where the injury would no doubt bruise — but it could have been worse.

Would have been if it hadn't been for the Nightblood. Dev stole a glance at Templar — the Terizkandian prince looked exhausted, his mouth set into a thin, hard line.

194

"You cast using Sul'eldrine," Dev commented as they walked. While he knew a few minor spells himself, he wasn't a sorcerer by any means. Nonetheless, he was aware that most battle spells were cast using the Night Tongue, or one of its many dialects. Only priests and healers used Sul'eldrine for their spell casting.

Templar breathed heavily, his yellow eyes catching the torchlight, blazing unnaturally and reminding Dev uncomfortably of the man's dark heritage.

"Magic can be cast using any language — or even silently," Templar replied. "It's just a matter of fixing the magical energies into the correct patterns. For me, Nightspeak works best."

"But Sul'eldrine is what priests use," Dev pressed. "And a spell to create sunlight . . ."

"My grandfather wanted me to serve in the Temple of The Redeemer, hence my name," Templar told him. "I studied some when I was younger. Wasn't particularly suited for it — that doesn't mean I didn't learn anything."

"But a Night Dweller shouldn't be able to use such a spell," Dev pressed. *It's unnatural.*

"Are you really a Night Dweller?" Nikki asked hesitantly, having overheard their conversation as he followed behind, still holding the reins of their horses. The smooth tenor of his voice was laced with trepidation. The horses trotted dutifully behind him. Dev noticed the furtive motion the young man made with his right hand. *Wants to make the Kharakhian warding sign against evil — but he's afraid of offending Templar. He likes him.*

Templar pushed his dark hair back from his face with one ring-studded hand and flashed a sardonic look at the young Deldano. "The eyes aren't a dead giveaway?" he

195

asked. "Worse than those Deldano green eyes of yours — everyone knows instantly who I am. What I am."

"Oh, no . . . I just meant . . . I mean I had wondered . . ." Nikki sputtered.

Templar waved away Nikki's attempt to apologize. "My father freed a Night Dweller from imprisonment long ago — he had no actual connection to the creature, but he found the circumstances of his imprisonment distasteful. In gratitude, the Night Dweller claimed him as a member of his family, made him his blood brother. The trait was passed on to my sister and me. My grandfather wasn't very happy about any of it." He turned to fix a pointed stare at Dev. "I am still half-human you know. Sul'eldrine may not come naturally to me, but it's not going to turn me to stone either."

He hopes, Dev thought to himself but he said nothing and let the subject drop as stablehands ran up to help Nikki with the horses. Dev went to retrieve his personal belongings from his horse's saddle.

"We are not a horse!" Kyr yelled out a moment later, catching all their attention. Dev looked up in time to see the half-elvin boy throwing himself from Tormy's saddle. He snatched the cat's trailing shoulder straps from a stableman, who had taken Tormy's saddle as a sign that the cat should be stabled along with the horses. But Kyr misjudged the leap, and his frail body crashed against the startled man. Worriedly the man instinctively bent down to help the boy up.

"It's all right," Omen called out, rushing over to them. "I'll take it from here. My brother's still shaken from the fight. And I'll unsaddle Tormy."

"Yes, sire," the stableman answered and left them with a

quick bow.

Dev saw Omen dust Kyr off, checking him for injury and inspecting the hex mark on his hand. The burns had healed, but Dev could see that the mark had continued to grow. Last he looked, it had reached the boy's elbow. *He never complains about it though, not unless Omen directly asks.*

"Gather your things!" Kadana called. "The orclets might be back any minute!"

Two young girls dressed in leather breeches and studded armor too big for either of them ran at Kadana.

"Caia! Tokara!" she shouted in delight and scooped both of the girls up in her arms as if they weighed nothing.

"Kadana's daughters?" Dev guessed, aiming his question at Omen who was pulling the saddle from Tormy's back. "They're taller than I expected — I thought they were younger."

"Caia is six," Omen replied. "Tokara had her tenth birthday last winter. The Deldanos are all tall." He called out to them, and the two girls ran to greet him enthusiastically — though Dev noticed their attention was primarily focused on the large orange cat and the small orange kitten who was currently sitting on the top of Kyr's blond head.

The girls were tall, lean, green-eyed, and honey-blond like their mother. Their gangly bodies reminded Dev of long-legged colts. But instead of Kadana's wavy curls, both girls had perfectly straight hair, which they wore identically — loose and grazing the tops of their narrow hips.

"My granddaughters were brave and honorable," an older man said as he stepped from the shadow of the gatehouse. Though tall and strong looking, he had silver hair and a weathered face deeply lined with age. He gave a stiff

197

nod to Kadana.

The man, Dev guessed, was Diatho's father — Yoshihiro. Avarice had written him notes on Kadana's family, briefing him on their history. He knew Diatho's family hailed from Shindar, and old Yoshihiro looked every inch the Shindarian warrior.

Yoshihiro wore traditional Shindarian armor, each darkened piece of plate armor molded to his body. He'd forgone the traditional face mask and helmet, but laced plates protected his shoulders, arms, waist, thighs, and shins. He'd traded the Shindarian split-toe foot wrappings for hard leather boots studded with metallic rounds.

Yoshihiro gripped his single-edged Shindarian blade close to its squared guard. The slender long sword curved moderately. Another sword, about half the length and more curved, hung suspended parallel to the ground from his left hip.

Dev knew Yoshihiro had been a sword master in his prime, and while he'd only been to Shindar once in his life, Dev knew enough to understand what the term "sword master" meant in that land. *The Shindarians have elevated sword fighting to an art form.* He wondered if he would have a chance to observe the old man use his impressive skills.

"The kas'injin came with the setting sun," Yoshihiro told them as they moved from the courtyard toward the main house. A tall soldier wearing the Deldano livery guarded the large double door to the main castle structure. He pushed the heavy door open with effort, letting them through.

Kadana's two girls walked alongside the enormous Tormy, staring at him in awe. Dev could tell they wanted

198

desperately to pet him. *No doubt he'll take full advantage of their eagerness and get well-brushed this night.* To his surprise, Yoshihiro gave Tormy a respectful bow of his head as he passed him.

"Not just any kas'injin," Kadana pronounced the Shindarian easily. "They are orclets," she explained. "I don't know if you get them in Shindar. Here they hatch from peapods grown on trees in the Autumn Lands. The first pods generally start appearing in early autumn, but the orclets are tiny at that point. You probably never noticed them because they only come out at night. Bright light burns them. They shrivel up and turn into fallen leaves when sunlight hits them."

"These aren't tiny," Nikki said with a shudder. "Some were the size of wine barrels and weighed nearly as much."

All eyes turned to the young man. *Knows a lot about wine barrels, does he?* Even in the darkness, Dev detected a blush creep over Nikki's cheeks.

"Grew up in a tavern," the young man mumbled.

"Is he . . ." Tokara started to ask, turning to her mother.

"Yes," Kadana cut her off. "Another nephew, girls. Come and meet him." She drew Nikki aside to meet his young aunts while they moved deeper into the castle proper.

The entrance hall of the main house was lit with oil-lamps, the door to the hall wide enough for Tormy to pass freely inside. Kadana led them into a large hall with an enormous dining table and a huge fireplace. A fire roared despite the fact that it was the height of summer.

Solstice is only two days away, Dev reminded himself. He could see signs that the denizens of the castle were already preparing for some sort of summer solstice festival

199

— the hall was decorated with a wide assortment of weaponry and suits of armor from numerous locales, as well as long sprigs of green tree branches and flowering bushes. He knew that here in Kharakhan the summer solstice was often celebrated with large sporting events and tournaments followed by elaborate feasts. It was also common for local leaders to meet to discuss issues — and he supposed that this solstice Kadana would have a great deal to discuss with her people. No doubt the sporting events would be abandoned in light of the imminent threat.

"I've read about these orclets," Shalonie said as the rest of them dumped the packs they'd taken from the horses onto the table, unburdening themselves from the journey.

Kadana crossed the room to remove a number of weapons from where they hung on the walls — large maces mostly. *Good weapons to bash orclets.* She carried the arsenal over to the table while Shalonie talked.

"By the autumn equinox," Shalonie explained, "the orclets are full grown orcs, intelligent and quite dangerous. They typically top out at about five feet tall. Tend to be more numerous as well as that's when the pods are fully ripe. In most lands, the orcs only appear on the night of the equinox when the Autumn Gates are opened. They are only usually dangerous however during the week before and after the equinox. Prior to that, they are more of a nuisance than a threat. People tend to avoid them by staying inside after dark, since the orcs naturally avoid light, and prefer the hunting grounds in the Autumn Lands over our world."

Dev chuckled silently to himself as the girl spoke, looking around at the others as they hung on to her every word. *Shalonie is better than having a library of books following us around. No wonder Avarice told me to keep an eye on*

200

her. I can think of a dozen people who'd gladly kidnap her for her knowledge. He moved off to one side of the room and seated himself on a wide stone bench near a suit of armor. He pulled open his own pack to rummage through it. He had a number of poisons inside that if mixed with the correct ingredients might prove useful against the orclets.

"That's why people light balefires during autumn," Shalonie continued uninterrupted. "And why you don't go out after midnight. The balefires tend to keep the orcs away. After the equinox, their numbers begin to die down, and they disappear entirely by the time winter sets in.

"Occasionally there are unusual years where their numbers are extremely high — and they become more of a swarm. This is similar to years when you might have an abundance of frogs or locusts that swarm and then quickly die out."

The cats stared at Shalonie. Tormy was stretched out on one of the table's benches — nearly too big for the narrow resting place — his long plume of a tail trailing on the ground. Tyrin was seated on the table itself beside him, tiny tail curled neatly around his paws. "You is saying all those words in the right order," Tyrin said reverently. "That's &@$#*! incredible."

Dev choked back a laugh. The little cat's foul tongue never failed to amuse him, though he could see the rest of the group wincing at the sound. Omen threw a wary look at the two young girls listening so attentively to the cats.

"Shalonie is being very smartinessness," Tormy explained to Nikki, who seemed transfixed by the woman's lecture.

I don't think it's her brain that's cast a spell over the boy, Dev thought.

201

"We've had a few orclets here over the last week," Kadana's eldest daughter, Tokara, said. "I saw them by the river, but I've never seen so many all at once."

Orclets only come out at night. What was the kid doing by the river at night?

Kadana arched her eyebrows quizzically.

"I took the girls fishing for midnight carp at the weir," Yoshihiro said before Kadana inquired further. "These orclets seem to have purpose. Seem to be directed. The young Melian lady is correct — these orclets should not be hunting in our lands."

"And they're really hungry too," Caia added. "They ate up all the carp and didn't leave us any."

Kadana's face twitched in a way that suggested to Dev that she wasn't pleased to hear of her daughters' late night outdoor excursion. *Kadana is definitely going to ask about that fishing trip.*

"That is being very sad," Tormy agreed sagely with the child, and both Kadana's girls turned adoring gazes toward the cat. "I is liking carp on account of the fact that they is fishies, and fishies is tasting like salmon which is the bestest."

"The very bestest," Tyrin agreed.

Caia eyed the little kitten with intense longing as if she couldn't wait to hold him in her small hands.

Dev chuckled.

The little girl threw a shrewd look at Dev, knowing he was watching her. "We had to lock our dogs up in Tokara's room," she explained. "My puppy, Howler, chased a big fat orclet through the stables and almost got bit. So, now I can't have him with me."

"Grandpa said hunting dogs don't stand a chance against

kas'injin," Tokara agreed fiercely. "He said all the dogs would be safer upstairs."

Dev noted an oddly faraway look on Tokara's face.

There's a story there, he thought, but let it go.

Kadana clasped her hands together and gave Yoshihiro a formal bow of thanks. "There's a good chance the orclets will be back," she proclaimed quickly. She turned to glance around, coming to rest on Templar who was sitting not far from Tormy at the table, long legs stretched out before him.

Judging by the weary look on Templar's face and the way he was rubbing his forehead, Dev guessed the Terizkandian had not recovered from throwing his spell.

Maybe he will turn to stone yet.

"Templar, any chance you can use that spell of yours again?" Kadana asked.

Templar hesitated, his gaze moving briefly to Omen as he contemplated what to say. *He's worried about letting Omen down. Let's hope he's smart enough to realize that bravado is not what we need right now — honesty is the only option when planning out a defense.*

"Probably not," Templar admitted, surprising Dev with his candor. "I can try, but don't count on it. Like I said, spells like that aren't easy for me. . ." He broke off with an apologetic wave of his hand.

Kadana clapped him on the shoulder. "We'll manage." She motioned toward the weapons she'd left on the table. "Omen, Nikki, Liethan — best arm yourselves with something more suited to fighting orclets."

Nikki hesitantly picked up one of the maces, holding the spiked weapon awkwardly in his hand. "I've never actually trained . . ." he started to say, but Omen patted him firmly on the back as he took one of the other weapons for himself

— an enormous two-handed maul that he held easily in one hand.

"Doesn't take much skill to use these — just bash away at anything that moves," Omen replied.

"And don't hit yourself," Liethan added, taking two smaller club-like weapons and spinning them expertly in either hand. "That hurts."

"And we'll get some . . ." Kadana said more to herself as she moved toward another wall and removed a leather coat bound with black, studded scales from one of the many armor displays lining the wall. "Here, Nikki, try this on. This was Beren's. It should protect you from the claws and teeth of the orclets well enough." She held it out to him. It was designed to slip on much like a leather jacket, buckles at the front to keep it fastened in place. Nikki took the leather and shrugged himself into it; it fit well across his broad shoulders.

I guess all the Deldanos are of a similar build. Dev cast a practiced eye over the armor, which showed signs of wear but looked well-kept. *Elemental-steel, from the looks of it. Beren must have used that for dragon hunts. Resists fire and frost both — wonder if Nikki realizes it's worth more than his mother's entire tavern? Probably bespelled as well.*

"Good," Kadana declared her approval as she buckled up the straps at the front of Nikki's armor. "And we'll see about finding you some greaves. What about the rest of you?"

She scanned the room. Templar, Omen, and Liethan were already armored in fine gear — Templar's embossed black leather was of Terizkandian design, the faint sigils covering it a sure sign it was enchanted. And the lightweight Lydonian silverleaf scales Omen wore beneath his knee-length leather coat would be impervious to the claws of the orclets. Liethan's leathers were studded with black rivets of Nvrelian onyx, no doubt also bespelled by his sorceress aunt Arra. And while Dev and Shalonie wore only basic hardened leathers, Dev noticed that like him Shalonie had a number of rings on her hands and several studs in her ears that were likely ensorcelled with various enchantments to turn back blades.

If Avarice made that coat of Kyr's, it likely has protections woven into it as well, Dev noted. "Could use some more arrows," Dev called out. "And a large vat of sulfur if you have it. Yellow sky-rock, dwarven red-stone or elv-in-salt will work as well." He held up a silver vial he'd pulled from his pack, curious to see if Kadana would know what it was.

"You mean to make acid bombs?" she asked.

He inclined his head, impressed. "If you have the containers for it — glass or ceramic will do. I have enough Death-worm poison to make a fair few bombs. Might help with the defenses."

Kadana tapped her youngest daughter on the shoulder. "Caia will help you find everything. And Tokara, you'll get arrows to everyone who needs them. We also will need—"

"Orclets!" The warning cry from outside was clearly heard through the open door of the hall. "Attack!"

"They're climbing the walls," another cry rang out.

Kadana rushed toward the open doorway, snatching up a large mace in mid-run. "Come on!" she shouted to the others. "We need to fortify the gate!"

Dev tensed and rose to his feet as Templar, Liethan, Nikki, and Shalonie raced after Kadana. They were followed closely by Tokara and Yoshihiro; only Omen, Kyr, Caia, and the cats remained behind. Omen held Kyr by the arm with a firm grasp, his other hand holding a fistful of Tormy's shoulder fur to keep the cat in place. "Tormy, you stay inside and protect Kyr. I'm counting on you!" he told the cat. "Kyr, you stay here, stay inside!"

The boy quickly snatched up Tyrin and held the little cat tightly to his chest. Omen threw Dev a warning glare. Dev tilted his head in understanding, releasing Omen to charge after the others.

Dev shoved the flask of Death-worm poison into his belt as he moved across the room toward Caia, Kyr, and the cats. While Avarice had sent him along to keep Omen safe, he knew Omen was more than capable of handling himself. Kyr, on the other hand, was far more likely to be injured, and Dev wasn't certain Tormy possessed the mental capacity to understand the responsibility Omen had just given him. *Not to mention, I'll be a lot more help if I can just find the right ingredients to make the bombs. If Kadana has any wyvern blood in the castle I can make a gas that can wither even the tangler vines in the Terizkandian swamps — bound to have some effect on these orclets if they're hatched from peapods.*

"Caia," Tormy purred sweetly as he turned toward the little girl waiting anxiously beside them. "Where is being a good place to hide a Kyr?"

"Yes, please," Tyrin added. "A place with warmness and comfortableness."

So maybe the cats do know what they're doing, Dev mused.

"Well, our dogs are upstairs . . ." Caia said with a little lisp and narrowed her eyes at Tyrin, weighing the consequences. "But baths are a good place to hide and get warm too," she said quickly.

Dev eyed the oversized leather armor the girl was wearing and the sword at her side, guessing that as young as she was, she probably had more experience with a blade than Kyr. While Kyr was a few inches taller than the six-year-old, the boy was unnaturally thin, and likely weighed less than the healthy Deldano child.

"And we can get your stuff too, sir." Caia gave Dev a gap-toothed smile. "We can get dwarven red-stone in the smithy. And I think we even have elvin-salts too in the apothecary." She turned her gaze toward the cats. "I'll take you down to the baths first."

"Baths?" Tormy looked skeptical, and Dev recognized the stubborn look that entered the cat's eyes.

"Baths mean water," Dev explained to the girl. "Felines don't like water." Outside he could hear shouts of battle, Kadana's voice rising above the others as she barked out orders. Kyr flinched at the noise, and Dev hoped he wasn't going to fall into one of his odd stupors and start spouting prophetic nonsense.

"Unless the water has salmon in it," Tyrin supplied quickly. "Do your baths have salmon in them?"

Caia giggled, her blond hair bouncing with the motion. "No, but our baths are really warm. Momma had the baths lined with sun stones."

"With what?" Dev coughed. *Sun stones! What are these Deldanos doing?*

"Sun stones." The little girl's eyes sparkled. "They're very warm and—"

"I know what sun stones are," Dev cut in a little too fast. *Wars have been fought over sun stone mines. Any sorcerer worth his salt can turn them into weapons.* Dev had seen a necromancer use a single sun stone to burn men alive on the battlefield.

"We have a whole wall of them," Caia said easily.

Kadana has a wall of sun stones? We may not need the bombs — surely Shalonie or that Nightblood can figure out a means to use sun stones against creatures vulnerable to sunlight.

"Come on." The little girl waved her hand.

Tormy, Tyrin, Dev, and Kyr followed closely behind Caia who swiftly raced from the hall and down another passageway that led deeper into the castle. She skipped through the stone corridors, mindless of the shouts of battle coming from the outside, or the soldiers running about as her home was besieged by magical creatures.

They passed through one well-appointed room after another, the wealth displayed within the castle a testament to Kadana's successful adventuring career. *Impressive,* Dev appraised the castle as he followed the girl. *Intricately worked stone pillars. Chandeliers crafted by giants. That furniture is faerie-made. I am certain.*

A wide stone staircase wound its way to the lower parts of the keep. Tormy had to duck a little as they passed through the rounded arch.

Dev considered the change in architectural design. *The castle's exterior is far older than the inside. This has all been updated. Recently.*

The stairs were wide enough for Caia to walk alongside Kyr. The little girl had taken the boy's hand as if sensing his unease. *He doesn't like being separated from Omen even with both cats beside him.* Kyr kept glancing behind them as they walked, though they were deep enough into the castle that the sounds of battle were no longer audible. Dev brought up the rear.

"Something is tickling my nose," little Tyrin squeaked and let out a tiny sneeze.

"It's the minerals in the water," Caia said sagely.

"Hot springs?" Dev asked.

"From the depths, it rises," Kyr blurted out. "They are fleeing from it."

"Is you being all right, Kyr?" Tormy asked, taking on Omen's protective role, Dev realized.

"Who is fleeing from what?" Dev hoped the boy would answer. In the last few weeks, he'd come to realize that whatever nonsense the boy spouted, it likely had some deeper meaning. He studied Kyr's profile in the light of the glimmering wall sconces. The boy was assuredly half-elvin. There was a slight point to his ears, and his skin glimmered like the white of a bleached skull. His hair, fine and straight, nearly glowed like the white shine of fresh snow during a new moon.

But as frail as he is, is he really as helpless as he seems? Dev wondered. *If he truly is Cerioth's son, then there is no telling the depths of his resourcefulness and strength. And most of the crazy things he's said have been real — one way or another.*

"The peapods," Kyr explained simply.

"From sunlight?" Dev pressed. "They're fleeing from sunlight?"

The boy stared at him in confusion. "It's night out," he reminded him. "She's going to have to cut deep. It will have to be blood."

"Watch your step, Kyr," Tyrin warned from the fold of Kyr's coat pocket. "Don't trip and fall in the drink. I is not wanting to get wet."

They'd emerged from the stairwell into a large room that contained three mineral pools and three tiled baths that were fed by waterspouts jutting from a natural stone wall. But Dev's eyes fell immediately on the far wall, which rose to a cavernously high ceiling; it was inlaid with glowing orbs, each about the size of a man's fist.

"How pretty," little Tyrin whispered. "Your wall is flaring like the sun at high noon."

"And it gets warmer, the closer you step," Caia said and waved her hand at the sparkling wall.

Top to bottom sun stones. Dev didn't want to believe his eyes. *A king's ransom! In their baths!*

"Your mother had enough sun stones to cover a whole wall?" Dev still felt perplexed.

"Oh, no." Caia replied blithely. "Momma had ever so many more, she found a whole mine of them. But she said that putting the stones on the other walls would make the room too hot."

"Did you say you have more? More sun stones?" Dev dared to hope. "Are they all set into other walls?"

"No, they're loose," Caia said innocently. "Mostly."

"Show me!" Dev tried to contain a laugh. "We just might have a way to hold back the orclets."

Caia's eyes grew big.

"We is going to be &$%@#! heroes again," Tyrin crowed.

Caia's eyes grew even bigger at the imprecation.

"Don't repeat Tyrin's potty words," Dev shot out. "Now, where are those stones?"

"Some are in the washing tubs," Caia said. "Some are in the kitchen, some are in the stables and the hen house,

210

some are in our living quarters, but the closest ones are just right there." She pointed to the tiled baths.

At the bottom of two of the tiled baths, Dev spotted arrangements of loose sun stones which caused the water to glitter with light.

Without further consideration, Dev lay down flat on his stomach and reached for the sun stones at the bottom of the pool.

"Oh, I is good at scooping," Tormy hollered with great enthusiasm.

With a mighty splash, the giant cat hopped into the middle of the bath seeming to forget his distaste for water in the excitement of the hunt. "Scoop. Scoop. Scoop," he sang off-key. "It is being as easy as scooping up salmon from the river. And in a little while I is having all the warmy stones. Scoop. Scoop. Scoop."

Dev snatched up a sun stone. It was nearly too hot to hold, but the heat stayed steady and didn't increase. He knew that the right magical spell could cause the stone to burn out all its energy in one powerful burst. Left alone they would emit a steady heat and light for centuries, but twisted by magic they could be turned into deadly weapons until the power inside of them was spent. He took the basket little Caia gave him, and dropped the stone into it, collecting the others Tormy retrieved from the bottom of the pool.

"I have to get these back upstairs," Dev told the two children and the cats, wondering if he could trust them to stay put. He doubted either Omen or Kadana wanted Kyr and Caia anywhere near the battle.

"I is all wet!" Tormy protested, climbing out of the pool. "I is not liking all wet!" The cat shook himself violently, water splaying out in all directions and causing Tyrin to shriek in protest.

"All right, hold still!" Dev commanded as Tyrin's voice started to echo off the stone walls. Though Dev was no sorcerer, he knew enough magic to cast a quick drying cantrip over the lot of them. Tormy's fur fluffed instantly and both cats started to giggle.

"What about the bombs?" Caia asked. "Aren't we going to make bombs?" The girl looked hopeful, and Dev frowned. *Definitely Kadana's daughter.*

"We may not need the bombs," Dev explained. "We can use the sun stones. You four stay here."

Four pairs of insulted eyes turned toward him at the command, and Dev recognized the start of a rebellion. He knew better than to underestimate any of them. *Never hear the end of it if something happened.* "All right, fine. Follow if you must. But stay inside the castle. And if anyone asks, I left you down here in the baths where it's safe."

Caia looked bewildered by his words. "You're going to lie?"

"Yes," Dev proclaimed quickly. "I'm very good at it."

To his surprise, the foursome looked impressed. Tormy cocked his head to one side, whiskers twitching. "We is going to follow," he admitted with the blatant honesty Dev had come to expect from the cat. "We is going to be naughty."

"We is not naughty!" little Tyrin protested, tail lashing. "We is being heroic!"

"Heroically naughty," Tormy corrected, and Tyrin's ears perked.

"Heroically naughty! I is liking that!" the little cat proclaimed.

"Just make certain you aren't heroically dead! You wouldn't like that," Dev warned sternly, hoping that at least one of them had some common sense. He turned and headed back up the stairwell, hearing the pitter-patter of paws and feet behind him as the two children and two cats followed.

Chapter 14: Spell

SHALONIE

They had been trying to duplicate Templar's sunburst spell since Liethan had beckoned them to the top of the flanking tower. Templar had accessed every last bit of his magic and was completely exhausted. The latest attempt had left both of his hands blistered with deep burns. Shalonie's experiment to use Omen's psionics to boost Templar's spell had only succeeded in knocking Omen flat on his back.

"Sorry, Omen!" She tapped at Omen's cheek with her hand until he opened his eyes, looking dazed. "It didn't work." *Brilliant idea, oh genius!* she scolded herself. *You managed to injure both of them!*

A group of warriors ran past them toward the far side of the wall, answering calls for help.

Templar, looking pale and drawn, stared at the burns on his hands. "Would you look at that. I think I was just smited by the gods," he joked halfheartedly.

"The gods didn't smite you," Omen groused as he pushed himself upright. "That was me. I don't know why my psionics reacted like that — my father can do this without needing Cypher Runes. Why didn't it work?"

"It takes years to learn how to join your power with someone else's," Shalonie explained. "No two people think the same way, so getting the energy to flow into the same pattern is almost impossible. I thought the Cypher Rune would solve the problem." *Guess I can't solve every prob-*

lem with math!

From their turret perch, Shalonie watched as Kadana's archers fired into the rampaging horde on the ground below. She heard the distant squeals and snorts of the marauding orclets. Kadana's voice boomed through the caterwauling. It sounded like Kadana and her men-at-arms were holding the line in front of the gatehouse with brute force. Shalonie knew that Nikki was down there with them.

How long can they keep that up if the orclets just keep coming? At least the beasties have mostly stopped scaling the walls.

Batches of scalding oil dumped through the machicolations at regular intervals had dissuaded the creatures from climbing the four towers any longer. The few that were still trying to come over the battlements were easily bashed back to the ground by Liethan.

"We have to try again," Omen insisted. "Templar's spell is a good one. It just needs more power behind it." He looked at Templar's blistered hands, and Shalonie found herself wincing in sympathy. She knew Templar's inhuman heritage would allow him to heal preternaturally fast, but the burns still had to hurt horrifically.

"You good to try again?" Omen asked his friend.

"Sure," Templar inclined his head. "What's a bit of smiting between friends? We can tell my grandfather I attempted to conjure sunshine and butterflies with the power of the gods when we get back home. He'll be delighted."

But Shalonie waved her hands in denial and tossed down the silver tipped stylus she'd been using to draw the Cypher Runes. "It didn't work — it's not going to work no matter how many times we try it," she said, angry at herself for wasting time inking the Cypher Rune on Omen's skin. She

215

thought of Nikki battling in the fray below. *He's not a trained warrior.* Fear snapped at her heart.

"We can't just give up!" Omen protested.

"We have to try something else!" Shalonie insisted. *If the equation is wrong, no amount of trying is going to make it work.* "I have to think of something else!" She racked her brain for a solution — just about everything she could think of would require hours if not days of preparation. *There's no time.*

"The imps are starting to dig under the lower curtain walls," Liethan shouted as he fired his crossbow down toward the ground beyond the castle walls. "Look at those little claws go. And I'm running out of bolts." Young Tokara had been making regular runs back and forth along the walls, carrying arrows to the archers and crossbow bolts to Liethan, but she'd warned them they were running low.

"How bad is it?" Omen called up to the Corsair.

The look Liethan threw down to the three of them wasn't encouraging. "Probably ought to think of something soon," he warned. "Judging by the movement I can see in the forest, there are thousands of these things out there. Sooner or later, Kadana's people are going to be overrun by sheer numbers alone. They can't fight forever."

"Dawn is still many hours away," Shalonie murmured to herself, panic clawing at her throat as she listened to the shouts of the soldiers below.

"Shalonie!" The voice of Dev Machelli caught their attention, and they all turned to see the young man racing up the stairwell along the inner wall that led to their perch on the tower turret. He was carrying a large glowing basket in his arms. Both Omen and Templar struggled to their feet as he approached.

216

"Sun stones!" he exclaimed, holding out the basket. "I found a dozen sun stones in Kadana's bath!"

"What were you doing in Kadana's bath?" Templar snarked. "I'm being smited, and you're bathing?"

Shalonie had to laugh despite herself.

"Take these." Dev ignored him and pushed the basket at Shalonie.

Omen reached for one of the stones, gingerly touching it a few times before picking it up. He was wearing leather gauntlets, but Shalonie knew the stones would still feel warm in his hands. The sun stones cast a golden glow over all their faces.

"You can use them against the orclets, right?" Dev insisted.

Shalonie stared into the basket, her mind moving frantically as she tried to reevaluate the situation in light of the new factor Dev had introduced.

"We can't use these blasted things!" Templar protested. "You push magic into sun stones, and they'll burn everything in a fifty-foot radius, including us."

"No!" Shalonie shoved the basket into Omen's hands, and then turned on her heel to pace back and forth as she latched onto a glimmer of an idea. "We don't need their heat; we just need their light! I see where you're going with this!" She shot Dev a brilliant grin and then continued pacing while the others watched her impatiently.

"Shalonie?" Omen sounded perplexed. "Templar's right. These things burn. We have one in our oven back home."

"No!" Shalonie waved her hand as if scribbling down a note, her gaze focused inward with deep concentration. "They burn and they emit light. If you indiscriminately trigger them, they'll do both uncontrollably until they burn

217

themselves out. But you can control it, and all we need is their light, not their heat. It's actually the frequency of the sun's light that destroys the orclets, not the heat. All we need to do is control the output."

She thought of every means she'd ever heard of controlling the stones. "I could put them in oculerns, and then we could control all of them with an oculumni except I don't have time to make any of those. I could use a Cypher Rune — a tattoo on a dozen different people — they could hold the stones and surround the castle — but they'd have to stand there all night, and tattoos take a long time to make. A linking spell then — something to link them together and control the flow of power — the light frequency is just a mathematical calculation but they still have to be linked to each other and the magical source. So I'll need—"

"Will cutting someone help?" Dev asked abruptly, interrupting her tumble of thoughts. She looked up to regard all three men. They were staring at her with bafflement as if she were crazy, until Dev's words sank in.

Templar threw a sharp-eyed look at Dev and let out a Terizkandian curse.

"Dev!" Omen exclaimed. "Why would you say something like that?"

A dark look crossed Dev's face. "I didn't," he growled. "Your crazy Kyr did — and since half of what your brother says turns out to be right, I thought I'd mention it. He said 'she'll have to cut deep' along with something about blood."

"He probably just meant that Kadana would—" Omen began.

"Blood would work!" Shalonie snapped elatedly, cutting him off before he could finish. Dev's words had given her an idea. She'd already used Omen's psionics to power one of her Cypher Runes successfully. *This is the same idea only it won't require Omen to be in contact with the stones continuously.*

"Blood?" Omen said, disconcerted.

Templar stared at her. "Blood magic? Are you sure you want—"

"Omen, I can use your blood to tie the stones to each other and you, and use you to power the Cypher Rune — but that will mean the Rune will have to go on you. . ." she trailed off momentarily, a thought occurring to her. "And that means I'll have to cut it into you." *He won't allow that.*

"Your turn to get smited, Omen," Templar joked tepidly.

"Great." Omen's grin was weak at best. "But I'm game — if you think it will work."

"Really?" Shalonie couldn't hide her surprise. "You're going to let me cut you? Just like that? I'm not even sure this will work."

"It'll work!" Omen said definitively, apparently having more faith in her than she did herself. "And it's not like I can't handle a bit of blood. Now, what do we need to do?"

"We need to put the stones somewhere their light can reach a circular area around the castle," she explained.

"You mean like all along the walls?" Templar asked.

"No, they have to stay together." She cast her gaze around the ramparts. "The more spread out they are, the harder it will be to control their magic."

"What about up there?" Dev pointed toward a narrow center tower at the very top of Kadana's main keep.

Shalonie recognized the make of the tower — it was meant as a signal watch — a tall spire that loomed high over the entire area. It had four wide archways at the top that led out to a narrow balcony that surrounded it entirely.

Supposedly signal lights lit atop the tower could be seen from other distant towers — though when it had last been used for such a thing, or if those other distant towers even still existed, Shalonie did not know. However, at the very top of the conical roof of the tower was a large metal crucible with a wide ringed edge where they could place the stones — provided they could climb to the top of the tower. Shalonie assumed at one point in time there must have been a scaffolding of stairs to carry wood to the top of the platform — it had long ago either been removed or crumbled away.

We'll have to climb onto the steep roof itself.

"That will work," Shalonie reasoned, looking from the tower to the walls. *The angle looks about right.* "It's high enough that the angle should allow the light to hit just beyond the walls. The orclets nearest the walls won't be affected, but it will prevent any more from approaching. All Kadana will have to do is get rid of the ones hiding in the shadows."

"The roof is slate," Templar gauged, looking at the spire. "Slippery. Watch your step. Liethan and I will let Kadana know what you're planning. You three get to the tower."

"Hurry!" Shalonie urged. Then she clapped Omen on the shoulder, and the two of them followed Dev back down the stairs. He led them through the main corridor and past the large chamber where they'd been earlier. As they passed, Shalonie saw the faces of the two cats, Kyr, and Kadana's youngest daughter peeking out behind a curtain. She also noted the swift motion Dev made with his hands for them to hide. All four shrank back guiltily. Shalonie hurried along as Dev moved deeper into the keep.

They had several sets of stairs to climb before they

reached the one that would lead up to the top of the center tower, but Omen knew the castle well enough to guide them through the torch-lit halls without difficulty. As they ran, they passed a number of servants huddled together in various corners, terrified by the attack going on outside. They were all armed with weapons of some sort, but Shalonie guessed that few of them were fighters. The warriors were already outside defending the walls.

The raucous bray of an excited dog pack echoed through the halls, adding to Shalonie's tension. *Caia's hounds,* she thought absently.

"Here," Omen called when they reached the top floor. The entire area was dim and dusty. Dev had grabbed a burning torch from a sconce and lit their way. Omen pulled on a decrepit wooden door, the rusty handle nearly crumbling in his hand. The opening revealed a dark, dingy stairwell beyond. It wound upward, the stone steps uneven and worn. Shalonie guessed that the tower had not been used in decades — possibly centuries.

Dev went first, holding the torch in front of him. Omen followed, the basket of glowing sun stones pressed to his chest as they climbed upward. Shalonie came last, working out the Cypher Rune in her head.

It's actually a simple equation — just the variation for the light frequency minus the heat emission. It should work — theoretically. She didn't like the fact that so much of what she'd done on this journey had been guesswork — theories she came up with on the fly. She would have preferred to work out the details first — wanted the security of her methodical approach rather than the "come up with it as you go" method Omen and Templar seemed to thrive on.

It will work! she tried to assure herself. *I hope.*

They reached the top of the tower and emerged onto the narrow balcony. For a moment Shalonie made the mistake of looking down. The truly dizzying height made her stomach flip, and she thought she would vomit. She swallowed the bile and pressed herself against the tower wall, looking up into the star-filled sky to steady herself.

"You all right?" Omen caught her by the arm.

She squeezed her eyes shut for a moment. "Just don't like heights."

"We're going to need to climb onto the roof to put the stones in place," Dev reminded her.

"I'll be fine," she assured both of them. "I just won't look down — it'll be easy." She didn't sound very convincing, even to herself.

Dev set the torch into an aged wall sconce, and then leaped nimbly up onto the ledge of the narrow balcony. He grasped the edge of the slate roof, testing its firmness with a couple of sharp blows of his fist. "Sound construction," he assured them both and then lifted himself effortlessly up onto the sloped roof.

Shalonie closed her eyes again. She heard his boots scrape against the slate as he tried to find purchase on the angled surface.

"Shalonie, you better go next," Omen urged, setting the basket of stones down. "I'll hand the basket up to Dev once you're on the roof."

Her eyes flew open wide. "Right," she said and took a deep breath. Quickly unstrapping her sword and setting it on the ground, she grasped Omen's outstretched hand. Cautiously, she clambered onto the balcony railing, forcing her eyes to focus solely on the stones themselves and not the incredibly far drop. Omen kept a tight hold on her arm as she stood, turning to face the roof, her back to the long drop behind her.

Once Shalonie stood up, the edge of the roof was only a short distance away from her and all she had to do was reach out and grasp the edge — then pull herself up. But as she'd guessed, the angle was incredibly sharp. Dev crouched only feet away, his right hand held out to her, both feet planted on the slates. "It's fine," he told her. "Just move slowly. There are metal bracers on the crucible that we can hold onto once we climb up to it."

Steeling herself, she grabbed the roof's edge and lifted herself across. Her boots slipped several times against the slippery slates, but Dev caught hold of her and held her in place until she felt secure enough to pause and catch her breath.

"Climb up slowly." Dev motioned toward the bracers. Sure enough, she could see metal rings that must have held the long-missing outer stair scaffold in place at the base of the metal crucible. Despite the years, the metal — dwarven black iron — was rust-free and in good condition.

Shalonie climbed slowly upward while behind her Omen and Dev lifted the basket of sun stones onto the roof. Omen joined them on the slanted surface. Shalonie grabbed one of the black iron rings at the top and held on tightly, feeling at once more secure. She watched nervously as Dev and Omen made their way up to her. Omen had left behind his sword and stripped off the leather coat he wore over his silverleaf armor. Moments later, they all huddled around the crucible, each holding onto a ring.

"Now what?" Omen asked.

"Now the painful part," Shalonie told him honestly. "I'm going to cut the marks into you — and we need to get your

223

blood on all the stones. In theory that should connect you, the stones and the Cypher Runes."

"Let's do it then." Omen unbuckled the straps of the silverleaf bracer he wore around his left forearm and yanked off his gauntlet. Dev pulled a thin dagger from the sleeve of his own coat and handed it across to Shalonie while Omen undid the laces on his undertunic to bare his forearm.

Shalonie took a sharp breath through her gritted teeth as Omen held his bare arm out to her.

"Don't worry about hurting me," he told her. "Just ignore everything else and do what you have to."

She bit her lip, feeling sick to her stomach again; guilt gnawed at her. She filled her lungs with a deep steadying breath, and then raised the dagger, placing the tip against Omen's arm. She pictured the runes carefully in her head. The dagger Dev had given her was deadly sharp and cut deep the moment she touched it to flesh. She cut the marks as quickly as she could, grateful that Omen made no sound as she did so despite the well of blood rising from the wounds. She made several marks — some with quick sharp slashes and two with tight curves that would have been impossible to cut had the knife not been so sharp. Blood welled in all the lines and began dripping down the sides of Omen's arm, onto the slate roof.

When she'd finished the last of the marks, she motioned quickly to Dev. "Get the stones under the blood — we have to get blood on all of them."

He handed over the basket, and Omen held his bleeding arm over the opening. The blood hissed as it struck the heated stones and, despite the fact that the rune had not yet been activated, the stones glowed brighter upon contact with the blood.

Divine blood! she realized in alarm. *Cerioth! I keep forgetting Omen's parentage.* She held her breath, fearful that she'd miscalculated. If the stones reacted too strongly to the inherent magic in Omen's blood, the spell could go disastrously wrong.

When there was no further reaction to the blood, Shalonie finally let her breath out and glanced up at Omen and Dev; both men were watching her like a cat watches a mouse. "If I did any of this wrong, we're going to burn," she said slowly. "You know that, right?"

Dev winked at her. "Wouldn't be the first time someone tried to light me on fire. And it beats getting eaten alive by thousands of tiny monsters — which is what those creatures are going to do if we don't stop them."

"I'm not worried, Shalonie," Omen encouraged her. "What now?"

She looked upward toward the metal crucible. "We should place the stones around the edge of the crucible first."

Dev pulled himself upright — half standing, half kneeling on the steeply slanted roof, while Shalonie handed one blood-drenched stone at a time up to him. He placed them on the lip of the crucible in a ring until the basket was empty, then waved down toward her.

"That's it, Omen," Shalonie said. "Just like you did on the ship — push your power into the mark as if you were going to heal the cuts. One of the Leiran Patterns if you can manage it." She knew the Leiran Patterns were the most common psionic patterns used to knit flesh back together.

"As much power as I did on the ship?" he asked uncertainly.

Remembering the unexpected result of that, Shalonie

225

blanched. "Maybe not quite that much. Can you control it?"

"I can certainly try." He inspected the bleeding mark on his arm, his eyes narrowing as he focused his mind.

A moment later, Shalonie felt the distinctive tingle of power in the air, the waves of force brushing up against her own psionic shield in a rapid pulsing pattern. Only in that moment did it occur to her how easily Omen could rip through her shield if he wanted to. She'd always prided herself on having strong mental defenses. Sundragon Geryon had taught her the defensive shielding patterns when she was a small child, and she'd taken to the lessons as easily as everything else she'd ever done. But the power Omen raised made her realize exactly why the Daenoths were feared.

"It's working!" Dev's voice drew her attention, and she looked upward.

The sun stones had flared to life, light radiating out from the ring along the crucible and growing brighter and brighter with each passing heartbeat. And then, all at once blinding light burst out in every direction, lighting the area up like the noonday sun. The light struck out with brilliant force and illuminated the ground beyond the castle walls.

Shalonie heard the swell of a great cheer as the light seared the approaching orclets without mercy. As the magical sunlight hit, she witnessed the creatures' instant transformation from raving monsters to dried-up autumn leaves that fluttered harmlessly to the ground.

"Grab him!" Dev shouted.

Shalonie turned in time to see Omen pitching forward, the effects of the combined magic having stunned him. Instinctively, she reached out to grab him — her right hand closing over his wrist as her left hand tightened around the metal ring attached to the crucible.

But Omen weighed far more than she'd expected, and her left hand was wrenched free of the metal ring. His weight pulled her forward and downward toward the deadly drop below them. Her booted feet scrambled uselessly against the steep tile roof to hold them both in place. But before she could slip away, Dev caught hold of her flailing left hand, anchoring her in place, and for one brief moment the three of them hung there suspended — Shalonie grasping Omen's bleeding arm, Dev grasping Shalonie's left while simultaneously holding the weight of both of them with his own grip on the metal crucible.

"I can't hold him!" Shalonie shouted, shaking with panic and gripping Omen's wrist with all her might. Her hand felt like water as if all strength were gone from it and clamping her fingers down was merely a mental exercise. His hand was completely lax, and she realized he had lost consciousness — unaware of the danger.

Is he dead? she thought irrationally. She tried to ignore the wrenching pain in her shoulders as she was pulled in either direction. Feeling her grip weakening, she tried to wrap her legs around Omen, thinking she could help anchor him in place long enough for Dev to pull them up. But her jagged movement just wrenched her arms harder, and she felt something tearing in her shoulder. She could hear shouts off in the distance — though perhaps she was screaming as well.

Suddenly, a bright orange and white glimmer splashed in front of all of them. The strain on her arms lifted, and she saw Tormy rising above the edge of the rooftop — fur blowing back and paws landing soundlessly against the slate roof as he caught hold of Omen with his mouth — his teeth closing firmly on the leather belt at his waist.

Tormy's flying! Shalonie thought in amazement as the giant cat disappeared over the side of the roof with Omen. A second later, the large furry face appeared over the edge again — ears perked forward as he stared at Shalonie from where she still hung, held in place by Dev.

"I is getting you too, Shalonie!" the cat chirped. "I is catching you!"

Not understanding at all what was happening, Shalonie yelped and slid forward. Dev had moved, releasing his hold on the metal ring and allowing them both to slide down toward the large orange form. While Tormy didn't exactly catch her, he did stop her from sliding over the edge — placing one enormous white paw on her chest and holding her in place. She realized with a start that the cat was standing with his hind legs on the edge of the balcony below, front claws clinging to the roof — as fearless and steady as he would have been on the ground.

"Grab his fur and slide down his left side," Dev instructed. "You should be able to drop right back down onto the balcony."

She did as he instructed, and a moment later she was sitting back on the balcony within the confines of the tower openings. Omen was beside her — barely awake. He groaned in pain. Dev dropped back down beside them as Tormy turned to look over the edge of the tower balcony wall. "It is being all fair and fine!" he called down to the people below on the ground. "We is all being safenessness! And we is being hungry! Dinner time!"

Shalonie heard rousing shouts and applause from the courtyard, and she leaned back against the tower wall, exhausted. Her hands shook uncontrollably, and she felt cold as ice. *Saved by the cat!* she thought happily as her arms hung limply at her sides, both her shoulders aching from the strain she'd put on them.

Beside her, Tormy started to purr as he licked Omen's face. The young man, only vaguely aware of what was happening, reached out to pat the cat. "Yeah, Tormy," he muttered. "Good cat."

"I is being heroically naughty," the cat informed them. Dev looked as exhausted as Shalonie felt. The two of them exchanged wordless smiles before Dev reached out and patted Tormy's flank.

"Good cat," he agreed.

Chapter 15: Portal

OMEN

O men groaned as Dev helped him to his feet. Beside him, he saw Shalonie struggling to rise, looking like a broken wreck, pale and visibly shaking. An intense headache hammered away behind his eyes. "You all right there?" he asked the girl.

"Sure." Shalonie gave a weak smile, though the way she was holding both her arms belied the word.

"Kadana has a healer on staff," he told her and glanced down at his own arm where the Cypher Rune had been cut. While his arm was still smeared with blood — there was no sign of the wounds themselves. Either his psionics or his inhuman nature had healed them already, leaving not even a scar behind.

Tormy sniffed at his arm, before turning his attention to his face and smothering him with licks and nudges. Omen laughed and patted at the cat. "Thanks, Tormy," Omen barely got the words out through the blanket of orange and white fur. "You saved me."

"I is flying again, Omy." Tormy rubbed his face against Omen's chest.

"We is helping," Tyrin's little voice added, and Omen looked up to see Kyr standing in the shadows of the tower stairwell, Tyrin in hand, young Caia beside him. He guessed the four had followed them up the tower.

"Are you still green, Omen?" the boy asked with trembling anticipation.

"Yes, Kyr," Omen reassured his brother. "I'm fine . . . green. Nothing to worry about."

Awkwardly, they made their way back down the tower stairs and into the castle proper. While Dev seemed unhurt though quiet, Shalonie was moving gingerly as if in pain. Omen's head pounded with each step he took. *Need that healer,* he thought.

Led by Caia, they made their way back down to the lower levels, and then through the castle to the courtyard — now brightly lit by the light shining from the top of the watchtower. It was strange to see the castle so illuminated when the sky itself was still black as night. As they emerged from the castle, the courtyard erupted in a booming cheer — servants and workers relieved to put down their weapons. Kadana's garrison was still moving about, dealing with the orclets that were hiding in the shadows, avoiding the light.

Kadana crossed the courtyard at a half-run, the round metal plates of her studded leather armor clinking as she moved.

Unceremoniously, she pulled Omen into a fierce hug.

"That was stupid and reckless!" Kadana's face was flushed from battle. "Thank you. Thank you for being stupid and reckless." She turned to catch a glimpse of Shalonie standing just behind Dev. Shalonie looked mildly guilt-ridden, Omen noted. *Like Tormy when he's eaten all the cookie dough.*

"You came up with this plan?" Kadana demanded.

Shalonie looked at all the gathered people, the men-at-arms, the servants, the craftsmen, the visitors, her companions, Kadana's family . . . Nikki. Her face turned beet red.

"Well . . ." she began hesitantly.

231

"It is being all my idea!" Tyrin announced. "I is asking Caia where is warmness and then we is finding the sun stones."

Kadana burst out laughing at the tiny feline's confident pronouncement. "Well done," she said, voice full of praise as her gaze swept over all of them. "Well done, you lot. All of you." She clapped Omen, Shalonie, and Dev on the shoulders.

"Werton!" Kadana called her captain of the guards. "Set watches. Keep eyes on the tree line, we don't want any other surprises before dawn." Omen watched as Kadana's castle dwellers went about the business of getting back to business. *They're pretty unflappable. Must trust Kadana.*

From across the courtyard, Templar and Liethan came to join them, Templar's eyes zeroing in on the streaks of blood still on Omen's arm.

"I think Shalonie could use a healer," Omen told his friend before he could say anything.

"I'm fine," the girl protested.

"Nonsense." Kadana turned her attention back to the group. "You all need checking on, and a hot meal in your bellies."

The cats meowed with enthusiasm.

Still cats.

Kadana didn't stop there. "And you need to get some rest — you'll have an early day tomorrow."

"What about the orclets?" Liethan cut in. "There are still a lot of them in the woods — and there's bunches hiding in the shadows of the walls."

"How long will that spell of yours hold?" Kadana asked Shalonie.

"Weeks, probably," she admitted. "The stones can keep

glowing like this for years — but eventually the last of Omen's blood will wear off and the spell will break. If we get a hard rainstorm, it will happen quicker."

"Then you lot get inside," Kadana urged. "Get some food and some rest, and we'll talk in the morning. Tokara —"

"Caia and I will take care of everything," Kadana's daughter broke in before Kadana could say more. "Don't worry, Mother."

"Good girls!" Kadana cheered in approval, and then stormed off to see to her garrison.

❖

Hours later Omen was awakened by the gentle shaking of Kyr's hand. He opened his eyes to see his brother standing beside his bed, already dressed for the day. Tyrin was seated on top of Omen's chest, staring down at his face as if he'd been studying him in his sleep, and Tormy was draped across Omen's legs, pinning him down with his weight.

"We have to eat breakfast," Kyr explained. "We're to follow the girl to the kitchen, and you're to come too. The solstice is tomorrow."

Tyrin hopped off to one side of the bed and climbed into Kyr's coat pocket.

"Tomorrow." Omen sighed.

The Summer Gate would be open, and with the Autumn Dwellers invading the world, he wondered what ill would come. He looked at Kyr's left hand, which was no longer bandaged — the blisters caused by his earlier blunders had all healed. The hex mark twisted around all of Kyr's fingers, wrapped around his wrist, and then disappeared beneath the sleeve of his coat. "How far has it reached?" he asked the boy.

Kyr's gaze flicked away uncomfortably, but he dutifully pulled back the collar of his coat. Omen's heart tightened when he realized that there were now black tendrils beginning to wind around the boy's pale throat. Another blunder from him and Kyr's entire arm would burn and blister. Fierce determination swamped through Omen. *I have to take care of this as soon as possible.* Khylar had to be found — and Indee had to lift her hex.

"Does it hurt?"

Kyr bit down on his lip and shook his head.

"It's growing. You didn't tell me." Omen felt sickness swirl in his stomach.

"It's all right, Omen," Kyr said mildly.

"&^$@%^!" Tyrin groused, reflecting Omen's mood.

Awake now, Omen dressed quickly, preparing himself for the day. Once ready, they left the room. A large servant woman waited for them in the hall; she was holding a covered basket in her arms.

"This is being Hessaby," Tormy supplied. "We is going to follow her to the kitchen where we is going to eat lots and lots."

"Hessaby," Omen greeted.

She curtsied low, inclining her head. "Begging your pardon, my lord," she greeted. "I'm the pantler's assistant. Your lady grandmother is saying to feed all of you up well and good."

"What is being a pantler?" Tormy asked as they followed after Hessaby. Omen quickly explained to him that a pantler was the person responsible for the room where all the castle's food was stored.

Both cats looked intrigued.

"Hessaby," Tyrin spoke up. "You must be knowing a lot

about where the places is where, say . . ." the tiny cat pretended to draw an example from midair, "the salmon and the cream is being waiting for me."

"The cream is kept in the buttery, not in the pantry," Hessaby corrected.

"You don't have to tell him where the salmon is," Omen said quickly. "It may be better to keep Tyrin in the dark about food storage."

The woman smiled and bowed her head.

They arrived in the kitchen to the hustle and bustle of breakfast being prepared. Several cooks busied themselves with pots and kettles hung over three different, large fireplaces. A whole pig roasted on a spit while a young kitchen maid basted it with a long, flat brush.

"Mistress Olema," Hessaby addressed an older woman Omen guessed to be the cook in charge. The woman had her hair efficiently wrapped in a scarf and wore a clean, coarse full apron over her Deldano green tunic.

"Why are you bringing folk to my kitchen?" Olema seemed more harassed than angry. "We are very busy."

"The lady bade me tell you, the family will join their company down here for breakfast."

Olema didn't miss a beat, confronted with what was no doubt nerve-racking news.

"Please, the long table." She indicated a long wooden table with benches at the far end of the kitchen. "Please, sit and be welcome."

"There are more of us," Omen warned. He could already hear the others approaching and turned in time to see Templar, Shalonie, Dev, and Liethan entering the kitchens, led by young Caia who ran ahead to greet the two cats.

Mistress Olema just tutted and ushered them all toward

the table. She turned to Hessaby. "Give our guest the seed cakes to start."

Hessaby ducked her head and scurried off toward a large door with an iron grating.

"Is that being my pantry?" Tyrin contorted his body in order to see the door and nearly fell to the ground.

"No," Dev lied swiftly, catching the little cat before he could leap from Kyr's pocket. He set the kitten down on the long wooden table next to a plate of buttered rolls which Tyrin happily swatted at, stealing one from the plate and sinking his tiny teeth into it.

The group all sat down around the table, the sounds of Kadana's kitchen making Omen feel restless.

"You want to cook something, don't you," Templar said. It was a statement not a question.

"Kadana is bound to have phenomenal spices." Omen craned his neck to see what all was happening around him, curiosity riled. "She travels all over the world, you know."

Templar pressed a hand down on Omen's shoulder, preventing him from stepping away from the table and joining in the culinary fun. "Too many cooks, they say—"

Kadana entered the kitchen, followed by her father-in-law, Tokara, and Nikki. Kadana had changed from her armor to a Deldano green hooded robe and looked slightly more the noble lady than the warrior, though Omen spotted boots peeking out from under her hem. The girls were both in leathers, and their grandfather had stripped off his armor and appeared in a pale Shindarian jacket and pants. Nikki, Omen noticed, was once again wearing the armored surcoat Kadana had given him, looking every inch a Deldano. He smiled brightly when he saw Shalonie and slid in next to her. She handed him a fresh seed cake.

236

"Eat, everyone." Kadana sat down on the bench between Omen and Templar.

A servant hurried over with steaming mugs of buttered tea and bowls of milk thick with cream tops for the cats.

Tyrin scrambled around the table and hopped to the larger of the two bowls. "I is thinking Tormy will be needing more than that." He nodded his sharp little chin to the small bowl that had obviously been intended for him. Then he plunged his whole face into the cream, slurping up Tormy's helping quickly and messily.

"Right away." The serving girl ran back toward the buttery, grabbing a larger vessel in mid-sprint.

Tormy frowned as much as his fuzzy face allowed. "I think I is being hoodwinked."

"Don't worry, Tormy." Omen patted his cat's broad back. "She'll be right back. Why don't you sit down a little."

The big cat straightened out his front legs, stretched his back and flopped down on his stomach. He hid his white paws under his ruff and waited patiently.

"You two feeling all right?" Kadana asked then, her gaze sweeping over both Omen and Shalonie. Omen had known a good night's sleep would cure his headache, but he looked to Shalonie with reawakened concern. He knew she'd hurt herself when she'd tried to save him on the roof — both her arms getting wrenched by the strain of holding his weight.

"I'm fine," she assured them with a gentle smile. "Your healer saw to me last night. Just a few torn muscles is all."

"Aster is very good," Kadana agreed. "Especially with bumps, bruises, and broken bones. I am glad it wasn't any worse."

"While we are on the subject. Thank you," Omen told Shalonie. "You were extremely brave and cool under pres-

237

sure." He tilted his head toward Dev to include him in the thanks. "If you two hadn't been there, I would have fallen."

Shalonie blushed, looking uncomfortable at the reminder of what had happened.

Dev just waved a hand dismissively. "Would have been a lot harder to continue spying on you if you'd cracked your head open on the ground," the Machelli quipped.

Despite the galling reminder, Omen had to smile. "You told my mother, didn't you?"

The mischievous twinkle in Dev's eyes told him everything he needed to know. "Don't worry, I made you sound heroic," he assured him. "Not as heroic as Tormy and Tyrin, of course."

Tyrin looked up from his cream, ears perked forward. "Heroically naughty!" he protested. "We is heroically naughty. The naughty part is being very important."

"Yes," Tormy agreed as if dispensing sage advice. "Avarice is saying that stealing cookies is naughty, even when I is telling her it's heroicallyness, and we is liking cookies, so the naughtiness is very important."

"Oh, don't worry about any of that," Dev assured the two cats. "She knows exactly how naughty you two are — trust me."

Satisfied, the cats went back to their breakfast while Omen endured the amused snickers coming from the others. Even Kadana joined in.

The servants brought over several more plates filled with crispy bacon, fresh peaches, and steaming bread straight from the oven.

Kadana studied the fare in satisfaction. "We cleared out the orclets around the castle," she told them between bites of peaches and sips of tea. "And your spell is holding —

the light is keeping the ones in the forest from even approaching the castle. But come nightfall, they'll move again and head for the villages away from the sun stones."

"We can help protect the villages," Omen offered immediately.

"I know you would and could." Kadana studied their faces, one after the other. "But there's far more at stake than just one castle or a few villages."

"No one is safe until the Autumn Gate is closed," Shalonie said quietly.

"You will have to close the Gate. All of you." Kadana looked at her newly discovered grandson. "You too, Nikki."

Nikki gave a stoic nod. *I have a feeling he was planning on following Shalonie regardless,* Omen thought, gladdened. *Can't hurt having him keep an eye on her.*

"I would go with you," Kadana said, studying her cup. "But my responsibility is to my immediate surroundings. My family. My people. The tenants of my land. The villagers I've sworn to protect. And those orclets, I can only hold them off for so long. I've never seen so many of them."

"You could eat them," Tormy suggested.

The servant girl had returned with a large bucket of milk, and Tormy dipped his tongue into the creamy liquid, looking very pleased with himself.

Omen served both cats large slices of bacon.

"Eat them! That is being a &$#@%^&! great idea," Tyrin threw in his support. "I is thinking they is turning to leaves in the light — so they is probably a fruit, and fruit is being deliciousnessness when you is pouring cream on them."

Kadana ignored the cats. "You'll have to leave for the

Mountain of Shadow right away, and I'm sorry to say, you'll have to go the fast way."

"You mean a portal?" Shalonie caught on before Omen did.

"That sounds like fun." Omen toasted Liethan whose face lit up with delight.

"You said riding the portals was dangerous," Nikki cut in.

"What's a little danger when life as we know it hangs in the balance," Kadana countered. "We avoid them unless we have no choice. This is one of those times when it's worth the risk — it's going to have to be."

"Which portal?" Shalonie questioned. "And how will we find one that leads exactly where we want to go?"

Kadana poured herself another mug of tea. "There's a portal nearby in the forest — it's one of the more stable ones in Kharakhan — been there as long as I can remember." She motioned toward Liethan and Omen. "Your mothers and I used it frequently when we were younger — before we stopped. It's what we always referred to as a fixed portal — it always went to the same place, generally at least."

"What do you mean generally?" Shalonie asked with a clipped tone.

Omen exchanged antsy looks with Templar and Liethan — while he understood all of Kadana's warnings about portals, he couldn't help but feel pure excitement at the thought of using one.

Kadana reached across the table for a slice of thick bread. "It always leads to the Mountain of Shadow — the problem is, the Mountain of Shadow isn't stable. So the exit is never the same — never know what is waiting for you on the other side, save for the fact that it will be somewhere in the Mountain."

"A cave then?" Shalonie pressed.

"Cave, cavern, ancient ruin, chasm, dead forest — could be anything," Kadana replied. "The Mountain of Shadow isn't like other places. Realms — thousands of them — seem to converge there at that point. The Mountain is one of the most magical and unpredictable places you'll ever find. My guess is that since you'll be entering it so close to Summer Fest, the most likely place you'll end up is in the Summer Lands themselves. If you find the Gate closed, that's when Omen should play the lute."

Omen thought back to the ridiculous song he'd played for the Bower Dames. *Better put some thought into this.*

"How do we find the Autumn Gate?" Templar asked.

They all looked to Shalonie for the answer.

The girl gave them an annoyed look. "How am I supposed to know? I've never been there," she reminded them. "I'm sure we'll figure it out." She pulled out a notebook from the pouch at her belt and flipped through several pages before laying it down on the table and turning it toward Omen and Kadana. "I have a number of diagrams of the pathways in the Mountain," she explained. "Beren and Arra have repeatedly attempted to map it, and they gave me access to their notes about a year ago."

"Can't be mapped," Kadana stated definitely. "They kept trying — but they kept failing."

Shalonie tugged thoughtfully at her golden braid. "Yes, but I'm fairly certain I've worked out some basic patterns. The Mountain itself seems to respond to the intent of those who enter it — so if you're trying to get somewhere specific, there's a good chance that's where you'll end up. It's a form of sympathetic magic."

"Or you'll end up in the exact opposite location of where you want to go," Kadana corrected her. "It may respond to intent — but it isn't always friendly. The Mountain can be very vindictive."

"Are you saying we shouldn't go?" Liethan asked.

Kadana laughed at that. "No, way I figure it, it's the best option you have for finding the Autumn Lands. Just telling you to be careful. Now finish up your bacon — we should get started as soon as possible. We'll be taking the tunnel under the castle to the portal."

Tokara and Caia's joint squeals interrupted their mother's sentence.

She gave them a stern look, and they sat up straight and didn't make another sound.

Don't want to lose their chance at going into the tunnels, I guess. Omen had heard of the tunnels under his grandmother's keep but had never been there before. *Looks like I get to go to a lot of places I've only heard about — just hope I figure out how to come back in one piece.*

❖

After breakfast, they gathered their belongings, servants resupplying them with food for the journey. But unlike before, they would not be taking their horses — and had to carry what they needed. With the exception of Kyr, they all shouldered backpacks. Tormy dutifully let Omen strap the saddle onto his back, to which more bags were attached. And then they headed down into the cellars of the castle to the promised tunnels.

They stood in front of tall metal double doors, laboriously pushed open by Kadana's seneschal. The older man, Kadana had referred to him as Gollis, was reluctant to unlock the gate to the underkeep, as he called it. Far from arguing with the lady of the castle, however, Gollis did as he was asked, but his hands shook as he placed a ridiculously large key into the rusted circular lock. Distantly, Omen noted an ostentatious golden ring with the head of a lion on the man's index finger.

Bet there's a story there.

"I will have the garrison at the ready, my lady," Gollis said, his otherwise pleasant voice stiff with worry. "The underkeep has been quiet for many years, but that does not mean it is sleeping. It may well lay in wait."

"I know, Gollis," Kadana said lightly, her decision made. "We shouldn't keep it waiting."

Gollis swallowed so hard, Omen was concerned the man would choke on the additional words of warning he was too mannered to utter.

"What's under the keep?" Dev asked with a frown.

"A maze of tunnels," Tokara said. "Momma says the tunnels extend all the way to Dysartha."

Kadana shot her daughter a stern look. "You are not ever to go to that city, by tunnel or any other way."

"Yes, Momma," Tokara and Caia said with small voices, their enthusiasm damped only slightly.

"The tunnels," Kadana explained, "are very old. I don't know the exact reason for them, but I guess they go back to the time of the giants of the earth."

A coterie of liveried servants handed out torches to each person in the group.

Templar spoke a quick word, which lit his torch.

Kadana huffed approvingly. "I always thought those domestic cantrips were handy." She touched her torch to Templar's; the pitch caught fire immediately.

"Careful with the torches, girls," she told Tokara and Caia. "Don't get the fire near any person and be very careful you don't accidentally bump the torch into Tormy."

"I is going in the back, behind all the torches," Tormy squeaked.

"Good idea," Omen agreed. "That way you can watch our backs too."

Kadana's girls and Yoshihiro were in the rear as well, but many strides in front of Tormy, who walked with measured steps, his ears swiveling at the merest suggestion of a sound. Kadana led the way, Omen and Templar side-by-side only steps behind her. Kyr stayed close behind them, the kitten triumphantly riding on his shoulder.

Kadana led them through the maze of tunnels confidently, turning without hesitation whenever a tunnel diverged.

"You know these tunnels well," Omen said.

"I spent a few months trapped down here," Kadana said with a wry tone in her voice. "Courtesy of Beren's father. Got to know the place really well."

Omen wondered if this revelation was an accidental slip or an invitation to probe further. All he knew was that Beren's father was both of the line of the elder giant Straakhan and that of a lady of the faerie, though Omen did not know of which court. He decided not to ask.

"We've never been able to clear the forest as far back from the castle as I've wanted to," Kadana said. "There are too many wood spirits and ancient wild things who call the forest their own. None of them take kindly to any clearing efforts . . . which I found out the hard way.

"I think at one point the tunnels were the only means of getting around the forest without running into its inhabitants. And I noticed that several of the tunnels shorten travel time.

"I've never tried it, but a few of my friends, your mother included, Omen, insist that they managed to get to cities a day's ride away in a mere hour . . . Not that we're going to try that." She shot another stern look over her shoulder.

Omen was certain the warning was meant for her daughters, but he was also certain everyone in the group who had a mother felt admonished. Certainly, he'd heard similar warnings from his mother over the years. *You don't argue when she's using that tone.* He noted the unsettled look on Shalonie's, Liethan's, and Nikki's faces as if they were recognizing their own mothers in the tone.

The tunnels were dusty, cobwebbed and smelled of dank earth, but despite Gollis' dire prediction, nothing attacked them or got in their way.

"Are there more dangerous routes in this 'underkeep?'" Shalonie asked what was on Omen's mind.

"I've spent a lot of time clearing the tunnels," Kadana explained, "though not for a few years. If you are wondering, Gollis was correct to be concerned. But I think this route is going to be safe."

After a while, Omen thought he heard water and noticed a stream of light up ahead.

They scrambled past several boulders to arrive at an iron gate set over a cave mouth that led out of the cavern and into the world beyond. The back of a waterfall splashed down in front of the gate. They'd have to step through the waterfall to reach the forest beyond the cavern exit.

"I is not getting wet." Tormy's voice quavered.

"Don't think you have to worry, Tormy." Templar stepped up to the gate. "It's an illusion, isn't it?"

Kadana smirked. "I commissioned the waterfall illusion

along with the gate when I first secured the underkeep." She drew a long-shanked key with a thin ribbon from around her neck, worked the lock, and swung open the iron gate smoothly and quietly.

Kadana stepped through the waterfall without hesitation, disappearing from sight. The others began following one by one, vanishing through the very real looking water.

Omen caught hold of one of the straps on Tormy's saddle and gently pulled the large cat through the water.

Tormy, ears flattened against his head, tail fluffed as if terrified, insisted on closing his eyes. "It is just being too horrible, Omy," Tormy whimpered. "Water is falling down upon my head."

"Stop being a baby," Omen said, feeling a little embarrassed in front of the others. "It's not even real water."

"&%*#!@$!!" Tyrin grumbled softly, no happier than Tormy, though he rode through the water illusion on Kyr's shoulder without any further complaints.

"This is fascinating," Shalonie called out.

Omen took his eyes off Tormy and glanced around the small clearing. Shalonie was standing next to a large square stone that rose a few inches up from the mossy ground of the forest clearing. The stone was large enough for a dozen people to stand upon and was intricately carved with symbols of interlocking circles and triangles. The moist silvery sheen of morning dew coated the surface and made the sigils gleam in the light. Around them, tall ancient trees wove a near canopy overhead, blocking out the piercing sunrise. In the muted light Omen could see the faint glimmer of a curtain of blue emanating upward from the large stone. Magic permeated the air around them.

It wasn't cold, but Omen felt a shiver run through him.

An uncomfortable thought passed through his brain. *Anyone or anything can come through that portal — and it's right next to my grandmother's home!*

Kadana stood nearby, warily watching the woods around them, one hand on the hilt of her sword. Dense, black forest surrounded them ominously. Omen noted a few deer paths shooting off in several directions. *Too narrow and low for a human. No wonder she has such a large garrison in the keep.*

Templar joined Shalonie at the stone platform, both of them edging carefully around it while they studied the sigils and the shimmer of light above the stone.

"What is that?" Nikki blurted out. He stared at the stone in amazement.

"So, this is a fixed portal," Shalonie said.

"It is." Kadana took a deep breath. "Or as fixed as they ever get. From here, this portal leads to the Mountain of Shadow . . . Last time anyway."

Liethan tried to tame his grin, but a small whoop escaped his mouth regardless.

"You said, 'last time?'" Dev asked plainly.

"I spent a good number of years riding the wild portals without anything ever going wrong," Kadana explained. "And then something went wrong. I've tried to avoid them since then. Felt like my luck had run out. Didn't want to chance it after that."

She shot a sharp look at Omen and Liethan. "Your parents stopped around that time too," she told them. "Felt like they had too much to lose."

"It can't be naturally occurring," Templar remarked, moving his hands over the sigils on the stone. "Someone created this."

Kadana gave another wary look around the clearing before replying. "Not all the portals have such stones — I always assumed the portals came first and that stone was just placed as a marker." She turned her attention to Shalonie who was scribbling something in her notebook. "Are those Cypher Runes — are they what created the portal?"

Shalonie looked up from her work. "No, these aren't Cypher Runes — they're Sul'eldrine Script. The Divine Tongue, Sul'eldrine doesn't actually have a written form — or at least none that we know of. Normally it's just written down phonetically in the local alphabet. But over the years there have been numerous attempts to create a universal scripting language — this one was prevalent here in Kharakhan many thousands of years ago. This one marks this land as sacred — I'm not sure the stone and the portal are even connected. But I'd have to do more research to confirm one way or the other."

"We should hurry!" Kyr spoke up suddenly, his gaze focused on the portal. "We'll miss the doorway if we don't go soon. And we should probably go before they start growling louder."

Accepting that Kyr likely saw something the rest of them didn't, Omen turned to his companions, meeting their gazes as he looked from face to face. "Kyr's right. We should get going," he said. "But not all of us have to go. If any of you want to stay, I'm certain Kadana will be happy for your support in holding back the orclets and anything else that may be coming out of the forest."

Even as he said the words, he knew none of his companions would choose to stay behind. Shalonie was drawn by the mystery of the portals themselves, and would likely have gone alone. Templar's and Liethan's loyalty to him was unquestionable, even without the draw of excitement both were feeling for the trip ahead. Nikki was determined to prove himself, and even Dev, who'd been hired to join them by his mother, had proven more than once that he'd risk his life for all of them. And, of course, he didn't question the cats or Kyr who'd follow him anywhere.

"This is the mark of the man," Kadana said, "Or the woman. You step into that portal, even if all goes well, you will never be the same. Each act of courage makes it easier to drive ahead and harder to stay behind."

She set her eyes on her daughters and her father-in-law. "I wanted the girls to see this, but it's time for us to go back . . . Just remember what I said, Omen. Hit 'em hard."

She patted Tormy's flank.

Omen took hold of Tormy's saddle strap, and then wrapped his other hand around Kyr, pulling his brother to his side. He motioned to the others, and they all surrounded the portal square.

"On three," Tyrin announced from Kyr's shoulder. "One, two, three . . ."

Omen took a step forward. His foot met nothing, and he felt like he was again falling off the roof of Kadana's keep.

Air rushed around him, pulling at his clothes and whipping through his hair. Sounds flew past him in a clamoring rush. He felt waves of burning heat and icy cold course through his body. Colors assaulted his eyes as light streamed and spread out before him in painful bursts.

His feet met solid ground again, and he stumbled to one knee. He tried to shake off the dizzy feeling.

Tremendous roars assaulted his ears from all sides, and he forced himself to his feet.

He saw nothing past a shimmering kaleidoscope of hues

in front of his eyes, but his nose picked out the acrid smell of blood, urine, and char. Releasing his hold on Tormy and Kyr, he shrugged off his backpack and grabbed the hilt of his sword. He'd carefully drawn the blade from its scabbard before his eyes cleared.

"Omen!" he heard Kyr's panicked voice overlapping with Tyrin's scream of, "&$#^*@! wyverns!"

Want more?

Follow Omen and the gang into the Faerie realm of the Autumn Lands as they try to save the missing king in AUTUMN KING (Book 5).

❖

If you've enjoyed HOLLOW SEASON, please consider telling a friend, or leaving a review. Help us spread the world Of Cats and Dragons. And, as Tormy would say, that is being greatlynessness!

More OF CATS AND DRAGONS tidbits and artwork are waiting for you at:

OfCatsAndDragons.com.

Join our adventurers by signing up for the OF CATS AND DRAGONS Newsletter.

For Audiobook Lovers! Listen to OF CATS AND DRAGONS on Audible

Thank you!

Carol

My days are still a struggle, and my writing could only continue with the support of my friends and family. I want to thank my parents for their tireless care and constant encouragement. I wouldn't be able to get through all this without you.

The same goes for my siblings and their beautiful children. Their support and love is endless and keeps me going each day. And Camilla keeps me bolstered and grounded with her visits, and her willingness to just sit and talk to me when I'm too sick to do much more than lie there and listen.

And thank you to all our fans. The positive reviews we've gotten for all our book fill me with hope. I'm so grateful to have my writing to keep my mind busy while I'm fighting through this terrible disease. God bless all of you.

❖

Camilla

P.J. —

This is another one I've only been able to finish because you gave me time and space. If it weren't for you and your unwavering support, I would still only dream of being a writer. You've given me the freedom to create. You've given me the freedom to finally be who I was meant to be.

Bob and Terry —

Thank you for letting me visit and spend time with Carol. You are incredible caretakers. Carol and I would not have been able to complete SUMMER'S FALL, HOLLOW

SEASON, and AUTUMN KING if you hadn't been willing to let me invade your home on a monthly basis.

Bonita —

My fellow Empyrean Press paladin. From DOG BREATH to BLOOD & BONES, you've always had my back. You are tireless, honest, steadfast, and kind. You've always been exactly who you were meant to be.

Jo Bozarth of HerProcess.com —

Thank you for giving me the opportunity to talk about my collaboration with Carol, our friendship, and what the last year has been like. Our talk came at the very moment I was starting to feel lost. You put me at ease and let me clear my head. Onward . . .

The Friends OF CATS AND DRAGONS Facebook Group —

What would I do if I couldn't share goofy cat pictures with you? It gives me such joy that you love the stories I love. And, as Tyrin would say, that's &$#@ awesome!

❖

We also want to thank all of our friends who continue to listen and throw nothing but positive energy and love our way as the tale of the tale unfolds.

And a big thanks to everyone who keeps asking, "What's next?"

About the authors

Carol E. Leever:

Carol E. Leever, a college professor, has been teaching Computer Science for many years. She programs computers for fun, but turns to writing and painting when she wants to give her brain a good work out.

An avid reader of science fiction and fantasy, she's also been published in the Sword and Sorceress anthologies, and has recently gotten into painting illustrations and book covers. A great lover of cats, she also manages to work her feline overlords into her writing, painting and programming classes often to the dismay of her students.

Camilla Ochlan:

Owner of a precariously untamed imagination and a scuffed set of polyhedral dice (which have gotten her in trouble more than once), Camilla writes fantasy and science fiction. Separate OF CATS AND DRAGONS, Camilla has written the urban fantasy WEREWOLF WHISPERER series (with Bonita Gutierrez), the mythpunk noir THE SEVENTH LANE and, in collaboration with her husband, written and produced a number of short films, including the suburban ghost story DOG BREATH and the recent 20/ 20 HINDSIGHT. An unapologetic dog lover and cat servant, Camilla lives in Los Angeles with her husband actor, audiobook narrator and dialect coach P.J. Ochlan, three sweet rescue dogs and a bright orange Abyssinian cat.

Get in touch

Visit our website at OfCatsAndDragons.com
Like us on Facebook @OfCatsAndDragons and join the
Friends Of Cats And Dragons Facebook group.
Find Carol:

caroleleever.deviantart.com

Find Camilla:

Twitter: @CamillaOchlan
Instagram: instagram.com/camillaochlan/
Blog: The Seething Brain

Or write to us at:
meow@ofcatsanddragons.com

Made in the USA
Las Vegas, NV
07 January 2022